PENGUIN BOOKS

TWISTED RIVER

SIOBHAN MACDONALD was born in Cork in the Republic of Ireland. She studied in Galway and worked as a writer in the technology industry in Scotland for ten years, then in France, before returning to Ireland. She now lives in Limerick with her husband and two sons.

TWISTED RIVER

Siobhan MacDonald

PENGUIN BOOKS

PENGUIN BOOKS

An imprint of Penguin Random House LLC
375 Hudson Street
New York, New York 10014
penguin.com

LIBRARY OF CONGRESS CATALOGING-IN-PUBLICATION DATA
MacDonald, Siobhán.
Twisted river : a novel / Siobhán MacDonald.
pages cm.—(A Penguin Mystery)
ISBN 978-0-14-310843-6
1. Families—Fiction.   2. Home exchanging—Fiction.   3. Americans—Ireland—
Fiction.   4. Irish—United States—Fiction.   5. Psychological fiction.
6. Suspense fiction.   I. Title.
PR6113.A2618T87 2016
823'.92—dc23
2015018810

Printed in the United States of America
1   3   5   7   9   10   8   6   4   2

Set in Dante MT Std
Designed by Elke Sigal

For Neil, Jamie, and Alasdair.

ACKNOWLEDGMENTS

I would like to thank the following people who proved themselves invaluable in bringing *Twisted River* into being: My husband Neil for his support and editorial eye. Sarah O'Donoghue—my first and loyal reader. My sons Jamie and Alasdair, for their humor. My agent Isobel Dixon for her support. My lovely editor Emily Murdock Baker and my friends and relatives who provided much encouragement along the way. You know who you are.

TWISTED RIVER

Oscar

She would never have fit as neatly into the trunk of his own car. He presses two fingers against her beautiful neck. Just in case. No pulse. The blow was fatal. He looks at her one last time and closes the trunk.

Her blood is all over his hands. Oscar stares at the curious patterns forming on his pale skin. No latex gloves this time. He tries to think. In the cold he hardly moves, watching the tiny pearls of red slide down the coarse hairs to his wedding band. The burning in his stomach spreads upward to his chest. His control is slipping, his panicked breath forming small clouds in the dark. Oscar is in turmoil. From man to shivering animal in the space of three minutes.

Across the road, water rages over the falls. Oscar has felt like this before. It was a long time ago but the memory is vivid. In fourth grade, he punches Annabel Klein so hard in the stomach that she vomits. Another memory flashes before him. This time he's standing over Birgitte, watching her die. Up the road, the church bells sound a mournful chime. What's done is done.

There comes the sudden beat of wings. Looking up, Oscar sees an arrowhead of swans slicing through the night sky. A splutter of rain starts to fall, the drops making a tinkling sound on the plastic bags scattered at his feet. Shards of glass from a smashed jar of peanut butter mingle with exploded bags of popcorn. There's a squashed banana—the flesh pulped from its skin—and a packet of brownie mix daubed in blood.

Should he look in the trunk of the car one more time to make sure?

He fumbles for the catch. It isn't like his BMW. This is a VW sedan. The car they'd agonized in, attempting to sort things out. He'd so wanted to straighten things out. His fingers slip left and right, searching for the catch. The VW badge is smeared with blood. There it is. He squeezes with his thumb and forefinger.

"Dad?"

He freezes. He hadn't seen the kids pick their way across the gravel.

"Elliot?"

His nine-year-old is shivering in pajamas in the driveway. Jess, his twelve-year-old daughter, is behind him.

"You've been gone a long time, Dad," says Elliot.

It's more a question than a statement.

Jess stands there, perplexed, eyes innocent and wide. He sees her scanning the debris of the grocery shopping all over the driveway. His children cannot know what just happened. They must be protected, no matter what. The roaring in his ears begins to build again. He wills his mouth into a smile, pulling his lips over his teeth. He hopes it looks convincing.

Jess's face drains of color as she edges toward him. The sound in his ears is almost unbearable.

"What is it, Jess?"

He can see her mouth is moving. She is asking something.

"What did you say?" he shouts.

"Where's Mom?" she shouts back.

Kate

Kate could never quite make up her mind whether she loved or loathed September. A flurry of withered leaves danced over her feet as she scurried down the steps of the Clare Street campus and set off briskly for home. Snatching a quick glance at her watch, her heart skipped a beat. She was cutting it fine. She quickened her step. She had to make it home before five. Not a second later. It was a new routine, now that summer break was over. It had been harder with all the idle time this year. Things had been different when they'd had the beach house.

Today had been difficult. Once upon a time Kate would have jumped at the chance of becoming assistant head of the Visual Communications Department. She would have been thrilled to bits. But that was before there were other demands on her. She should have been elated at being offered the position so soon after her return to the workforce. Instead, she felt a bittersweet sadness at having to turn it down. Life was about choices and this was a choice she had to make.

Simon Walsh, the head of department, had looked at her in disbelief.

"This is a windup. You're teasing me, right?"

With a heavy heart, Kate shook her head.

"But, Kate, you're the best person for the job," Simon protested.

"You know that. I know that. I know you're only just back but you've got the talent and you know this department like no one else."

"I know that, Simon. And I'm flattered. Really, I am. But things at home, you know . . ." She hesitated. "It's just not that easy. The job I have now I can manage. Assistant head is a whole other proposition. Extra responsibility, more time here on campus. I have thought about it. Believe me."

Realizing she was serious, Simon ran a distracted hand through his long hair. "There has to be a way. I was so looking forward to having you as my wingman."

Again, Kate shook her head. She'd made up her mind.

"I'm sorry. There'll be other equally suitable candidates. Anyway, surely the job has to be openly advertised?"

Disgruntled, Simon had taken off, shoving his hands deep into the pockets of his crumpled linen jacket.

Already Kate was at the Abbey Bridge and a gust of wind pulled at her slackly fastened chignon, threatening to loosen it. A man on a bicycle swept by, close to the curb. She smiled to herself. It appeared he had every worldly good he owned in his pannier. A black and white dog with attitude sat in the basket up front. Again she looked at her watch. There were scarcely fifteen minutes left. Would she make it? In the old days she might have taken the car but they had only one car now and Mannix had it today. Her laced-up boots started to chafe against her skin as she broke into a jog.

Suddenly, Kate heard the pounding of feet from the rear. Two guys with white hooded tops ran past her. It wasn't clear if one was the quarry and the other the prey or if they were running together. Moments later a squad car screamed through the evening traffic pursuing the two fleeing creatures until they disappeared through an alleyway and out of sight. Unperturbed, Kate continued her journey, the satchel full of papers clapping up and down on her hip.

This was a city where the haves lived side by side with the have-nots. A city whose messy bits were not hidden from view. Even though these encounters were common enough, Kate was always cautious making her way home past the inner-city housing schemes by the old walls of the city. She was panting now. She glanced again at her wrist. Five more minutes to go.

Once she got to the ancient walls of King John's Castle, Kate could just about see her house across the river. She could imagine it in her mind's eye, just around that bend of houses that overlooked the falls. Kate liked this part of town. She liked the fact that it had probably looked largely the same over the span of centuries. Thomond Bridge with the falls on one side, the low humpbacked rolling hills on the other. The whalebone-white arches of Thomond Park Stadium in the distance. The Treaty Stone with the somber bulk of St. Munchin's Church across the road. The boardwalk.

She scurried over Thomond Bridge, her calves hot and sweaty and her hair eventually escaping and swishing about her face in the wind. Her mouth had gone dry. Why the hell had she not ended that last lecture just five minutes early?

Rustling through sheaves of papers and the crumpled tinfoil of hastily eaten sandwiches, Kate searched for the jagged clump of keys at the bottom of the canvas bag. She managed to stumble through the front door just as the church bells began to chime five. She'd made it!

"Fergus? . . . Izzy? . . . I'm home."

Kate clambered up the stairs to the kitchen, heart in her mouth.

There, curled up in a blue fleece blanket in a corner of the chaise longue, staring intently at the clock on the wall, was Fergus. He looked from her to the clock and back again. The TV flickered busily at the other side of the room.

"See, I told you," said Kate, out of breath. "I told you, five o'clock. Home by five."

"I see that, Mum. It's five o'clock now. But you're very *nearly* late . . ." He turned back to the TV.

"Whew!" she mouthed to Izzy, who was leaning over the breakfast counter in an apron.

Izzy knew only too well the consequences of her mother arriving after the agreed time. She too had witnessed that thinly veiled anxiety, seen it erupt and spew out great torrents of anger and confusion, blistering the remains of an evening. And yet this evening, Fergus's response didn't register the relief it normally did when Kate walked through the door.

This evening there was something else. Something else was eating him. Kate's fingers itched to ruffle his curls but Fergus hated being touched on the head. Instead, she laid a hand on his shoulder.

"Good day?" she said to the back of his head.

Izzy looked up from her homework on the counter, looking grave.

No response from Fergus.

"Good day, Soldier?" she asked again.

"All right, I guess . . ."

It was then that Kate noticed the familiar hairy creature hulking its way across the screen, mammoth knuckles scraping the pavement, the anguished roar of frustration as it beat its breast in pain.

"*King Kong*?" Kate looked at Izzy.

Izzy nodded.

So it had been a bad day. *King Kong* always made an appearance after any unsettling incident or unhappy encounter. The great lumbering creature seemed to act as a salve. What did Fergus see in him? Was it the primal anguish and confusion of the beast?

Kate filled with dismay. This was the second time this week already. In fact, *King Kong* had graced their TV screens more times this term than all of the previous year. Shoulders slumped, she went to the hallway and hung up her purple jacket and the satchel of project proposals that now seemed doomed to remain unseen for the evening.

Returning to the kitchen, she put her arms round Izzy, squeezing tight. None of this was fair on Izzy. Kate had to constantly remind herself and others that her daughter was only eleven. As the money had slowly dried up, Izzy never questioned, never complained, accepting every new cutback and economy with stoicism. Music lessons gone. Ballet classes gone. The only thing left was Girl Guides.

Izzy tried hard. "Don't worry about us, Mum, I'll mind Fergus when you go back to work"; "I'll walk Fergus home from school";

"I'll help Fergus with his homework." Inasmuch as anyone could help Fergus with his homework, Izzy tried. She tried her little heart out.

"Is Dad home for dinner? He promised to take me to Guides tonight." Izzy undid the apron and handed it to her mother.

"He'll be on his way," Kate responded with more conviction than she felt. Mannix's behavior had been erratic in recent months, but he had a lot on his mind with the new job, and anything was better than all those months of unemployment.

Alone in the room with Fergus, Kate set to chopping peppers and onions. Every now and then she looked over at the velvet chaise longue that she had personally reupholstered. Fergus was cocooned and fetal under his blanket.

"Today not so good then, Soldier?"

Fergus's face suddenly blotched up and he bit his lower lip. Kate stopped chopping.

"There was writing," he said. "On the wall." Dislodging his glasses, he screwed a fist into an eye socket.

Kate's heart sank. "What do you mean?"

"Writing on the wall in the school yard over by the wheelie bins. They were all laughing. Everyone was laughing . . ."

He rubbed the other eye now, desperately trying to keep in the crying.

"I don't care," he said. He twisted the blanket.

"What did it say?"

How stupid of her! How incredibly stupid! How could Fergus tell her what it said? He could scarcely read. Even after five years of learning support, reading did not come any easier. They were going to have to go private. She knew that. She'd known it for some time. But it was the money. Always, the money. They'd do their own research, find their own therapists.

"*Who* was it, Soldier?" she asked this time. "*Who* was it that wrote on the wall?"

Fergus looked at her as if she already knew.

"Frankie?"

Of course.

"It was Frankie, wasn't it?"

Silence.

A tough kid with a shock of lice-ridden carrot hair, Frankie Flynn was a latchkey kid. In the beginning, Kate tried tolerance. Frankie Flynn didn't have it easy. His mother discarded her fluffy dressing gown only to go to her evening job in the off-license, and it was said she was paid in kind.

"I'll sort this out, Soldier," said Kate calmly. "I'll take time out tomorrow and go to the school."

Fergus shot up.

"No!!! You are NOT to go to the school," he screeched. "If you go to the school I will NEVER EVER talk to you again. EVER. And stop calling me Soldier!" He ran from the room dragging his blanket behind him.

Kate was stunned. Onion fumes mixed with tears of hurt for her child. She needed a moment to think. Going to the window, she edged herself into the wicker seat suspended from the ceiling and looked out at the river. An elderly couple huddled over the handrail in the riverside park. They were throwing scraps to the swans below. A young mum pushed her toddler in a miniature car propelled by a long plastic handle. A couple of joggers ran past in conversation and continued on up the boardwalk. Some pleasure craft had moored on the far side of the river, over the weir outside the seventies LEGO-like office block that hung somber and gray over the water. The silhouette of buildings on the far side of the river was a curious mélange of old and new. Striking and gauche. Elegant and unremarkable. A microcosm of the city at large. It was a view Kate had grown to love as much as she loved this house with its upside-down layout.

Their house had been the place to be at on New Year's when fireworks rained down against the castle walls and bled in multicolor on the water below. Kate stared out now at the late evening sunshine, a golden glint on the ripples over the falls. The tide was ebbing and there would be fishermen out in the shallows later. Urban fishermen who pitched up with crocked bicycles and bits of old shopping bags. She often wondered if they ever caught anything.

She closed her eyes, feeling the soothing warmth of the low sun caress her eyelids. When she opened them again, the elderly couple was shuffling off, possibly uneasy with the appearance of a thin man pulling a mastiff terrier on a chain—the animal's chest broader and more menacing than its owner's.

Click. The turn of a key in the door downstairs. Mannix. Kate felt her chest grow tight. His steps were heavy on the stairs. One at a time now, not like they used to be.

"You look chilled . . ."

That smile—brilliant as always. That was what she had fallen for—his smile. His shirt still looked fresh and crisp against his sallow skin. In his hand he held his laptop.

She half-smiled, not wanting to start the evening on a sour note.

"The kids?" he asked, draping his raincoat over the back of a breakfast stool.

"In their rooms."

"Good. Good." He rubbed his chin pensively and took a few steps toward her. He stopped then as if he'd thought of something.

"All right?" she asked.

He took a few more steps and then sat gingerly on the edge of the chaise longue.

He cleared his throat. "Look, Kate, there's something I have to tell you . . ."

"There's something I have to tell you as well," she interrupted. She would have to get this out of the way.

"Okay, then . . ." He hesitated. "You first."

She told him about Fergus. About the episode in the school yard—the latest installment in a catalog of incidents that now seemed to be descending into a regular pattern of bullying.

"That little prick!"

Mannix shook his head, his face gripped by a spasm of anger.

"So, what's this? This is the third or fourth time since the new school year. So our Fergus is that little shit's latest punch-bag?"

Kate's stomach knotted. It was true. It looked like Fergus was set to be Frankie's target for the year. First, there was the disgusting incident with the sandwiches, then the sports bag soaked in urine, and now this.

"Fergus doesn't want me to, but I'm going to the school. I've decided." Kate stood up wearily out of the chair and padded across the polished floorboards.

Mannix shook his head. "And just what do you hope that will achieve? Come on, Kate. You know what we're dealing with here. Look what happened to that Polish kid's dad . . ."

"What Polish kid?" asked Kate.

"You know, the scrawny fella. What's this the kids call him? Oh, yeah—Polski Sklep."

"I know who you mean—what happened to his dad?" Kate remembered Polski Sklep being bullied and knew that his mother had gone to the school to complain. But she wasn't aware of any repercussions beyond that.

"Oh, Kate! You don't think his father's two broken ribs happened by accident?"

"What do you mean?" The knot in her stomach pulled tighter.

"Polski Sklep's father is . . . was . . . a bouncer at a nightclub in town. He got beaten up in the lane outside. That was down to Flynn's old man."

"I thought Frankie Flynn's dad was in prison."

"And you think that stopped him?"

Kate sighed.

"How do you know all this, Mannix?" she asked, her plan of action now looking futile.

"Spike."

Spike was Mannix's brother. The other half of the O'Brien brothers. As Kate tossed the vegetables onto the sizzling wok, her face set in a frown. Spike would know. He was in the nightclub business. Spike was in any business that he thought would make him money.

"Hi there, honey." Mannix's face softened at his daughter, who'd floated silently into the room. She was neatly dressed in her Girl Guides uniform. "Oh, shit . . ." he added.

"Aw, Dad, you haven't forgotten, have you? You said you'd take me to the Guides tonight."

"No, no, of course, Izzy, that's fine. It's just that . . . no, never mind. Of course I'll take you."

Izzy looked at her mother.

"You told him, then? About Fergus?"

"Yes, I told him," said Kate, doling out four equally sized portions into black patterned noodle bowls.

"What exactly did Frankie Flynn write on that wall?" Mannix looked at Izzy.

Izzy hesitated a moment as if she didn't want to say.

"Well?" said Mannix.

Kate held her breath.

"Do you really want to know, Dad?"

"I really want to know," said Mannix.

"'Fergus O'Brien is a fucking spastic,' that's what it said."

Kate felt like she'd been slapped across the face. For a few moments none of them said anything. Mannix's eyes narrowed.

"Did it, now?" he said eventually.

Izzy looked from Kate to Mannix, slowly drinking in their reactions.

"I hate Frankie Flynn." Izzy's voice was ice-cold.

"Don't you worry about that little bollocks," said Mannix, circling his daughter's waist.

"Mannix!" Kate protested, but noticed the profanity had softened Izzy's expression. She had the makings of a grin. Father and daughter were alike in so many ways. Quick to anger, quick to judge, impetuous.

"What are you going to do?" Izzy wasn't letting it go.

Kate squirmed, her parental authority under siege from the piercing stare of her young daughter. The truth was she didn't quite know. Not yet.

"Let's have dinner, Izzy," she said breezily. "It's not your job to worry about this. It's mine and Dad's. Go downstairs and get Fergus, will you?"

Izzy opened her mouth as if to speak but clammed it tightly shut again.

"K," she muttered.

"Sticks and stones may break my bones but names can never hurt me," rhymed Kate, but her words rang hollow and trite. Izzy turned her back, but not before Kate registered the look of disgust on her daughter's face.

The meal was stilted and awkward, Mannix trying to cajole Fergus without actually addressing the issue, Kate aching to smother her fragile eight-year-old with love. She'd give him anything she could to protect himself. Anything to boost his self-esteem. If Fergus could only walk into that school with his head held high, maybe then he wouldn't wear the mantle of a victim quite so readily. If she could just conjure up something to make him more resilient, more robust. Maybe then Frankie Flynn would move off to prey on someone else. It wasn't a noble solution, she knew, but at the moment all she wanted was Frankie Flynn to leave her son alone.

Even though she'd prepared the meal just the way he liked it, she half expected Fergus would leave his meal untouched. Surprisingly, in between monosyllables, he ate. He did his usual circle trick with the vegetables. He picked a yellow pepper from the yellow pile, a carrot from the orange pile, and then some onions. And back to the yellow pile to start all over again. He was trying his best to put on a brave face in front of his father.

Izzy ate her meal in moody silence. As Kate cleared the dishes she knew they were going to have to do something about Fergus, but for the life of her she didn't know what. Something would come to her over the course of the evening. She went out to the hall to retrieve her satchel in the hope of going over some papers.

Mannix passed her in the hallway carrying a flowery pillowcase.

"Domestic skills at last?" Kate raised an eyebrow.

"Oh, this—it's for Izzy, something for Guides, I think." His lips grazed her cheek as he breezed past, freshly showered and having swapped his suit for jeans.

"I turned down that job today, by the way."

Given the amount of agonizing she had gone through, she was surprised he hadn't asked her about it already.

"Job?" He looked at her blankly.

"The assistant head of department? The job that Simon offered me?"

"Oh, that . . ." he said dismissively. "Sexy Simon will have to look for his assistant elsewhere, I guess," he added sarcastically.

Kate felt hurt. It had been silly of her to expect any acknowledgment or recognition of what she had just turned down. Mannix had somehow gotten it into his head that Simon's interest in her was more than professional. But Kate couldn't help feeling let down nonetheless.

"Ready, Izzy?" Mannix shouted, going down the stairs.

At the bottom, he turned round. "Oh, Kate, by the way, I'm calling over to Spike for a bit. We'll talk when I get back, okay?"

"Spike?"

"Kate, don't start. Give the guy a break."

Her expression must have said it all.

"I didn't say a thing," said Kate. "Pints in the Curragower Bar, then?" She kept her tone even. It wasn't as if they could afford them.

"No, Kate. I'm going round to Spike's flat. See you later," he said, sounding resigned. He ushered Izzy out the door and slammed it a little too forcefully behind him. Kate sighed. She should have bitten her tongue.

Just before heading up to the study on the third floor, she looked in on Fergus's bedroom and was alarmed not to see him there. Not on the bed with his Nintendo. Not making models with his K'NEX. As she stood in the twilight she heard a heavy panting sound coming from the other side of the bed.

"Fergus?" she said tentatively, walking around the bed.

More huffing and puffing.

"What on earth are you doing?" Although it was perfectly obvious what he was doing.

He stopped then and propped himself up on one arm.

"Push-ups. Thirty tonight. And more tomorrow. I'm going to get up to a hundred a night."

"Isn't that a bit much?" He'd never shown any particular interest in gym work before. Still, she smiled, glad to encourage any new endeavor.

"It's not too much . . ." he huffed. "I'm going to be a beast!"

"A beast?" Kate laughed.

"Yeah. I'm going to become an absolute beast. And then I'm going to kick the living crap out of Frankie Flynn."

The smile froze on Kate's lips.

"Oh, but Fergus, that's not . . ."

He glanced up briefly, and then without answering he went back to his push-ups. Kate shut the door softly. She definitely had to talk to Mannix about this.

With a slew of papers spread out on the desk in the study, Kate tried to concentrate. She stared at the letter she'd received last week from Oberstown House, the young offenders' facility. They'd invited her to make a presentation to their further education students. Again, she was conflicted. The logistics were difficult. That was a trip the whole way to North County Dublin, a longer day at each end, and more up-heaval for Fergus. As much as she relished the idea of broadening their student base and making their courses more accessible, she knew where her priorities lay.

Next, Kate attempted to jot down some advice on the portfolio proposals her second-years had handed in. But the words swam around in a slurry of language. What advice could she offer her own child? She looked around the book-lined room and at the woven tap-estries hanging on either side of the long sash window. Darkness had now fallen and the lights from City Hall shimmered on the river.

And then it came to her. She spent so much time worrying about the future. Their future. Fergus's future. But the time was now. She needed to do something now. Putting the sheaf of papers to one side, she turned on the desktop and settled herself into the office chair. An hour must have slid by easily before she found what she was looking for.

"*Oooooowwww!!!*" came an agonized howl from down the stairs.

Good Lord—what had Fergus done now? Tearing down the stairs, she nearly went over on her ankle. There, in the gloom, was Fergus, doubled over, holding on to a foot.

"What happened?" She rushed to comfort him.

"My toe is all messed up," he said, sobbing.

"How did that happen?" His big toenail had split and blood was seeping out from underneath. On closer inspection, she saw that the edge of the toolbox was poking out from the cupboard door underneath the stairs. He had stubbed his big toe on the corner. She didn't doubt the pain and he was in full throttle now. The injury was the final straw in his day of humiliation.

"*Dad . . . I want Dad . . . Get Dad!*" he howled.

"Let's put a plaster on first. He'll be home soon, Soldier," she said, trying to placate him.

No go.

"Get Dad now! I want my dad now!"

The bleating descended into a pitiful moaning. Her heart went out to him. She wanted to scoop him up and squeeze him and cuddle the pain out of him. But it was no good. He wanted Mannix.

"Okay, okay, okay . . . hang on, I'll phone him."

The stark light of her mobile lit up in the gloom. "*Calling Mannix mobile.*" It went to voice mail. There was no point in leaving a message. Fergus wanted him now. She knew what she should do. She didn't want to, but she knew she had to. She'd have to call him. She'd have to call Spike.

"*Calling Spike mobile.*"

No answer. She'd try the apartment landline.

"Hi, Spike, it's Kate."

"Kate—my favorite sister-in-law!"

Kate squirmed. She was Spike's only sister-in-law.

"Can I have a quick word with Mannix?"

She heard his breathing and could almost see his languid movement as she heard him drawing on a cigarette.

"Sorry, Katie. No can do. Haven't seen my bro for weeks."

"Oh, I see . . . Oh, well, then . . ."

"But if he pitches up, I'll get him to give you a bell, all right?"

Spike was enjoying this—the fact that Mannix had lied to her.

"No problem—I'm sure he'll be home soon."

"I'm sure he will, Katie."

She hated being called that. And he knew it.

"Thanks."

Now she wished she hadn't called.

"Where's my dad?" Fergus said, sniffing, still in a heap on the floor.

"I don't know," she said snappily, sympathy for her son now replaced by a gnawing sense of unease. "I don't know where your dad is."

It was only then that she remembered Mannix had wanted to tell her something when he'd come home from work. As she coaxed a bruised Fergus upstairs with hot chocolate, she tried to dampen the worry that had lodged in her gut.

Where was Mannix? And why had he lied about going to Spike's?

Mannix

Things had been getting a little uncomfortable for Mannix. He'd always liked the view from the edge, it made him feel alive. But there were lots of balls in the air at the moment. Too many, in fact, and some of them needed to be taken out of circulation. He'd tried to do that tonight. It would take time before he knew if it had worked.

Sitting in the VW saloon, he felt as if he were skulking—like some of the other characters who drew up in the lay-by. They looked like they were waiting for something or someone. But Mannix's business was done. He was taking a breather, trying to cool down with the damp night air coming in off the river.

The passenger window had jammed halfway down. Like him, the car was beginning to show signs of wear and tear. It was a relic from his former job. They'd allowed him to keep it as part of his severance package, a little sweetener to make sure he'd go quietly in the end.

He hadn't seen that one coming. No, sir, not at all. Normally, his instincts were good, but he'd been caught off guard. It had been two years ago now, but he still winced at the memory. All those years in the same company, going in as a technician, Kate encouraging him to take night classes, and gradually rising up through the ranks. They'd become used to the pay rises, the bonuses, the stock options, the dividends. It had become the natural order of things.

Mannix had never been more pumped up and manic than during that time, investing and reinvesting. Like an addict, he'd enjoyed the rush it gave him. He'd started taking bigger risks. He started in on property. The apartments first and then the beach house. It seemed like the only way was up. Then one day it was simply as if someone suddenly called time on the party. It was over. He watched the wealth he had amassed fizzle away like air seeping out of a gaudy party balloon until it collapsed, all shriveled and sunken. He hadn't seen that one coming either. But he was not alone there. It was a global meltdown.

He looked at his reflection in the mirror without turning on the cabin light. The light from the streetlamp by the boat club was enough. In the amber half-light he looked clammy and shaken. His face was still blotchy and he'd have to somehow change his shirt when he got home. Examining the stains on the pale blue cotton, he became aware of a movement in the shadows to his left. He pulled the beanie farther over his head and slunk down in his seat, not wanting to be seen. But the figure hovering by the railings was not interested in Mannix. It hovered by the bouquet of flowers that was tied there and then crouched down to read the messages pinned to the torn cellophane. A tribute to a soul that the river had swallowed. After a few moments the figure got up again and shuffled off into the night. "Christ," said Mannix to himself. "No matter how bad things get I hope I never end up in the river."

A loud guffaw and the sound of chatter interspersed with the urgent wail of an ambulance making its way over the Condell bridge. Two figures were making their way out of the boat club and joking together.

Shit!

Mannix recognized them both. He thought the place would have been locked up by now. Everyone gone home. He slunk even farther down in his seat. He didn't need any questions about where he'd been the last few weeks. How come he wasn't training? His scull was on a rack inside. It hadn't been out on the water for months.

"All right there, sir?"

Mannix jumped. A garda car had pulled up alongside him, and a female garda was now looking at him disapprovingly.

"Yes, Garda, of course." He pulled himself into an upright position and smiled broadly. "Is there a problem?"

She looked at him as if she were trying to make up her mind. "Some of the residents . . ." She gestured to apartments on the other side of the road. "Some of them have rung in with complaints of soliciting . . ."

He laughed then, loudly. "Me? Soliciting?"

Fuck sake! He'd been accused of a lot of things but this was definitely a new one.

She didn't respond but looked wordlessly at a couple of long-legged women leaning against the trunk of a huge sycamore tree a few yards away.

"Garda, I assure you, I'm just enjoying the night air."

She looked at him dubiously, eyeballing him as her window wound slowly upward. The squad car crawled off, doing a three-point turn outside the boathouse, and crawled in his direction again. In the rearview mirror, he could see that it had pulled in to where the two women were now smoking. It was laughable. That was all he needed—a charge for soliciting.

Mannix turned the key in the ignition and the shiny green numerals on the dash read 9:55. He flexed his arms on the steering wheel. He could turn around and drive back up the strand, over the bridge, and home. He'd try again to tell her. He'd tried earlier but she'd deflected him. Maybe it was fate. He wasn't meant to tell her. But he knew that wasn't true. *He was definitely going to tell her . . .*

Or he could go to the Curragower Bar for just the one.

That's where she thought he was going to end up anyway. He wouldn't get any brownie points for coming home early, not with the mood that she'd been in these last few weeks. Preoccupied with Fergus and their finances. Still, he'd take her preoccupation over the explosive spats that had erupted out of nowhere when he'd been unemployed.

He was procrastinating. He knew that. He should go home but

the anonymous conviviality of the Curragower Bar was very appealing. It had been a long day. He succumbed to the lure of the bar.

"Mannix." His neighbor turned around and saluted him as he walked into the bar.

He wasn't going to get the anonymity that he had hoped for.

"Roger." Mannix jerked his chin, returning the salute.

Mannix scraped a stool alongside him. In the tiny bar there was nowhere to hide and there was no point in offending the man. There were only two other couples in the front bar and they were deep in conversation.

"Pint?" asked Roger.

"You're grand. I'll get my own," Mannix replied, signaling the barman, pointing at Roger's pint, and holding up one finger.

After a while, he smelled a faint tang of salt and sweat and felt embarrassed as it dawned on him that the waterproof running jacket he'd found in his kit bag in the back of the car probably hadn't been washed since the last time he was out with the club. He'd needed something to cover up the stains. Had that female garda noticed? Probably not in the dark of the car.

"I hear you're back in the saddle," said Roger by way of a conversation opener. It was the last thing Mannix wanted to talk about.

"Yeah, coming up for six months now." Mannix sipped from the creamy head.

"Tough going?" Roger addressed his query to Mannix's reflection in the mirror behind the counter.

Roger considered work of any description tough going. He'd been on the dole for years, and he wasn't called Roger the Dodger for nothing. In fact, he wasn't even called Roger. It was something more like Sean or Harry.

"Under the capitalist's yoke," said Roger, sighing, when he didn't get an answer.

"Well, it sure beats hanging around like a tool all day!" said Mannix, who was beginning to regret coming in now. Roger irritated him, coming over all superior as if he were somehow against work on the grounds of some high-minded ideology or principle. Roger was a lazy arse and that was the holy all of it.

"Ah, I dunno," drawled Roger. "Where else would you want to be on a sunny day apart from sitting on the deck out front here, looking at those mad young fellas trying to canoe up the falls?"

He turned then and looked directly at Mannix, his hooded eyes slowly blinking, lizardlike. It was then that Mannix noticed the curl of the lip and realized that he was being taunted.

"Feck off, Roger." Mannix smiled, thinking that he should really relax a bit. Not let things get to him so much.

"Well, I'm not exactly living the dream, I'll give you that," said Mannix, opening up. "My new boss is twelve years younger than me, what do you make of that?"

What did he expect Roger to say? How could he really expect Roger to commiserate? To empathize? What would Roger know of Mannix's belittling daily grind? Of how it felt to bite his tongue and rein in the caustic comments that bubbled to the surface in the face of constant corporate drivel. It was a job. That was all. He should be grateful. And Mannix knew he just had to grin and suck it up.

"That's what happens, you see, Roger . . ." The dark sticky liquid was beginning to hit the spot. "When you're back into the workplace after a break . . . you have to start at the bottom all over again."

"I suppose . . ." replied Roger, talking again to the mirror.

"You know what this kid asked me the other day—my boss, bearing in mind that this kid is barely out of braces . . . asks me where I see myself in five years' time. Asks *me* what my short- to mid-term goals are, what my long-term career plan is. And all the while I'm sitting there like a spanner, staring at the downy fluff of the baldy beard he's trying to grow."

"Oh, sure, I know where you're coming from . . ." said Roger, with conviction.

Like fuck, Roger knew. He couldn't possibly know the daily humiliation Mannix faced.

The couple in the corner looked over in Mannix's direction. He was talking too loudly. Far too excitedly. The other couple must have made a silent exit, slipping out unseen into the night.

"Ever think of joining that brother of yours?" Roger was swilling the dregs of his pint around in a circle.

"Spike?"

"Yeah, Spike . . ."

"Oh, I thought about that one many a time . . ." Mannix grinned ruefully. When he lost his job it seemed like a no-brainer. The most obvious thing in the world to do. But he hadn't made much progress with the idea. A brick wall would not be putting too fine a point on it.

"Was chatting to Spike in here last week," said Roger, gulping the last foamy dregs and slapping the glass back down noisily on the counter.

"Spike likes the pint in here, same as me," said Mannix, also finishing his drink.

"Yeah, haven't seen him at all this week." Roger paused. "A couple of guys came in here looking for him last night . . . the Bolgers, I think." Roger addressed the mirror again, casual as you like.

"Is that right?" said Mannix, slipping off the stool and putting his beanie cap back on. Suddenly he felt uncomfortable again. Time to go.

"You off, then?"

Roger seemed disappointed to be curtailed in his line of questioning. "You won't have another?"

"Can't afford it, mate," said Mannix, heading for the door. As it was, he shouldn't even have had any. But after the night he'd had . . .

It was quiet enough when Mannix entered the street. The tide was gurgling over the rocks, and as he headed around the curve in the road he heard the swish and plop of a fisherman's line. Lately, when he couldn't sleep he'd thought about joining them, but then he didn't want to give Kate any cause for further consternation. He hoped she'd unwound a little over the last few hours. *He wanted to get this over with.*

As Mannix neared the house he looked up to see a glow coming from the top floor. Kate was in the study. She must be working late tonight. The rest of the house was in darkness. He carefully opened the front door and entered the stillness of the house. The kids' bedroom doors were shut, not a sound coming from either.

He sniffed. Mixed in with the lingering smell of stir-fry was a musky vanilla scent wafting down the stairs. Kate had lit a candle.

As deftly as he could, he turned the knob of Fergus's room. In the sliver of light cast from the hallway, he could make out a small tuft of Fergus's white-blond hair poking out from underneath the Spiderman duvet. His wire-rimmed glasses were neatly placed on the bedside locker. The duvet rose and fell softly under the haunted face of King Kong on the poster above the bed. Fergus was in the refuge of sound sleep. A rustling sound came from beside a pile of neatly folded clothes in the corner. Darrow—Fergus's guinea pig—scrabbled about in his cage.

Pushing the door a little wider, Mannix made out a collection of figurines on the floor beside the bed. Fergus hadn't played with those in a while. They were normally kept in the large toy chest in the hallway. A shiver coursed down his spine.

The pageant that played out on the board disturbed him. Each assembly of figures scattered around the board depicted a scene of combat. Okay, so the figures and models were soldiers and tanks, it was to be expected. But these were not the usual scenes of sentry duty or sniper positions—the collections of figures were now cast in scenes of carnage, mounds of soldiers heaped on top of one another. He'd even fashioned a rope and hung one soldier upside down from a tower. The figure dangled eerily in the draft of the doorway. Mannix shivered.

He must have stood in the doorway for a good few minutes or more, brooding, when a muffled cough interrupted his rumination. So Izzy was awake next door after all. Poor Izzy, forced to grow up too fast for his liking, too sensible, the childish giddiness she was entitled to slowly squeezed out of her.

"Izzy? You awake?" he whispered.

No answer. Yet he swore he heard her cough and click her bedside lamp. The room was in darkness save for a chink of yellow streetlight coming in through the curtains and glowing eerily on the cast of Izzy's arm. She'd made it with her mother in the Art College, and the white plaster of Paris model was now proudly mounted in a wire frame on her chest of drawers.

Mannix stumbled on a discarded shoe as he edged closer to the bed.

"Izzy?" he said, more loudly this time.

She sat up in bed with a jolt, turning on the bedside lamp.

"What's wrong? Is something wrong?" Her dark eyes were wide and anxious.

"No, sweetheart, why would anything be wrong?"

There was plenty wrong, but nothing that Izzy needed to worry her young head about.

"Oh, it's just that . . . well . . . I thought. Oh, never mind. Good night, then, Dad."

She retreated, sliding beneath the duvet.

"Night, night, Izzy."

He closed the door and had that horrible feeling that once again he was failing his children. Fergus and Izzy were a long way from happy campers.

His legs felt heavy going up the stairs. In the kitchen a candle flickered on the breakfast counter. A freshly ironed shirt hung over the kitchen doorknob.

Shit!

He'd been distracted by the kids. He almost forgot. Making his way quickly downstairs again to the bedroom, he unzipped the whiffy nylon running jacket, putting it in the wicker laundry basket in the en suite shower room. He tugged the shirt over his head, not bothering to unbutton it. That could not go in the laundry basket. Those stains were never coming out—he knew that. Pulling on fresh boxer shorts and the T-shirt that he slept in, he opened the front door quietly and made his way to the wheelie bin around the side of the house.

Upstairs, on the top floor, he found Kate deep in thought, staring at the computer screen.

"Drink?"

He offered her the glass he'd brought from the kitchen. He'd opened a bottle of the cheap wine she'd bought last week. She might want it when she heard what he had to say. But Kate didn't even look up. She didn't even acknowledge that he had entered the room. *Tap, tappedy, tap, tap, tap* went the keyboard. So it was going to be like that, was it? He might think the better of telling her anything just yet.

"Fergus stubbed his toe . . ." she said casually.

"Oh . . ."

Hardly a 999 call in the grand scheme of things, he thought.

"He was pretty upset."

He kept his mouth shut. She was going somewhere with this.

"Like *really, really* upset, Mannix. You know the way he gets?" She looked up this time. Accusingly. "I-want-Dad upset, I-want-Dad-now-this-minute, that kind of upset . . ."

"Poor Ferg has had one shitty day," said Mannix.

Her gaze was steady. "So I called your mobile, and when I couldn't get you, I called Spike. At home. Spike said he hadn't seen you . . ."

Now was his opportunity. The door was wide open. He should tell her now. He felt his pulse quicken. Her eyes searched his face for an answer. He opened his mouth to speak.

"My mobile . . ." He hesitated. "Must have left the bloody thing on silent. A problem with one of the servers tonight—we had a patch release, there were bugs, and guess who they call?" He grinned widely, amazing himself at how readily the lies tripped over his tongue. How easily they came to him now. It isn't what he had meant to say, not how he'd anticipated the conversation going, but once more she'd thrown him off course.

"You were at work?"

Her tone was assured. She gave little outward sign of not believing him. Her question innocent. But this was how things had been lately. Tiptoeing around each other. Yet it represented an improvement.

"Yup. No rest for the wicked . . ." He tried another smile and once again proffered the glass of wine. This time she took it, her fingers softly brushing his as she clasped the stem.

"I want you to take a look at something . . ." Taking a sip, she looked back to the screen.

Oh, Christ, what had she found?

"Come here." She leaned back, pulling up a curvy chair she'd bought at a college end-of-year show during the good times.

His heart was in his mouth. But what he saw surprised him. Confused him. He leaned forward to get a closer view of the screen. An estate agent's website displayed a shot of an elegant wood-paneled sitting room with a large marble fireplace and an ornate over-the-mantle mirror. Three oversized windows dominated the room, one recessed in a high-ceilinged alcove. It wasn't an estate agent he recognized.

They'd spoken briefly about downsizing, but neither of them had had the stomach to mention it since. They loved this house. Selling the beach house had been wrenching enough. As for the apartments in Bulgaria, he didn't give a fiddler's, but this house was different. It was their family home. The bank couldn't take that. But what Kate was showing him was definitely not a downsize. Quite the opposite, in fact.

"What . . . ?" He looked at Kate.

"Just a minute," Kate responded. "You'll see . . ." She proceeded to scroll and enlarge each of the thumbnail shots on the screen.

There was a well-appointed kitchen with a center island and ice-white floor-to-ceiling cabinetry with eye-level glass-paned cupboards. Saucepans and other kitchen utensils hung from a rack over the island.

"Mmm . . ." Kate murmured her approval at the stylish room.

"But, Kate . . ." Mannix tried to interrupt.

"Hang on to your boxers, I'll explain," she said, and with exaggerated exasperation she proceeded to scroll through more photos. "The patience of a gnat," she muttered.

Mannix thought he'd better do as she had asked. After all, it wouldn't hurt to humor her. He found himself looking at photos of bedrooms. There was no doubt about it. This was the home of someone with taste. And equally obvious, it was the home of someone with means.

The bedrooms were large, the beds too, and built-in shelving and wardrobes kept everything neat and tidy. A kid's bedroom showed a poster of Harry Potter behind the bed. Mannix had often thought it odd how Fergus liked Harry Potter in a dispassionate kind of way—

not with the same all-consuming enthusiasm as other kids his age. King Kong was the man for Fergus. Poor ol' Ferg was immutable in his likes and dislikes.

"And the pièce de résistance . . ." Kate gave a final click and pushed the mouse away with a flourish. She sat back in the chair with the satisfaction of an artist who has confidently swept the last brushstroke on a canvas.

In the foreground of the photo in question was a balcony complete with outdoor furniture. It overlooked a park and a river. Tower blocks could be seen in the distance. Dublin? London? It certainly wasn't Limerick. Two glasses of wine sat invitingly on a glass-topped rattan table.

"I don't get it." Mannix shrugged as he swatted a tiny fly determined to land in his glass. "What am I looking at? Have we won the lotto?"

"I wish," said Kate, smiling, and tried to sip her wine. The fly had switched its attention to her glass now.

"It's an impressive pad, I'll give you that . . ." Mannix eyeballed the screen, engaging with Kate in her flight of fancy. "The dude that owns that gaff isn't short of a few euros."

"A few dollars, you mean . . ."

"Oh . . ." Mannix looked again at the screen, squinting at the small type in a sidebar. The address was given as New York. Riverside Drive, Manhattan, New York. He now stared stupidly at Kate. Was he supposed to know what was going on? Was this a reference to some earlier conversation that he was supposed to have kept in storage, something he'd nodded and smiled at, pretending to hear while he was mentally working on something else?

"Am I missing something?"

"No." She laughed at his confusion, and leaning over, she put her head on his shoulder in a rare but welcome gesture of intimacy. He tangled his fingers in the blond waves. She didn't say anything for a second or two and he savored the moment. It had been awhile since she had openly sought any affection from him.

"I've been thinking," she said, straightening herself up and looking into the viscous yellow of the glass. "I've been thinking about Fergus and Izzy. And about you and me as well. But mainly about Ferg . . . We have to do something."

"I agree." Mannix nodded, unclear where the conversation was headed. What did a smart apartment in New York have to do with anything?

"We should go to New York. The four of us. On holiday. In the October school holidays."

She looked at him. She was deadly serious.

Mannix guffawed with laughter.

"Jesus, Kate, I have to hand it to you. You take the biscuit. Here we are slaving away to get ourselves back on track, you're always harping on about it, for feck sake, and now you want us to take off for New York! How the hell are we going to afford that? What planet are you on, my darling artist?"

Kate's expression changed to one of hurt. Like he had suddenly slapped her when they'd been building bridges. Immediately, he regretted his impulsive outburst. His big bloody mouth.

"I have an idea . . . a plan . . ." she said in a little girl voice, making him feel worse.

"You do . . . ?" He tried to look conciliatory.

"As I was saying, before you jumped down my throat—I think it would do Fergus a world of good to have something to look forward to right now. Something good to focus on. *King Kong* is his favorite movie in the world, right? The Empire State—his favorite building? Hence, New York. It'd be one in the eye for Frankie Flynn, at least—the only place that little delinquent is headed is a young offenders' institute!"

"Of course, but . . ."

"I know, Mannix—the money. There's the accommodation for a start. That's where this comes in."

She looked back to the PC screen. "It's a home-exchange site," she explained. "The people who own this particular apartment are looking for an exchange home in the Clare or Limerick area at the end of October."

Mannix raised his eyebrows, careful this time to bite his tongue. He'd been to the States plenty of times, California with Spike in their twenties, Cincinnati visiting relatives, with work in Texas, and latterly, only five, six months ago, in Boston on a training course with his latest job. But he found it pretty damned hard to fathom that someone with a luxury apartment in Manhattan would want an exchange home in Limerick.

"Just one question, Kate. Why?" He tried not to sound too skeptical.

Putting down the wineglass, she pulled in closer to the desk again and cupped the mouse.

"It says here . . . just a minute . . . I know I saw it somewhere . . . yes, here it is . . . Hazel Harvey." Kate looked at Mannix. "She's the owner, she's a native of Limerick, so she says here in the owner profile. Born and reared on O'Callaghan Strand just over the bridge!"

"Oh, I see . . ." Well, that might explain it, all right. "Mmmm . . ."

"Okay, I know," said Kate, anticipating his next remarks. "So, that's only one part of it. What about the rest? The flights? The spending money?"

"Exactly," said Mannix, wondering what she'd pull out of the hat next.

"Well, don't be mad at me . . .". The little girl voice again. "I've been saving. Not much. Just a little every week—in the credit union. For Fergus, you see—for private speech and language therapy, and there are other therapies I've heard of for kids like him. There's a place in Galway. Anyway, that's all by the by now. I really think we need to do something now. Something today. Our little boy's self-esteem is going to be in tatters if we don't do something soon . . . and short of getting Frankie Flynn with a baseball bat . . . Anyhow, the long and short of it is I have the money for flights and sightseeing. I vote we spend it now."

A wave of affection washed over Mannix. He'd always admired Kate's resourcefulness, her coping skills, especially in times of crisis. And, God knows, she'd needed that over the last few years. She looked at him now, earnest faced, waiting for a response.

His response seemed obvious. She'd conjured up a holiday out of nowhere. He'd never even known about the nest egg. And this wasn't any old holiday. This was the holiday of a lifetime.

"Well?"

She was waiting.

"I can only imagine the look on Ferg's face . . ." A ripple of excitement fluttered in his belly. Something warm. Something good.

"You're up for it?" A slow smile was beginning to spread across her face. Her face was a mixture of mischief, excitement, and happiness colliding into one.

"You betcha!" he answered, leaning over and kissing her full on the mouth.

It wasn't the way he anticipated closing the evening. Not by a long chalk. He'd anticipated screaming, disbelief, disgust—and worse. *But one thing was for sure—it was clear that he couldn't tell her now. The timing was all wrong.*

"Hopefully, we'll hear back soon," she mumbled in between kisses. "I put up all the best photos I could find of this house. And views of the river outside. It may not be the Hudson . . ." She laughed then as her hands crept underneath his T-shirt.

"Come on . . . bed . . . now." Mannix grinned.

The way things were going he could be in for a double whammy. Kate seemed elated by her scheming. Relieved that she had hatched a plan for Fergie's plight. She slipped her hand in his as they made their way down the stairs. He wouldn't squander this opportunity.

He was right. Kate wanted to make love. To feel him inside her again. As she wrapped her legs around him he couldn't help but feel dishonest, that he'd stolen her affection. Either way he was enjoying it, stolen or otherwise. But he wasn't a fool. Mannix O'Brien knew he was playing on borrowed time.

"Guys, I have something to tell you." Kate was fit to burst.

She must have phoned him at least five times today to keep him abreast of developments. And he made sure this time his phone was not on silent. Even Mannix, who liked to move fast once he'd made a decision, was surprised at how quickly and easily everything was falling into place. Twenty-four hours had not yet passed since Kate sent out her request, but the folks with the fancy Manhattan apartment were looking forward to coming to Limerick. They loved the look of the house overlooking the falls at Clancy Strand. They were a professional couple and their kids were roughly the same ages as Izzy and Fergus.

Fergus and Izzy looked up from their late-night pizza. Fergus looked mildly curious and Izzy bored and disinterested. According to Kate, she'd hardly spoken a word all day.

The anticipation was written all over Kate's face. "I'm telling you now, because it's only a few months and you've got to start saving your pocket money."

The kids got precious little pocket money, but Mannix knew that this would all be part of the fun.

"Yeah?" Slight interest from Izzy now.

"You, Fergus, and Dad and I are going on a special holiday during the October school holidays this year."

That certainly grabbed Fergus's attention.

"On holiday? Where?" he asked, separating two slices of pizza stuck together with strands of cheese glue.

"We're off to the Big Apple!"

Fergus's jaw dropped, as did one of the pizza slices.

"New York?" came Izzy's high-pitched query. "You're joking us— New York? *The* New York?"

"Yes, Izzy, *the* New York."

Mannix reveled in his wife's delight at imparting such momentous news to the kids. He reveled further at Izzy's incredulity and glee.

"Oh my God, oh my God, I don't believe it, oh my God . . ." she kept repeating.

Fergus was speechless.

"Well, Soldier, what do you think?" asked Mannix.

"Absolute class. Awesome." Fergus looked stunned. "This is just the best day ever. Thank you, Mum. Thank you, Dad." He was grinning broadly now. Mannix's soul felt warm.

Pizza in hand, Fergus rushed at the two of them, hugging them tightly. He was not given to easy displays of affection. Mannix thought if he or Kate had had any misgivings about spending her nest egg, they were mightily dispelled now.

"So, my little soldier, when you go in to school tomorrow, you can tell everyone in your class how you are going to be on top of the Empire State Building in the October holidays."

"You bet," said Fergus, pushing his glasses back up his nose with a cheesy hand.

"Frankie Flynn included," Kate added, giving Fergus a knowing look.

"Dunno 'bout that, Mum . . ." Fergus looked dubious.

"Why ever not?" asked Kate.

"Frankie didn't come to school today."

"Oh . . . is that right?" said Kate.

"Yeah, they said he was in hospital all night. His arm's all banjaxed. Someone attacked him last night. Nobody knows when he'll be back."

Fergus picked off the onion from the last slice of pizza and then looked at his mother as he grinned. "So you see, Mum, it's been the very best day ever."

Hazel

Hazel winced at her reflection in the mirror. It hurt like hell when she touched there above the cheekbone. With her finger, she patted, searching gently at the back of her head. Where was it again?

"Ouch . . ." She'd found it. That hurt like hell too. The size of a conker, they would say at home in Ireland. Only this was not a glossy-coated chestnut but a bulbous contusion above the base of her skull. She hadn't been able to sleep on her back—even if she'd felt like sleeping.

She had wondered about going to the emergency room at Weill Cornell but this would be the second time in as many months. She didn't need the attention—or the incident reports. And anyway, some of those guys played squash with Oscar.

It was 6:15 A.M., still quiet, as she hovered over the twin sinks in their en suite bathroom. Oscar always allowed her these few quiet moments to herself. The penchant for the double sink had always mystified her. After all, who really wanted to perform their morning ablutions side by side, one shaving, another gargling, or spitting tooth-paste into the adjacent drain? Maybe in the first flush of a relationship or a marriage. Neither of which applied to Hazel and Oscar.

Leaning over the marble bowl, she edged closer to the mirror.

Blood bursts flecked her eye white, and the eyelid had swollen a mix of red and purple. The whole of her left eye socket was swollen, giving it a reptilian quality. Raising her fringe, she saw how the jagged gash his ring had made was crusting over. The fringe hid that, at least.

Brushing her teeth was agony, her jaw still aching and bruised from where she'd hit the wall. She opened her mouth as wide as she could and moved her jaw from side to side. It felt stiff. Even her neck felt sore as she bent to spit the spearmint saliva from her mouth. As she straightened up, a shadow fell across the room.

"Oscar."

She wasn't sure if she'd mouthed it or said it. His tall, wiry frame filled the doorway. The way things had been left, she wasn't sure if he was still mad.

"Hazel . . ." He looked at her face, shaking his head. "Let me hug you, my poor, poor Hazel."

She had her answer. He wasn't mad anymore. As she stood immobile, Oscar moved behind her, circled her waist, and dropped his head into the crook of her neck—a gesture of submission. Her nostrils filled with the smell of him, the musk of his gray-white hair, his slept-in T-shirt, and the faint odor of stale coffee.

"What has become of us?" he asked of their reflections in the mirror.

"Don't," she whispered, worried at the emotion that threatened to well up.

"Please, Oscar, don't." She bit her lip.

Releasing her, he took a step back.

"You're not going in today, Hazel? Are you? Tell me you're not going in." There was an edge to his voice.

But she had to do this. No matter what he said. She just had to.

"I must," she said quietly, examining her palette of eye shadow. Should she accentuate the purple or mask it?

"You can't go into a classroom looking like . . . like . . ." He faltered.

Funny that underneath it all, Oscar was conservative, cared what people thought. Something to do with his Anglo-Saxon heritage, perhaps?

"And you think I'm going to look so very different to the students I try to teach, do you?" she ventured—more bravely now. Taking the job at the Impact School, she knew she was heading for a challenging environment. But sometimes she just felt like an extra on the set of a war movie.

"I really don't get why you're being this stubborn, Hazel." His voice was firm, in control again.

She was beginning to wonder herself. She'd always thought of her stubbornness as a virtue, but it was looking increasingly likely it could as easily be her undoing. Hazel was always loath to admit defeat. She wanted to make things work. To turn things around. But she didn't want to argue again, to push him again. What Oscar wanted was for her to get a publishing job like she'd had before, to work in Manhattan and not trek off into "that ghetto" every day.

"Are you going to answer me?"

His arms still circled her, his breath hot against her neck. There was a tenderness now but underneath she sensed that lurking anger. She was trapped.

"Mom . . . my cell—have you seen it?"

Elliot shuffled into the bedroom, rubbing the sleep from his eyes. Hazel heaved an inward sigh of relief. Oscar was careful never to argue in front of the kids. Defeated now, he let her go and swung around to ruffle his son's pale blond hair, blocking Hazel from Elliot's view—as if he couldn't stomach his child seeing her like this.

"Good morning, sleepy head!" He mussed up Elliot's pageboy hair. But that didn't distract Elliot.

"Holy cow! Mom! What happened?" Elliot was perfectly awake now, eyes darting from Hazel to Oscar, looking for an explanation. Oscar opened his mouth to make an excuse but Hazel was there before him.

"A drunk on the subway," she said quickly, just the way she'd rehearsed. "That's all, Elliot. Looks worse than it feels." She chanced a smile through the lies. A shooting pain seared down her jaw.

Elliot looked at his dad.

"Thought you said the subway was safe. That Bloomberg used to take it every day when he was mayor."

"The subway is safe, son. But I can't guarantee it one hundred percent. It's certainly safer now than when I was a kid."

Elliot's face dropped. His father had told him something that appeared to be untrue. Poor Elliot. He idolized his father and Hazel was always reluctant to say anything to fracture that childhood faith.

"Whoa, Mom!! Look at you. What the hell happened?" Jess had joined them now, showered and uniformed, and, for once, interested in someone other than herself.

"Mom was attacked by some drunk on the subway," Elliot chipped in.

"For real?" Jess assessed the situation. "What did the cops have to say about it?" She flicked her hair. Jess's reaction to the assault seemed detached. Hazel could feel hurt but she knew that Jess was a slow burner. Sympathy would come later.

"No need for the police. I was in the wrong place at the wrong time, Jess. It won't happen again." Hazel had made this promise before, but this time she really meant it. Oscar was fiddling with his electric razor, avoiding her gaze.

"Jeez, Mom, you seem fairly chilled about all of this," said Jess.

"Enough, Jess," said Oscar. "Go see if Celine has put a pancake mix in the fridge and get started on breakfast. We have this under control."

Hazel wasn't chilled. She was in shock. It had been the sheer surprise of it. The force of the blow had stunned her, the depth of anger had left her reeling.

"Go on, then, guys . . ." Oscar shooed the kids out of the bedroom.

He turned to Hazel. "Celine still does that, right? Leave a pancake mix in the fridge?"

"Yeah, she still does that," Hazel answered mechanically.

Celine was their part-time nanny who came in afternoons for the children after school.

"You're determined to go in, then?"

"Please, Oscar . . ." She looked at him, almost pleading.

"Okay, then, Hazel, have it your way, but don't say I didn't warn you."

Riding down the elevator, Hazel tried to avoid looking at her reflection by following the paths of the spidery white veins in the marble floor tiles. As residents from lower floors joined the car, she took out her cell and pretended to read.

"Good morning, Mrs. Harvey, how you doin' today?"

Sidney Du Bois, the doorman, was upbeat as always. Hazel had long since given up on trying to get him to call her by her first name. He too liked to be addressed as plain Du Bois.

"Fine, thank you, Du Bois." She turned her head to the side as if to admire the flower arrangement on the stand. Just four more strides to the door.

"The children just about missed the school bus this morning, Mrs. Harvey. But I shouted at the driver to wait."

"Thank you, Du Bois." She looked at him now.

What could she do? It would have been rude not to.

"My pleasure, Mrs. Harvey," he said slowly, his expression hardly changing.

Du Bois—efficient, polite, and unfailingly discreet. By far the best doorman on the Upper West Side. She exited the air-conditioned lobby and stepped out onto the sidewalk, into the growing heat of the September morning.

She almost wished the season would change in that ridiculously schizophrenic way that summer could become winter overnight in this part of the world. She felt vulnerable in her light cotton blouse and linen pants. She'd have much preferred to hide under layers of coats and hoods, but there were probably weeks of hot, steaming, sticky weather left to go.

As she turned the corner at West Seventy-fifth Street and made her way the few blocks toward the Seventy-second Street subway station, she passed an assortment of smartly dressed office workers, joggers on their way to Riverside Park, and clusters of old ladies harnessed to poodlish-looking dogs on their way to the dog run. She found it hard to imagine herself old and retired in Manhattan, much less in a procession of elderly ladies looking after their pooches. It was convivial, healthy, and had a lot to commend it, but she just couldn't picture herself in that situation.

They'd retire out to Long Island, just like Oscar's parents had done—at least that's what Oscar had always planned. When Jack and Estelle Harvey had moved out to live in their second home in Sag Harbor, Oscar and Hazel had moved into their Riverside Apartment. But all that had changed now. Changed utterly.

As she came to the canopy-covered piles of fruit outside the Fairway market, she stopped and hovered over the oranges and lemons, inhaling their citrus aroma. She often stopped to pick up a bag of fruit for the day, but today she hadn't even managed breakfast. She couldn't imagine having an appetite anytime soon. She waited for the lights at the crosswalk. Across the road, a line of people had started to form outside the Beacon Theatre. A chat show host was performing there tonight. When they'd first moved to Riverside Drive, she and Oscar regularly went to the Beacon or to Lincoln Center, reveling in all the district had to offer. Oscar's sister, Helen, or Celine would stay over with the kids, and in a way it almost felt like a second honeymoon.

As she stood staring trancelike at the DON'T WALK signal, she remembered her first meeting with Oscar, at the opera in Verona. The vast jaws of the arena breathing out the heat of the day, bats and swallows crossing the paths of powerful spotlights. Armies of tourists clambering up and down stone steps. The smell of cooking dough wafting in from pizzerias. The orchestra tuning up. Dignitaries entering the arena on the red carpet. And she remembered a large man panting beside her, his breathing labored, sweating for Italy.

She thought he might easily have a heart attack, collapse, and flatten her. As the corpulent man swayed in the heat, on her other side, a voice said in her ear, "How you doing there?"

She turned around and looked into those eyes for the first time. Such crystal blue. She remembered the squareness of his jaw, his easy charm. His confidence. Oscar had shifted position to make more room for her. He called a nearby attendant and bought two fans and two red cushions. One each. The stone steps were far too uncomfortable, he said, she'd never last, she had to trust him. And she had.

"Move it, lady!"

She hadn't noticed the signal change. Gathering her thoughts, she walked across briskly and made her way down the subway station at Verdi Square. The train pulled up just as she made it to the platform. She was thankful that there had been only one flight of stairs, unlike the tube from her London days, when descending countless assortments of stairs and elevators into the bowels of the earth made her feel claustrophobic.

All the seats in the car were taken. As she raised her arm to reach for the pole, an elderly man made as if to offer up his seat. She nodded her head to signal that she was fine. Good Lord! How distressed must she look for an old man to offer up his seat? Suddenly, it felt as if everyone in the car were staring at her. Rather than gawk at her reflection in the darkened window, she concentrated on a tiny pebble that rolled around on the grimy floor, breathing through her mouth and trying to ignore the smells of sweat and feet.

Six stops later, the seat next to her was vacated and she shimmied in next to a bald man in a tie and short sleeves. He was reading the *Wall Street Journal*. As he scrolled through the pages on his tablet, a flashing ad caught her eye—a Discover Ireland tourist ad. She smiled. The collage of images might have been updated but it was the selfsame palette of photos over the decades—dusted off and recycled to show green fields, smiling faces, sheer cliff faces, and the ubiquitous pints of Guinness. "Come to Ireland for the craic," it invited. No mention, of course, of the empty coffers or the IMF being in town.

As the train swayed and shuddered, she shut her eyes, allowing the briefly glimpsed electronic images to take her on a journey back to Ireland. It was fifteen years since she'd left, not long after her mother's funeral, her sense of family blown away, disintegrated. She felt as fragile now as she did then. She remembered walking down that pathway from the house on O'Callaghan Strand, realizing that she was an orphan. The river was full that day, threatening to break its banks. She remembered getting into the taxi and looking over her shoulder one last time at the FOR SALE sign staked at the entrance. She had closed the door on one life and entered another.

"Stand back, sir! I am asking you one more time to stand back. You there . . . get in line!"

A zealous police officer was barking at the straggling line of students.

"Face furniture off," the squat officer shouted at Sabrina King. Nonplussed, Sabrina King stared straight ahead and tossed her outsize earrings into the plastic tray next to the metal detector. The plastic tray was already brimming with an assortment of potential classroom weaponry.

Behind Sabrina was Beatrice Obande, earnest and compliant. Hazel admired Beatrice for withstanding the aggravation she had to put up with. Hazel seethed with the deep unfairness of it all. Her own kids were attending a private, well-run, safe school. Beatrice wanted to learn, to better herself. She didn't want to end up in a penitentiary like her brothers. And this is how she got her education, going through a metal detector every day, treated like a criminal. There was no doubt about it. The regime at this Impact School was harsh, the penalties severe. Three strikes and you were out.

As Hazel hurried past the metal detector, flashing her ID badge, the police officer gave her more than a cursory glance. Jay Mahoney stared at her as he lumbered past. Hazel's pulse began to quicken. He stared at her in that sneering way he had, flint-eyed and fearless. She quickly ran through her timetable again in her head. She had Jay second period after lunch.

"Your old man keeping you in line, then, Miss Harvey?" taunted Gumbo Hernandez as he passed her on the stairs.

Oh, no!

How was she going to get through this day?

And yet Hazel had to remember why she did this. Why she taught in this school. Sure, she'd steadfastly ignored all the advice she'd received. But she had to have faith in herself, in her convictions. Gripping the handrail and taking the stairs more purposefully, she told herself again why she did it. For the kids like Beatrice Obande. And the kids like Tyler Black and Shauna Doherty, two more students she liked to think of as her protégées.

At first, Hazel delighted in the degree of latitude she'd been given with her lesson plans. But her early attempts had failed. *The Great Gatsby* was a total failure. She'd been naïve. What possible resonance could these students have with a version of ancient society that was all white, college educated, and swanned about in mansions? She'd tried Shakespeare, *The Merchant of Venice*. Would the notion of a money lender wanting a pound of flesh strike a chord with them? "Man, they sure spoke like faggots back in the day" was the response she got. Next they did *The Pearl* by Steinbeck. Surely these kids would identify with Kino, the poor fisherman struggling to pay the town doctor when his son is stung by a scorpion. What would they make of the greed and violence aroused in the locals when they discover the value of the pearl that Kino has found? Would they see parallels in their own lives? But her twelfth graders were not impressed. Her paraphrasing of the story engaged them only in spurts and starts, but in the main it proved a crusade against apathy. And in the end, the mistaken killing of Kino's child left them confused and deflated.

"What the fuck . . . ?" Danny Santiago had looked over his shoulder at Jay Mahoney. "Kino's child gets iced and that's it? He throws the pearl into the sea and it's over?"

"Miss Harvey, gotta tell ya, that ending sucks." Jay had thrown it out there in a challenge.

"Okay, Jay—the ending sucks. That's your opinion."

"Yes, Mizz Harvey. That is my *considered* opinion."

A titter had rippled through the classroom. Jay had stared, daring her to challenge him, yet knowing his hands were tied. Jay was in perilous territory. He already had two strikes for unacceptable behavior. One more and he was out. He'd leaned back in his chair, opening his legs wide with sexual aggression. Hazel had let it go, trying to defuse the tension that had slithered into the room.

All morning, Hazel kept it together, ignoring the knowing looks about her face. Ignoring comments about her old man keeping her in line, ignoring the cell vibrating through the sticking linen of her pants. She was a professional, she told herself. Yet every now and then her heart would race—reminding her that she was human after all.

By the time the afternoon came around, Hazel was beginning to think she just might cope. But she still couldn't look at her cell. *Oscar was checking up on her.* No longer angry. Just a concerned husband now. She'd taken two more anti-inflammatories and was feeling groggy. She just might be able to get through this. It was the class she'd been dreading. Second period after lunch. The twelfth grade. Her most challenging class.

Jay Mahoney sat six rows back, sullen, cradling some perceived grievance as usual, his spiky hair an outward display of his overall prickliness. As he muttered and bit his nails, she tried to ignore him. Blank him out. She didn't want any trouble.

"Have any of you suffered racial discrimination?" Hazel read from the script. Before she'd even finished the question, she realized her mistake.

"Seriously, Miss Harvey?" came one response.

"Is a frog's ass watertight?" asked another.

"I guess we don't need to debate that point," she conceded. "Okay, let's imagine that you had to go on trial for a crime you did not commit . . ."

From the corner of her eye she saw Jay Mahoney straightening up.

"Like a GBH or rape, Miss Harvey? Is that what you mean?" He dusted off his combat pants and stared at her, his eyes boring a hole right through her.

"For any crime, I'm not being specific here . . ." she addressed the class at large.

"Well, Miss Harvey, we know all 'bout that round here," interrupted Tyler Black, nodding vigorously. "Someone gets carjacked or mugged and the Five-O are straight on our asses like flies on shit."

It ended up being a long, drawn-out, tetchy class. Hazel had no idea how she managed to get through it and she was glad when it was over. She was also glad it was Wednesday, the day she usually met her friend Elizabeth, if Elizabeth was free.

"Oh my God, Hazel!" Elizabeth whispered in shock as Hazel sat down to join her in the diner.

"Gee, thanks, Elizabeth. It's not like I don't feel bad enough already," Hazel muttered.

"Honey, I'm so sorry, it's just that . . . Oh, Hazel, this just isn't right."

They usually met in the diner on the corner of Broadway and West Seventy-fifth or in the coffee shop with squashy sofas on Amsterdam. Today it was the diner. It was busy with the din of jabbering tourists and locals, the sound of food being prepared, and loud orders being exchanged.

"This does not look good at all." Elizabeth sat down and leaned over to move Hazel's fringe aside to better examine the damage. "Your eye? Is that eye okay?"

"It looks worse than it feels, believe me."

Elizabeth was her longest-serving friend in New York. Hazel had met her when they were both doing an internship with Reuters. Even though their paths had split, they'd always managed to stay in touch.

"You could have a detached retina. You think of that? I'm assuming you've had it checked?"

Elizabeth scrutinized her and sighed. "Hazel, you haven't had it checked?" She paused, sliding her heavy black-rimmed glasses back up her nose. "Oh, honey, I just don't know what to say. Really, I don't."

It wasn't often that Elizabeth was lost for words, and seeing her so made Hazel feel worse. Hazel was struggling to contain the feelings that washed over her. She stared out the window at a crew unloading sets for the theater next door while Elizabeth placed her order.

"Not that there's any excuse, but what exactly sparked it off?" Elizabeth asked gently.

"Oh, Elizabeth, do these things ever need to be about anything?" Hazel shrugged. "Some slight or other . . ."

Combined with the shock, it angered her that they should even try to find a logic to rationalize such behavior. Elizabeth leaned back in her chair as the waitress set down the strawberry pancakes.

"Thanks, Anita," Elizabeth said, smiling.

"You ladies okay for everything now?" replied the waitress.

"Yes, thank you, Anita," Hazel said, nodding. The waitress tried her best not to stare at the bruise again. But in her effort to ignore it, she made her curiosity all the more obvious. No doubt she'd liaise with Du Bois later. Anita was Du Bois's sister.

"Anita makes me feel like one of the clients in the soup kitchen," remarked Hazel.

"I assume you're not volunteering tonight?" said Elizabeth. "I know you want to go to school but you can skip the soup run, right?"

"Yeah . . ."

Hazel ran a finger lightly over the crusted gash on her forehead. She felt each knobbly granule along its path. She'd already decided to give the soup kitchen a miss. She didn't want to give Oscar another excuse to get worked up.

Elizabeth was cutting the strawberries into tiny pieces and wrapping each piece into a pancake fold. Hazel sipped at her Americano.

"Look, hon, I've been tossing and turning about this ever since you called me last night. There's nothing else for it. You're going to have to go to the authorities." Elizabeth dabbed a dribble of cream at the corner of her mouth.

"I think you're wrong, Elizabeth."

Elizabeth stared at her hard now.

"Hazel, are you saying you're not going to report this?"

"No." She paused. "I know you don't agree, but I've given it a lot of thought as well, and I think it would only make things worse."

"Hazel, hon, you're making a big mistake. The only thing that's going to make this worse is not reporting it. This has to be stopped. He's going to think he can keep on doing it. And what happens next time?"

"There won't be a next time." The strong coffee was kicking in now. She should really have had a decaf.

"Oh, Hazel, how can you be so sure?" Elizabeth wasn't going to let it go.

The truth was she couldn't. But she'd think of something. She always did. She was competent. Resourceful.

"Jess and Elliot? They shouldn't have to see you like this. What did you tell them?"

"That I was attacked by a drunk on the subway."

Elizabeth shook her head.

"And Oscar?" she said eventually. "He was happy to send you in to work like that?"

Hazel didn't answer straight away.

"No. No, he wasn't. In fact, he wasn't happy about me going in at all."

"I'll bet he wasn't," spat Elizabeth. "Damned sure, I'll bet he wasn't."

Hazel gritted her teeth, desperately trying to stay in command of the tears that wanted to come.

"I can't show him how upset I am." Her voice came out all quavery and sticking in her throat.

Elizabeth looked at her. Stern. Somber faced.

"And how is Oscar now?" She twisted the paper napkin into an ever tighter screw.

"Worried," answered Hazel. "Not mad anymore. Just worried, you know."

"Worried . . ." repeated Elizabeth. "Worried," she said again, and this time Hazel could see the curl of her lip.

Usually, she appreciated Elizabeth's advice, her forthright nature, but today she just wanted her to listen, not to scrabble about for a solution. Hazel would find one in her own time. She stretched her arms behind her head, lifting the weight of her hair to cool the back of her neck. The dead heat and stickiness of the day were oppressive. The air-conditioning in the diner needed to be turned up.

"Okay, then." Elizabeth pursed her lips. "If you're not going to the authorities, I think you should at least go to counseling."

Hazel fidgeted with her rings, twisting her large solitaire diamond round and round.

"Maybe. We'll see . . . yeah, I'll think about it."

"Good." Elizabeth squeezed out a small smile.

"And now tell me, how's the man in *your* life?" Hazel asked, tired of being the focus of the conversation.

"He's doing just great, thanks. Way busier since he became VP." A genuine smile this time.

"I've got to hand it to you, Elizabeth—you lucked out there. Zack is one of the good guys."

Mouth full, Elizabeth nodded her agreement.

Hazel steered the conversation away from herself by inquiring about Zack's publishing company and what was happening with the big conglomerates. As she spoke, little thought bubbles were floating about her head. Much as it pained her to admit it, perhaps Oscar was right. Maybe she should have stayed in that world, but it was all a bit late for regrets now. She'd burned her bridges there.

"You're looking good, Elizabeth. Toned."

The capped sleeve of Elizabeth's printed jersey dress showed lithe arms that had seen a workout.

"Still hangin' in there. Still going to the dance studio. I miss the fun we had." She looked up from her pancake. "You didn't need to leave, you know."

"Let's not go there, Elizabeth," Hazel said with a grimace. "Ancient history."

"I'm only saying . . ."

"Well, don't."

For the remainder of the conversation, they chatted about Zack and Elizabeth's new apartment on the Upper East Side, steering away from anything contentious.

"Yours?" asked Elizabeth, as they got up to leave.

She'd spotted something on the floor between Hazel's chair and the booth behind.

"Good Lord, how did that get there?" Hazel could have sworn she'd put the journal back in her bag before Elizabeth had arrived. Elizabeth was bending down to pick up the leather-bound book with its gold lettering.

"Still keeping a journal after all these years?" Elizabeth looked amused.

"Therapy, Elizabeth. Therapy after a crazy day up at the zoo. It helps me unwind."

"Well, anything that does that has got to be good, right? You really need to look after yourself, Hazel. And, please, please, think about all that I've said." Elizabeth handed her the journal and leaned over to kiss her on the cheek.

"See you ladies Friday?"

Anita knew their routine by now. Other staff had come and gone but Anita had worked in the diner for as long as they'd been meeting there.

"Friday." Hazel smiled, hoping to God the bruising would at least be easier to camouflage by then.

Walking home, she was assailed by the stench of rotting garbage but also by a sense of dread. She walked past the secondhand record store that was one of Oscar's favorite weekend haunts. And suddenly, she doubled back. She'd had an idea.

"Bob Dylan?" she asked the wilting assistant, who was fanning himself with a faded Coltrane sleeve.

"Follow me," he said, perking up and shuffling over the uneven carpet-tiled floor to the back of the room.

"Down there." He pointed to the bottom shelf. "You'll find some Dylan down there."

She wasn't crazy about Dylan herself but Oscar was a big fan.

"Nasty bruise you have," remarked the assistant, handing over her change.

"Shit happens, I'll survive," she said blithely, and closed the jangling door behind her.

The vinyl cover felt dusty and clung to the perspiration on her palms. But Oscar would be happy with her choice. He used his iPod for jogging in the park or in the gym. But in the evening, he liked to open the French windows, sit on the balcony, listen to vinyl, and sip a California white while watching the sun go down on the Hudson.

She knew she shouldn't pander to Oscar. If anyone should be buying gifts around here, it should be him. He was the one who should be buying her flowers. But she was stubborn. She wasn't going to give up so easily.

Anything to smooth the waters.

Oscar

He was concentrating now. Focused. This was the tricky part. The acrid caustic smell pervaded the room. Even though it was a sizable room—he'd gone for the best he could afford—the smell inhabited every corner.

He moved closer, seeing that flicker of fear in her eyes. He smiled, trying to reassure her. But of course she couldn't see it, he was hidden behind the mask. Carefully, he chose a different burr—smaller, sharper. The woman said nothing as he made adjustments. She lay there, prone, captive, vulnerable. Her fingers drummed the hand rests. He didn't know if she was usually a talkative woman or if the earlier chatter had been to hide the fear. Whatever the truth of it, she couldn't say anything now. She could only blink as he did the talking.

She'd told him she was a runner. So he spoke about his new route through the park. How he'd thought about training for the marathon but had left it too late for this year. He told her how he'd enjoyed swimming on Long Island during the summer but that they'd returned home early with warnings of a hurricane.

The vein in her neck was pulsing and he could feel her breath hot on his latex glove. In any other setting it could have been an intimate encounter. Not here. There were three of them in the room now.

"More composite?" asked Dana.

"Thank you." He reached over.

Dana was efficient, took the job seriously, and rarely spoke unless it was entirely necessary. She never joked and never saw the humor in anything. Before, Oscar and Susan found it fun to see who could prize a smile from Dana but this fruitless game fell to Oscar alone since Susan's departure.

"Curing light?" Dana asked a few moments later.

"Yes, yes." He shouldn't snap. Behind the mask, he gritted his teeth. It was her job to anticipate but he found the woman irritating.

His patient's eyes flashed between him and Dana. He winked as if to let her in on a joke. Dana was getting under his skin. She was the outsider in the room. But if he was honest, he knew what was really pissing him off. He needed sugar. At this point in the afternoon, he always craved it. Like he could devour a Hershey's bar in one single bite, and then another, and another. Instead, he'd send Dana out for a linseed snack bar and a fat-free latte. He couldn't afford to feel bunged up. He was meeting Harry later.

"There was a lot of decay?"

The woman looked at him, wide-eyed and relieved. He depressed the chair lever and slowly brought her into an upright position.

"It was in pretty bad shape, for sure." Oscar pulled down his mask, allowing the woman to see him properly.

"But don't worry. I've fixed it. That composite will last you a lifetime. Some dentists do a quick fix. Their fillings look good for a while, but a few years down the line they need to be replaced. I, on the other hand, stand behind my work—I'm confident you won't have any more problems with that tooth."

"That's good to hear." She edged out of the chair and onto her feet. "But just in case, I think I'll go easy on the Twizzlers from now on!"

"Really? You don't look like a woman who splurges on candy . . ." Oscar towered over his petite patient.

"Would you like to settle up at reception, Miss Housemann?" Dana shot him a look colder than a witch's tit.

Shit. He should be more careful. He was still learning. He hadn't meant anything by it. But Dana knew how to keep him in line.

With the room to himself, Oscar became aware that his shoulders and neck were tight now. He stretched an arm behind his neck, pulling back an elbow with his other arm. His triceps felt tight. He repeated the stretch on the other side.

With the door to reception ajar, he watched as Dana took the patient's insurance details, her heavy bosom resting on the counter.

"The other dentist gone?" asked his pretty patient.

"There's no other dentist here, Miss Housemann."

"Oh . . . but the last time I was here—a couple of years ago, I think, there was a female dentist—a tall, striking lady."

"I don't know anything about that, Miss Housemann. Before my time."

"Oh, I see . . ." The woman handed Dana a plastic card.

"You're new here, then?"

Jesus, the woman was a talker. It wasn't just the nerves.

"Not exactly. Been here two years."

Oscar smiled. The old battle-ax was getting tired of the questions herself. She wasn't a warm woman and he'd be up the Swanee if he was relying on her to generate any new custom. It was just as well he had a solid network of his own.

"That must explain it," said Miss Housemann.

Oscar twisted from side to side, loosening out his back.

"You want to look at our revised insurance plan?" he heard Dana ask.

She might not have been warm but at least she was good on the business side.

"Sure." The woman took the leaflet. "So, that female dentist? She moved to another practice?"

Oscar straightened sharply from his sideways stretch.

"Ma'am, she could have gone on the last Apollo mission for all I know. It's just me, Mr. Harvey, and the hygienist."

"Oh, I'm sorry . . . I didn't mean to . . . Thank you, thank you very much," said his patient, embarrassed, fastening her purse in a hurry.

Oscar was gripped by unease. As he stood at the window watching the woman emerge into the busy street below, he wondered if she could be a journalist. A private investigator, even?

Dana poked her head around the door.

"An extraction in another twenty minutes, Mr. Harvey."

"Okay, Dana. Thank you. Oh, and Dana, could you step out and get me the usual?"

Dana looked at her watch, settled in the folds of her wrist. "I think I have time for that, Mr. Harvey." And off she waddled, leaving him a few minutes' respite, alone in the office.

With Dana gone, he went to the computer on her desk. This is dumb, he told himself. I'm being overcautious. Yet, he held his breath as he called up the patient profile from the patient database. Ah, yes—there she was, Rachel Housemann. There was nothing out of the ordinary in her profile. Dana had listed her profession as archive assistant. He googled her. Leaning over the desk, he let out a long sigh when he saw her listed on LinkedIn. She was indeed who she said she was. An archive assistant at the MoMA.

Of course he'd overreacted. It had been an innocent conversation, after all. Sure, long-standing patients were going to inquire about former staff. It was to be expected. Still, he couldn't help but feel relieved.

Looking at the grandfather clock, he noticed that Dana was taking longer than usual. Was she gorging on a secret pastry? He'd caught her in the Lebanese deli before, hiding a slab of baklava in her purse.

He sat back in Dana's office chair and looked around the room. It was a pleasant work environment. Hazel had helped him decorate the reception area, choosing the elegant clock, the impressive sideboard with its neat piles of periodicals and glossy magazines, and the collection of Queen Anne armchairs. They'd had fun on those weekends, sourcing the furniture, antiquing upstate and staying in romantic inns. Hazel had been a lot more relaxed then.

Going to the coat stand, he checked his cell. Two missed calls from Hazel. He shook his head. There was no point in returning the calls, she'd be in class. It was a week now since the incident. He didn't like to think about it, but he knew he should. She was taking longer to recover this time.

His neck muscles were tensing up again. It wasn't Hazel's fault and he knew he shouldn't get mad, but Goddamn it, the woman was stubborn. Just like Birgitte. Birgitte had also found it hard to listen, to take any advice. There had been arguments as well with Birgitte.

"Lordy! But it's hot out there . . ."

Dana burst through the door bearing a cardboard tray with two polystyrene cups. There were damp patches under the arms of her tunic and Oscar was sure he could spot some sugary powder in the hairs around her mouth.

"A quick sprint round Central Park?" he inquired, barely masking a shiver of distaste.

"A simple thank-you would do nicely, Mr. Harvey," she said sharply, laying the tray on the reception desk with puffy hands.

"Of course, Dana. Thank you." He forced himself to smile.

God, it was a horrible thought, but sometimes she reminded him of his sister.

"What did the dentist say to the golfer?"

Harry was panting heavily now, even though it was cooler down by the river. A film of sweat shone on his bald patch. They were headed south on the greenway bike path.

"Dunno. What *did* the dentist say to the golfer?"

Oscar was loosening up. Getting into his stride.

"You got a hole in one!"

Harry Becker loved his own jokes. Oscar imagined him cooking them up, sitting at his large oak desk with its enviable view of Madison Avenue and the Midtown Manhattan skyline.

"Did you hear about the Buddhist who refused novocaine during a root canal?"

"I guess I'm about to . . ."

"He wanted to transcend dental medication!"

"Fuck, your jokes suck, Harry!"

"Okay, a failure to amuse—I beg your pardon, at White and Calhoun we aim to please . . ."

White and Calhoun was Harry's law firm. It specialized in bank fraud.

A curvy jogger bounced her way along the path toward them. Harry's breathing was already raspy, his short legs thudding loudly on the pathway.

"Incoming, incoming . . ."

"Easy, Harry, heel, boy," Oscar said.

Although, if he were honest and he were the one married to Nancy, he might well get excited about shapely women. It wasn't that Nancy wasn't a pleasant woman but she was a bit on the plain side for Oscar.

"You're a bit wound up this evening, my friend. Bad day at work? Or just the same-shit-different-day kinda stuff?"

Harry had stopped on the pretext of relacing his trainer. He was finding it hard to keep up with Oscar, who was in better shape.

"I've no reason to complain in particular. Just feeling a bit beige . . ." Oscar shook the droplets of sweat from his brow.

"How are the financials going?" Harry pulsed forward and backward, resting one leg on the railing and stretching out the hamstring of his stubby leg. "I know the business took a big hit."

"Making progress, I guess. It's slow. She took me to the cleaners, you know. It's coming up on two years now. We're not back in the black yet. It's gonna take time."

"Man, that bitch really stitched you up."

"You can say that again."

"Man, that bitch really stitched you up!"

"Get lost, Harry." Oscar laughed and continued to jog on the spot.

"You're right, though," said Oscar as they took off again. "When I think about that crap she pulled, my reputation, I'd never have worked again. Could have been a whole different ball game, for sure. Except for you, my man." He clapped Harry on his sweaty back.

"Hey, what are buddies for? Told you Donovan was one kick-ass attorney. That guy could make Silvio Berlusconi look like a saint. Easy."

Harry wiped his brow with the sweatband on his wrist.

"And if I say it once, I'll say it again—with a case like yours, it's always better to settle out of court. Too much collateral damage otherwise."

It took another twenty minutes to complete their loop, during which time Harry gave him the outline of some young gun he was defending who had worked on Wall Street. Harry loved the cut and thrust of white-collar crime. It was safer than the criminal stuff. And the rewards were infinitely greater.

"Squash on Thursday?" Harry looked like a round red rosy apple now.

"Yeah, should be able to make that. I've missed the last two weeks."

They were nearing the entrance to the Seventy-second Street dog run.

"You're sliding down the ladder, my friend. Pelmann's taken your place."

"You're kidding me . . ."

But Oscar wasn't really listening. He was staring at a bench in the dog park. Was that Hazel? Was it really her? What was she doing sitting in the dog park? They didn't even have a dog. The woman's head was bowed, reading a book. She wore a blue shift dress and had the same slender, petite frame as his wife.

"Pelmann will be delighted to have passed you out."

"What? Oh, yeah, I'm sure he is."

They jogged past the park, with Oscar looking over his shoulder every now and then, trying to catch another glimpse. No, he decided. The woman in the blue dress couldn't have been Hazel. Today was her day for staying late at school.

"So, Pelmann's leapfrogged me, has he?" Oscar eventually responded. "We'll have to see about that!"

"Yeah. Didn't think that would wash well with you."

Pelmann was an anesthetist over at Weill Cornell, and even though they were all friends, all Columbia alumni, there was nothing

Harry liked more than to stir up a little competition between them all. That was fine with Oscar. He'd knock the spots off Pelmann.

"And Hazel?" asked Harry.

"What about Hazel?"

"Just wondering how she was—that's all."

They had finished their run and were doing cooldown stretches. Kids on skateboards were whizzing past.

"She's good." Oscar hesitated. "Yeah, Hazel's good."

"Something up, buddy?"

"Nothing's up exactly. Just every so often Hazel gets an idea in her head, you know how it is. Sometimes she just doesn't know when to let go."

"Man, tell me about it. Nancy's on about both of us joining a salsa class. Doing more stuff together. Although, I hear there are some pretty hot women at those classes. Maybe . . ." He grinned lewdly.

"Jesus, Becker, you really do think with your dick!"

"That's harsh. A bit harsh, buddy," Harry said, feigning offense. "But hey, tell me, Oscar. What's eating Hazel?"

"It's no big deal. She's just a bit unsettled at the moment, that's all. Happens every so often. She's talking a lot about going back to Ireland."

"Ah, the lure of the old country." Harry sagely rubbed his chin. "But she doesn't have anyone there anymore, right? Her folks have passed—there's no one left?"

"Not really, there may be an elderly aunt here or there, but no blood relatives. I guess that can happen when you're adopted. Hazel has this bee in her bonnet, for sure. Maybe we should go . . . the kids have never been. And I guess they should know their roots, right? Hell! I've never been either. But I've never really had any reason to go."

"Why don't you guys come over on the weekend, Saturday night? We can talk about it then. Nancy is always asking after Hazel. We'll have some pasta and I have some of that really good California white that you like. What do you say?"

"Sounds good to me, Harry. But let me check Hazel's schedule first." He wasn't sure if Hazel would buy it. "Maybe we can get Helen to sit the kids," he added, as if he were giving it serious consideration.

"Good. Good." Harry seemed happy with this. "How is Helen these days?"

"Oh, you know, larger than life." The "large" part was true. "Still single."

"Aaah!" said Harry. "I love the smell of sibling rivalry in the evening."

Oscar grimaced. He wasn't going to rise to the bait this time. "She's a good aunt to the kids."

"She has a big heart," added Harry, with a glint in his eye.

"Yeah, *big* being the operative word."

"See you Thursday, then. And don't forget to run the weekend by Hazel. You can let me know Thursday."

"Will do. Oh, by the way—this guy you're defending, the one accused of rogue trading. You never said. You think he did it?"

Oscar knew that Harry trusted him. They'd kept many secrets over the years.

"Hell, yeah, buddy! I've never defended an innocent man yet. Why else would he have hired me?"

According to Oscar's Rolex, it was ten to eight when he entered the lobby of their apartment building. It had taken him longer than he thought to collect his BMW from its service at the garage. He got it serviced at this time every year, in preparation for the winter. But most of the time it stayed in the underground parking lot. The subway system was efficient and, contrary to the story Hazel told the kids, largely safe.

"Evening, Mr. Harvey."

Du Bois was behind his desk catching a game on his portable TV. Maybe it was Oscar's imagination but he thought the doorman had been a little cool with him lately.

"And a very good evening to you too, Du Bois."

"Me and Mrs. Du Bois really enjoyed the show."

"The show . . . ?"

What was the man talking about?

"The tickets you and Mrs. Harvey gave me for my birthday. Much appreciated, sir."

"Eh, no. No, not at all, Du Bois. You're welcome."

"Thank *you*, sir."

Hazel was such a soft touch! How long had she been giving Du Bois gifts to celebrate his birthday?

There was no doubt about it. The man had a soft spot for Hazel, for sure. A middle-aged crush. He didn't know why this should annoy him. Du Bois was only a doorman, after all. But annoy him it did. And he could have sworn the man had been wearing one of his Lacoste shirts the other day. The pink one that Oscar used to like. He'd searched high and low for it but couldn't find it.

Exiting the elevator, he made his way down the corridor and turned the key in the heavy oak door. He entered the large black-and-white-tiled hallway and put his training bag on the floor. It was silent. The apartment was in darkness. No sounds of happy domesticity. No whirring appliances, no entertainment consoles, no TVs. No kids arguing. Just silence.

"Hazel?" he called.

Where was everyone? He'd tried to call her earlier but the call was routed straight through to voice mail.

"Elliot?"

Elliot's room was empty.

"Jess?"

She could be draped over her bed ingesting One Direction on her iPod.

But no. And there was no one in the kitchen or the living room. Where had Hazel gone? And then it occurred to him, Tuesday night was her dance class. But that still didn't explain where the kids were.

An unwelcome thought entered his head. A horrible thought. A thought he tried to squeeze and squash. Too late. The thought had stung him. The sting now burrowing away inside him. *She hadn't, had she?* The very suggestion of it froze him to the spot. The last few weeks had been quite fraught, more challenging than he was used to. He'd underestimated her. He used to be able to talk her around.

Paralyzed now, his mind raced, chasing ideas and possibilities. He thought back to this morning, to breakfast, the passing conversation, and his usual hasty departure from the house. No, there was nothing different. It had been their regular morning routine.

Stricken by his horrible thought, he stood in the darkening living room staring at the sun dissolving over the Hudson. He needed to calm down. Not overreact. He would approach this methodically and think it through. As he talked himself down, he became aware of a sound other than the rhythmic thud of his heartbeat in his ears. The steady drone of the air-conditioning. *She'd left it on.* That could mean only one thing—that she'd stepped out only for a while.

Hazel would never needlessly leave the air-conditioning running. Never needlessly waste electricity. No, his wife was a regular little do-gooder. Always looking out for the environment, the disenfranchised, the needy. Only Hazel wasn't always best qualified at discerning the needy. Not at all. Oscar all too often felt overlooked himself, while his wife ended up looking after the scumbags.

He tried her cell again, but ended up at voice mail like before. Not to worry. They'd be back soon. He decided to wait one more hour before escalating matters. Happy with his decision, Oscar went to the fridge to see if Celine had left him anything. On the top shelf he spied what looked like a chicken salad, tightly covered in plastic wrap.

Sitting at the breakfast counter, chomping on the mango and chicken, he wondered again if he'd missed something. Was there some event he was supposed to be at? He really had no idea. He looked at his watch again. Another twenty minutes had passed.

What the heck! He'd make the most of it. He didn't often have the apartment to himself. Taking the plate, Oscar went back to the living room and opened the balcony doors. Placing his plate on the wicker table, he covered it with a magazine and retreated indoors once more. Crouching down on his haunches, Oscar thumbed through the covers. They were in alphabetical order so it should be about here . . . There it was. Sliding it gently from its faded sleeve, he blew on the shiny shellac, sending dust motes sailing into the air. Then Oscar placed the record carefully on the turntable and lifted the stylus to track three.

At the first strains of "Visions of Johanna," he felt a wave of tenderness wash over him. Hazel could be such a thoughtful woman. And she certainly knew the buttons to press. He'd been lusting after this one for a while. *Blonde on Blonde*. And she'd even managed the original release—on Columbia. It was just a pity how the gift had come about. But what was done was done. Turning the dial, he cranked it up and went out to the balcony to finish off his evening meal.

"Oh my God, it sounds like an old folks' home in here!"

They were back!

Jess was holding a can of Dr Pepper. Diet Dr Pepper, he was glad to see.

"Hey, young lady, this is a damn sight better than One Direction or Justin Bieber."

"Oh, Dad. Pleeease . . . Justin Bieber? I'm way too old."

Even though she was only just twelve, Jess thought she was way too old for plenty of stuff.

"Hey, where were you guys? I've been here all on my lonesome . . ."

He walked in from the balcony carrying his empty plate and a half-full glass of wine when Hazel appeared in the doorway between the kitchen and living room. She wore a loose-fitting long white linen coat. Her face was made up—you could hardly see the marks. She looked nice. She also looked serious.

"Where were *we*?" she repeated. "Where were *you*?"

That uneasy feeling again. He had a feeling he was going to come out of this badly.

"I was here. Well, before that I went to collect the car, remember? I tried to phone you. Your cell was off."

Elliot wandered into the room, clutching what looked like a family-sized bag of potato chips.

"We were over at the school. The parent-teacher meetings, *remember*?"

Oh, shit.

"Why didn't you remind me?"

Three pairs of eyes were staring at him now. One in annoyance and the other two indignant.

"I did remind you, Oscar. Twice last night, I asked you to sit with the kids and I would do the meetings. I also called your cell today."

"Sorry."

"Okay," Hazel said softly.

"Guys, I'm really, really sorry." He looked from Jess to Elliot.

"Like it's not bad enough that we're in there all day. Elliot and I had to hang around in the recreation room for two and a half hours."

He wasn't going to get off that easy.

"Yeah," said Elliot, mouth bulging with potato chips, "felt like we were never going to get out—like an episode of *Orange Is the New Black.*"

"*Orange Is the New Black*? When the hell have you seen *Orange Is the New Black*?"

What was going on with his kids? The last he knew, Elliot was into *Harry Potter.* Where had the kid seen something as gritty as *Orange Is the New Black*?

Elliot already realized his mistake. His cheeks were crimson. Elliot was now the one in the dock.

"Luke's dad has the DVDs. We were only looking at the covers."

Luke was one of his buddies from school, that much Oscar knew.

"You should be very proud of your children, Oscar. Glowing reports for both of them!" Hazel was trying to deflect. To steer attention away from Elliot.

Oscar was prepared to be deflected.

"I'd expect nothing less," he said, and wrapped an arm around each child.

"Dad . . ." Jess wriggled to get away.

Hazel stood there smiling, eyes warm, looking at the three of them. The thoughts that had run through his head earlier now seemed ridiculous, stupid, even. He was seeing things that weren't there. First of all, thinking he'd seen her in the dog run. And then, thinking that she had . . . Well, all kinds of dumb stuff.

"So you missed your dance class tonight?" he shouted after her as she walked through to the kitchen.

She was filling the kettle.

"That's tomorrow. Decaf?" She pushed down the button and powered on the kettle.

"No, thanks." He held up his glass, showing his unfinished wine. "Thought your class was Tuesdays."

Reaching high for a mug, she turned around to face him.

"No, it's Wednesdays on Broadway." She cocked her head to one side. "The class I used to go to with Elizabeth was Tuesdays. Before I had to change."

"Sorry," he mumbled. "I forgot. The class with Elizabeth and . . ."

"Susan." She finished the sentence for him.

"I met Harry after work today," he said, moving the conversation on quickly.

"Still skinning the fat cats?"

"Yep. Nancy has been asking after you."

"That poor woman."

"We're invited over there Saturday. Said I'd check with you first."

"Christ, Oscar!" Hazel stopped stirring her coffee.

"What?" He tried to look innocent.

"Oh, come on. You know my feelings for Nancy and Harry. I can't sit there playing happy couples, knowing that the guy can't keep it in his zipper."

He knew he never should have told her about their last guys' weekend away. That had been a mistake.

"Come out to the balcony with me?" The kids were in the den and he needed to figure out what was going on with Hazel. She'd been acting strange ever since it happened. He wanted to know if they were okay.

"Just a minute."

Hazel kicked off her heels and started to undo the buttons of her coat. Oscar stared, surprised at first and then confused. Underneath she wore a blue shift dress.

"Why are you looking at me like that?" She took a step back.

"I saw a woman in the park earlier. Sitting on a bench in the dog run. I could have sworn it was you."

Suddenly Hazel started to shake, her eyes filling with tears.

"Hazel, what is it?"

She shook her head.

"Come on, tell me, honey . . ."

She flinched as he reached out to her.

"I . . . I haven't been feeling very well."

He watched the tears roll down her face. In her bare feet, she appeared even smaller. This time, she let him take her in his arms.

"I know, honey. I know. But we can work through this."

"I'm not sure, Oscar. I'm not sure this time. I've been on leave from school since yesterday." She looked up at him, eyes red, mascara running.

So it had been Hazel in the park after all. He hadn't imagined it.

"Is there anything that I can do? Anything at all?" His little sparrow was wounded.

"Really?"

She looked so vulnerable.

"Really." He took her in his arms again, enjoying the feel of her against his chest. He felt powerful, manly.

"I'm serious about going home, Oscar," she said in a small voice. "I want to go home to Ireland."

Kate

"Only nine more days, seven hours, and thirty minutes to go!"
Fergus had crossed off each day in alternate colors until the month of October now looked like a green and purple checkerboard. Brandishing a chubby crayon, he twirled round from the notice board next to the fridge. His pale face was animated and his blond curls were gelled up in spikes.

"That's right, Soldier—only nine more days to liftoff."

Mannix suctioned a strand of spaghetti, splattering tomato sauce onto his chin as it whiplashed into his mouth.

Next to the notice board was the blackboard with Kate's to-do list. She was steadily getting through the tasks. Keys cut. Clean oven. Clean fridge. Defrost freezer. Hoover under beds. Dust tops of picture frames. Polish brass door knocker. Clean windows. And then there were those jobs that could be done only at the last minute before leaving the house. Change bed linen. Clean bathrooms. Drop the guinea pig to Izzy's friend to mind.

"Are we selling up and moving out altogether?" asked Mannix drily.

"I can't have guests arriving from America to a slovenly house, now, can I?" she retorted.

She was feeling fractious at all the tasks that were falling to her. It wasn't as if she didn't have a job as well.

"Well, delegate, then," Mannix suggested, continuing to slurp his meal.

"Oh, I intend to, don't worry. Which reminds me—Fergus, can you tidy away all the models that are on the floor of your bedroom? And Izzy, you clear your floor as well, please. It's not as if you don't have a wardrobe. All your stuff—get it off the floor and into the wardrobe. Izzy?"

But Izzy wasn't listening. She was busy texting under the table.

"Izzy!"

"Jeez, Mum. Stop shouting."

"What have I told you about texting at the dinner table?"

"Don't text at the dinner table?" She shrugged as if she were guessing.

Mannix burst out laughing. Kate shook her head. Sometimes she felt as if she were mother to three children and not two.

"Are you putting on my Manchester United duvet cover for the boy that's coming?" asked Fergus.

Kate paused a moment before answering. This could be a flashpoint. Fergus exerted strong ownership rights over his possessions and she knew he'd been ruminating about another child among his things.

"I might." No definite commitment.

"Yeah. Yeah, I think the boy would like that," said Fergus. "I think you should put my favorite duvet cover on. Because even though we won't be here to see him, he's still kind of a guest, isn't he?"

Mannix looked up from his plate, looked at Kate, and raised an eyebrow. Kate's heart went out to her child. Fergus was trying really hard and he'd obviously been giving the exchange a lot of thought. The whole idea of the house swap was working wonderfully well on so many levels. Suddenly, all Kate's gripes about domestic tasks melted into insignificance. This was all about Fergus. And already it was working.

"It's kind of weird, though, isn't it?" Izzy slipped her mobile back in her hoodie pocket.

"What's weird, sweetheart?" Mannix wiped his chin vigorously with a paper napkin.

"You know. The idea of someone you've never met sleeping in your bed, eating in your kitchen, sitting on your toilet."

"Not particularly." Mannix was shaking his head at his daughter and flashed a look at Fergus. "We'll be doing exactly the same in the Harveys' apartment," he said.

Kate was surprised at Izzy's lack of tact. Normally Izzy was in tune with her brother's emotions. Although, if Kate were honest, she too found the idea of strangers in her bed and in her bathroom a bit uncomfortable. The idea of them being in the kitchen, or the sitting room, or upstairs in the study didn't bother her. But in the inner sanctum of the house—that was different.

Any niggling discomfort was a small price to pay for Fergus's improved standing in school. Word soon filtered through that Izzy and Fergus O'Brien were going to New York for the October school holidays. During the extravagance of the boom years, this wouldn't have caused a stir, but now there were reports of jealous looks and sighs. The injured Frankie Flynn had been forced to do some posturing.

"Frankie Flynn said more than likely, in fact, almost nearly definitely one hundred percent, that he's going to Spain for the midterm break," Fergus had told them.

"Spain, *my arse.*" Mannix scoffed. "I doubt that, Ferg. But let me tell you, even if that loser does—there's no Empire State in Spain."

Mannix later remarked in private that in the unlikely event that Frankie Flynn were indeed telling the truth, the only reason he'd be heading for Spain would be to one of his uncles, who was hiding out till the dust settled on some dodgy situation back home.

Kate tried not to think of Frankie Flynn. Ever since the decision was made to go to New York, there'd been a focus to their lives. Before this, Kate felt like they were all on a life raft taking in water. Bobbing along in the wake of the Celtic tiger, stunned, but still alive. Now the children were busy saving their meager pocket money. The holiday had given them all purpose.

"I could babysit to earn some more money. I'm old enough," Izzy had pleaded. Kate had no doubt, despite her youth, that Izzy was a responsible child. But a child, nonetheless. It was one thing leaving her watch over Fergus, but another person's child—she didn't think so.

"Oh, please, Mum. Think of all the Hollister I could buy. Please . . ."

But Kate would not relent. Even Mannix tried worming his way into Kate's affections, pressing her to forgo her reservations and let him do some weekend hours at the nightclub. "Kate, just think of all those outlets, all those bags and shoes that you could buy." His eyes twinkled, his face creasing into a grin. Kate remained firm.

"The lady's not for turning, Mannix. Anyway, this visit to New York is a cultural visit," she said. Kate didn't consider herself a consumer of high-street fashion, preferring instead to purchase pieces from fashion students at exhibitions or put together ensembles from charity shops.

She was grateful things had settled down with Mannix's new job. She should stop calling it his "new" job. He'd been there now since March, quite long enough to consider himself reasonably established. The calls and text messages that signaled many a hasty departure didn't happen anymore. Although Mannix was scathing about his boss and not enamored by the job, it paid the mortgage, and he seemed to be on top of things. He'd even gone back to circuit training with the rowing club, something he'd let slide earlier in the year.

Kate couldn't help thinking that since September, ever since New York was mentioned, their relationship had stuttered into calmer waters. It had been a while since they'd worked as a team, toward a common goal. The forces that had strained their relationship were receding, leaving behind a warm intimacy and a sense of rapprochement.

For the past few weeks, they'd been dog-earing pages from the Dorling Kindersley guide in bed at night, or printing off articles from the Web, and discussing them over a late-night glass of wine. Yes, she thought, as she filled the dishwasher after their meal, things had certainly taken a turn for the better.

And just as quickly, out of the blue, it all changed. It was two days later—when Spike turned up.

———————

It sounded like an argument. No—*argument* was the wrong word. A heated exchange, then. She was in the kitchen, looking for a clear plastic bag to put toiletries in for her carry-on luggage. Mannix had offered to go downstairs and get the doorbell. Curious when he didn't return, she went to the doorway leading out to the small landing and the stairwell. They were deep in conversation, Spike leaning back against the handrail, one foot wedged against the opposite wall. Mannix sitting on the steps almost at eye level with his brother. His back was turned.

Anxious not to be seen, Kate edged back a little, ears cocked.

"No, Mannix. This is serious hassle."

"Welcome to my world," Mannix replied.

"I'm being threatened, Manny."

"Well, that makes two of us," Mannix said again.

"Fuck it, Mannix. This is serious shit. They mean business. You can't honestly say that you'd really like to trade places."

"I suppose . . ."

"Anyway, I thought you had your situation under control."

Spike was whispering.

"That's what I thought."

"Look, they know where I am. I need to lie low for a while. They'll find another club. It's just that the way the Bolgers see it, it's time to return the favor."

"Fuck sake, Spike. It was a few lousy packages. I thought they'd forgotten and it's hardly a fair trade anyway."

Kate felt herself go cold. *The Bolgers.* A notorious criminal family. So Spike was involved with the Bolgers. Spike was gung-ho, but getting involved with *the Bolgers*—this was nothing short of insanity.

"Ask her, will you? For fuck sake, Manny. You're my brother!"

Ask who what? Kate held her breath.

"All right, all right!" Mannix hissed. "I'll ask her. But she'll probably go completely mental. She's already up to ninety about cleaning the house. We're off in a few days, you know."

The sound of a downstairs door opening.

"Oh, hi, Uncle Spike."

It was Fergus.

Poor Fergus thought his uncle Spike was really cool. Time for Kate to make her presence felt. She went to the top of the stairs.

"Oh, hi there, Spike. Come on up."

"On our way," said Spike breezily. As he straightened up, he managed to knock a photo frame from the wall behind him, sending it sliding down the stairs.

"Leave it. I'll get it later." She tried to hide her annoyance.

Back in the kitchen, Kate offered Spike a coffee. A beer and he'd be there for the rest of the night.

"So Spike, to what do we owe the pleasure?" She tried not to sound too catty.

"Just thought I'd call around and see what you wanted me to do for your American guests." Spike was smiling broadly. "It's next Friday you're off, isn't it?"

God, he was smooth. She wasn't sure who was smoother—Mannix or Spike. She should really have listened to her mother.

"Only seven more days and eleven hours to go, Uncle Spike." Fergus was cutting himself some cheese squares.

Kate would take him up on his offer. "Well, if you wouldn't mind showing them around the house, show them where the central heating controls are—that sort of thing. I've made out a list. It's on the notice board."

Spike was smirking now. He thought her far too organized. Too uptight. "And what about keys? House keys, car keys?" He looked at her over the rim of his coffee mug. "I could drive out in your car to get them, and drive them back here to Curragower Falls. *Céad míle fáilte* and all that."

"Well, if you're sure . . ." She hesitated.

"Consider it done."

"Are you staying to watch the match, Uncle Spike?" asked Fergus. "Man U?"

"Who else?" Fergus grinned.

"I've no electricity in my flat, so I'd love to."

"No electricity, what happened?" Mannix asked.

"Dunno. Sparky says it could take a couple of days."

"Well, you obviously can't stay there in the dark, now, can he, Kate?"

Jesus, they were some double act. Both looking at her now, innocently.

"Of course not." Okay, she'd play their stupid game. "Of course you can stay, Spike," she said through gritted teeth.

"You're some woman, Kate. Mannix is a lucky man," said Spike.

Really, what chance did any unsuspecting woman have against Spike? He was utterly convincing. And just how many unknown little cousins did Fergus and Izzy have out there now, she wondered to herself. Kate left them to their match, Fergus wedged between his two idols, happy with his bowl of cheese squares.

Kate retreated to the stairwell and set about dusting the photo frames and rehanging the one that Spike had knocked over. It was the one of their wedding, with bridesmaid, best man, and her mother on the edge of the bridal party, trying her best to manage a smile.

Kate balanced the frame on the picture hook as she scowled at Spike's dimpled face grinning back at her. Unable to find the hammer, she'd tapped the nail as deeply into the wall as she could with a spanner. She hoped it would hold. There was no point in asking the men for help. They were busy bawling at the TV screen. Cries of "Send him off!" "The ref's a bollix!" "You absolute muppet!" and "Come on, Man U!" were coming thick and fast from upstairs.

As she worked, only one name kept going round Kate's head. *The Bolgers*. Whatever was going on, Mannix was mixed up in it, and all evening she'd been asking herself, did she really want to know? What had she gained by eavesdropping? All she'd done was disturb her newfound calm. Whatever it was, the brothers could sort it out for themselves. This time, she was going to bury her head in the sand. But she wasn't going to be taken for a fool.

Later that night as she turned over to go to sleep, she looked at Mannix, who was poring over a New York guidebook.

"I'm not stupid, you know, Mannix."

"I know you're not, Kate," he replied.

Seven days later, at 2:30 P.M. local time, Aer Lingus flight 102 touched down at JFK. It was Mannix's second transatlantic trip that year, having been in Boston on the training course in March. Kate had been as excited as the kids about the flight. The last time she'd been on a plane was three years ago when she and Mannix went to see the rugby in Rome. Her mother had moved in to look after Fergus and Izzy. Her mother didn't come to the house at Curragower Falls too often and she'd been glad of the opportunity to get to know her grandchildren.

During the flight Kate had watched a movie, but her mind kept wandering and she tried not to fret about the Harveys and their holiday.

Of course Limerick couldn't be compared to New York. Oranges and apples, her mother had said. But she hoped that Hazel Harvey would be pleasantly surprised by the many positive changes in the city over the last fifteen years. Unlike Mannix, Kate didn't feel a blinkered passion for Limerick, but she did bristle when outsiders criticized the city. And she certainly loved her own little pocket of it, that sliver of shore by the Shannon.

Once they'd cleared immigration, Mannix led the charge to the luggage carousel. Caged for six hours, he was now suffering a surfeit of energy. He marched ahead, with Kate, Fergus, and Izzy trying to keep up. Kate had enjoyed Mannix's attention on the flight. He knew how much work she'd put in over the last week and how she'd suffered Spike's company for six long days. It was true what her mother said. Guests were like fish. After three days, they go off. What had annoyed Kate most was Spike adding his boxer shorts to the family wash without even asking. He had no idea of boundaries.

Halfway through the flight Mannix brought it up. "Kate—thanks for Spike . . ." He'd rubbed her hand, which was on the armrest between them. "It was a tough few days."

"I assume he got the electricity back?"

"That's all sorted now."

"Strange, wasn't it," Kate had remarked, "I mean how the night-club downstairs was grand and the flat upstairs kaput?"

"Different circuits, I guess," Mannix had said.

Now, as they hovered over the carousel, Mannix shuffled from foot to foot looking impatiently for their luggage. He ran his hands through his hair, fidgeted with his phone, and shot it repeated looks of irritation.

"Found a mobile provider?" asked Kate.

"Not yet, it's scanning."

"You're not having withdrawal symptoms already—what's the panic? We're on holiday . . ." Kate linked his arm and leaned her head against his arm.

"No panic, Kate. Just a few little niggles at work . . ." His fingers mauled the phone.

Mannix reported to a guy he considered to be inferior to him in almost every way. Add to that the fact that the guy was younger than him, and it was a recipe that didn't do much for Mannix's ego. He'd bemoaned the fact that he had to dumb down his résumé to get the job in the first place. But it was the times they lived in. Too many over-qualified people looking for too few jobs.

As Fergus helped his father pile the suitcases onto the trolley, Kate suddenly felt uneasy.

"We *can* trust Spike to meet the Harveys at the airport? He wouldn't mess that up, would he?"

"No, of course not," Mannix snapped, the sibling bond between them now invoked.

Another thought then struck her.

"God, he wouldn't try to hit on Hazel Harvey, would he?"

"Oh, come off it, Kate!" Mannix pushed the trolley through the sliding doors.

"Why ever not? She's good-looking—blond, petite . . ."

"That's daft, Kate. Why on earth would Spike do that? From what I saw on Skype, she looks just like you!"

Kate raised an eyebrow. "And what does that mean? That I'm not attractive enough for someone else to hit on?"

"Of course not. Stop fooling around, Kate. Anyway, for one thing he's not into blondes." Mannix waved for a taxi. "Brunettes and dark-skinned girls are more to Spike's liking."

If only Mannix knew, she thought to herself as she got into the taxi.

The driver of their yellow taxi had quite stilted English, and had only recently arrived from Damascus. Still, he managed a stab at a commentary as they drove through Queens.

"It's just like on telly," said Izzy, looking at the wooden houses with open gardens.

"Flushing Meadows, sir . . ." The driver pointed it out to Mannix. But Mannix was still grappling with the phone.

"You like Federer, sir?" the driver asked him.

"Yeah. Yeah, he's great." But Mannix wasn't really listening.

"A legend," Fergus joined in from the back, next to Kate and Izzy. "Federer is an absolute legend."

Awhile later they drove over the Harlem River. The driver was now directing his stilted commentary to Fergus, who wanted to know the landmarks.

"Can we see the Empire State? Can we see it yet?" Fergus edged forward, straining the seat belt.

"No, sir. We're uptown, in Harlem. The Empire State is in Midtown."

Lackluster blocks were characterized by dull red brick and functional cheap signage over the commercial units. Groups of people straggled the pavements, moving with little sense of urgency or purpose. They looked like they were hanging out rather than going anywhere.

Ten minutes later, the character of their surroundings changed.

"Broadway," announced the driver, looking in the rearview mirror.

Mannix was still texting. Finding herself irritated, Kate leaned forward to speak through the opening in the Perspex partition between the driver and the backseats.

"This is Broadway, Mannix!" she said with exaggerated enthusiasm.

"Fantastic, isn't it?" he said without looking up.

These buildings were beautiful in a way she hadn't expected. Huge, ornate, imposing. In European terms, New York was in its infancy, and yet these buildings had all the grandeur and elegance of ancient Paris.

"Wow, awesome," said Fergus, head craning back. "Look how high that building goes!"

"Are we nearly there?" Izzy whispered urgently in her ear. "I'm dying for the loo."

"Is there far to go?" Kate asked the driver.

"Nearly there, ma'am."

They entered a narrower street and immediately the neighborhood changed again. The street was darker, leafier, and numbered canopies graced the entrances to the buildings. The feel was residential. They cruised past a pocket of restaurants and a café. The steps leading up to the grand brownstone buildings were decked out with hollowed-out pumpkins and Halloween decorations. The taxi turned right and seconds later they pulled up outside a five-story apartment building across the road from a tree-lined park.

A uniformed doorman emerged from the canopied doorway and bustled about as Mannix paid the taxi driver.

"The O'Brien family, I presume?" said the doorman, smiling broadly. "I'm Du Bois."

"You okay with that, young miss?" He took Izzy's suitcase.

"Welcome to Manhattan," he said once inside the airy lobby with its wood paneling and marble desk. "The Harveys are on the top floor. I'll take you up—a very nice apartment too."

Kate felt sure this was something of an understatement. She looked at Mannix, raising her eyebrows.

"The toilet?" came Izzy's strangled tones as Du Bois pushed open the heavy oak door to the Harveys' apartment.

"The restroom is down the hall, fourth on the right, young miss."

As Izzy jiggled down the hallway, Du Bois showed them around. The space afforded was at least three times that of their house in Limerick. The home-exchange site hadn't done it justice, unable to capture the generous scale of the rooms or the height of the ceilings. The apartment was even more tasteful and elegant than it appeared on-screen. The French windows that led out to the small balcony provided a panoramic view of the park, the river, and what Kate surmised were New Jersey skyscrapers in the distance. Kate wondered at the cost of such an apartment with its open aspect in this vertical city. She worried even more now that the exchange seemed unfairly balanced in their favor.

As Du Bois escorted them from room to elegant room, the heavy scent of fresh-cut flowers lingered in the air. There, in a simply cut crystal vase on the island in the kitchen was an artful arrangement of long-stemmed tiger lilies. An envelope leaned against the vase. Kate suffered a sharp pang of regret. She thought back to the bottle of supermarket wine and the welcome card she'd left on her own kitchen table.

Opening the envelope, she quickly scanned the headed notepaper:

> *Dear Kate, Mannix and family,*
>
> *What a pity I won't be here to meet you. From our conversations I feel like I know you already. By now Du Bois will have shown you around. He will be only too happy to oblige with any queries or advice—he's my right-hand man!*
>
> *I've left a list of restaurants on the sideboard in the hallway together with the car keys should you choose to travel farther afield. By the way, the Italian on West 74th is a great neighborhood restaurant. Nothing fancy, but it does a great calzone.*
>
> *Am so looking forward to our trip to Ireland. I haven't been back in fifteen years.*
>
> *Have a wonderful time! And don't forget the Circle Line—highly recommended.*
>
> > *Best wishes,*
> > *Hazel*

"What a lovely welcome," said Kate, comparing it with the bald welcome card she'd left at home. She should have made more of an effort. "She seems like such a warm person. Oh, I really hope she enjoys her time in Ireland."

"Not as much as me . . ."

"What's that, Du Bois?" Kate turned round.

Du Bois was picking a hair from his lapel. His expression was solemn. "No one deserves a vacation more than Mrs. Harvey."

Kate flashed a look of concern at Mannix. But Mannix wasn't listening.

Before she could say anything else Du Bois had turned on his heel and made for the door as if already regretting what he'd said.

Mannix

He was doing his best to enjoy himself. He really was. Cracking jokes, jollying everyone along, trying to say all the right things. But his heart wasn't in it. Every now and then shards of anxiety cut through him. *Why now? When he was on the other side of the ocean?* He thought it had all been sorted out.

"You okay?" Kate asked, her eyes locking onto his, like the grand inquisitor she was. He knew she smelled blood.

"Of course," he answered casually. "That's some size of a bath in there. Big enough for two," he added, winking.

"That's the third time you've been since we arrived, Mannix."

"Good God! Can't a guy go to the bathroom in peace? If you must know—I've been feeling dodgy ever since that airport sandwich. I thought it looked funny."

"Take it easy, I was only saying."

It was Kate's turn to look aggrieved now but he needed her off his case. The truth was, while he did feel queasy, the bathroom was the only place he could text in peace.

"Okay, then, I'm good to go now—everyone else ready?"

It looked chilly outside. He tightened his scarf and tucked his mobile safely into his parka pocket. It was set to mute.

The kids were in overdrive now, awed by their surroundings, reveling in every new experience. Fergus was bug-eyed with tiredness. Izzy, stoic as usual, was drawing on her stamina.

"Not too far on our first night, okay, Mannix? Maybe that Italian that Hazel Harvey mentioned?"

"Maybe. Maybe not. We'll see," he said, bustling everyone out the apartment door.

Nothing irritated him more than strangers or people of passing acquaintance proscribing how he should spend his holidays or his free time. He remembered an old school report card—*Mannix does not take kindly to instruction*. You could chalk that one down.

"Fergus has been poring over the map," Kate whispered, on her tiptoes. Her breath felt warm and damp. "Fergus is going to direct us, isn't that right, Ferg?" she said loudly.

Fergus nodded, all business, holding on to the shoulder straps of his holiday backpack.

In the lobby, Kate engaged the Du Bois guy in conversation—asking him where they should go for breakfast. Were there any bakeries nearby? The sort of thing they could easily figure out for themselves. That too irritated Mannix. Could they not just head out on the street and find this stuff themselves? There was no need to ingratiate themselves with this guy.

"Your new best friend?" he asked as they hit the pavement. Almost instantly, he regretted his surliness.

"Oh . . . don't be such a grump!" Kate said pleasantly. "You know what, kids? I think someone is hungry and just a little tired."

Kate looked to Fergus for support, but he was Daddy's boy. Recriminations were not forthcoming. Mannix linked his son's arm and pulled him close in the cold.

"Careful, Dad!"

Fergus switched the map from one hand to the other as if it were the key to some ancient treasure. Kate threaded her arm through Izzy's and the two of them walked ahead together, chatting and laughing.

It was true Mannix was withered from traveling but his short temper was due in larger part to the unsettling text messages. There had been only the odd one over the past few weeks but now there was a steady trickle. He could block the number but something told him he should play along for now.

"Three blocks down before we turn?" Kate shouted over her shoulder. She cut a vibrant figure in her ocher velvet coat.

"Three blocks downtown and four blocks east," said Fergus with authority.

"Spoken like a New Yorker," said Kate.

Mannix felt heartened at this little exchange. Fergus was relaxing into his new environment, delighted to have a job to do, easily able to decipher the neatly laid out streets with their grid system and numbering. His son might be a poor reader but he had a facility with numbers.

As Mannix watched his wife happily chatting, he felt a burst of affection and admiration for her. Instinctively, Kate knew how to stroke Fergus, how to make him feel good. But her razor-sharp intuition was something to be feared. Kate knew something was up. He'd tell her soon. Perhaps here, while they were on holiday. He'd tell her some of it. He'd probably only confirm some of what she already suspected. However, it should be enough to keep her at bay. For now.

Kate inspired in him a feeling to do better, to be a better person. Much as he tried, he all too often felt he let her down. He knew she'd married him against her mother's wishes. He also knew that it had taken a lot for her to do so. Sometimes, the debt of loyalty and gratitude he owed her felt too onerous. Too burdensome. He simply wanted to go back to loving her as he had in the beginning. But that was the trouble about beginnings. There could be only one. Still, where they were at today was way better than where they'd been at a year ago. He should stop tormenting himself and connect with the present and his surroundings.

Once they crossed Broadway, they found themselves on a residential street decked out with Halloween decorations. Mannix began to feel that he'd drifted onto the set of a Batman movie. Gotham City. Swirls and puffs of steam escaped from grilles in the ground. They spewed out white clouds that curled and vanished into the night air. Hollowed-out pumpkins cast a mellow yet eerie glow. Sirens screeched close by. Mannix imagined Batmobiles swooping out of the sky.

"One more block." In the gloom Fergus consulted the map.

"Well, you managed to get us here, Ferg," said Izzy a few minutes later as they descended the steps to the restaurant.

"Dough balls, here I come," said Mannix, patting his stomach.

The restaurant was perfect. Absolutely fit for the evening's purpose. Not stiff or formal, which Mannix loathed, but low lighting, low chatter, and low-key.

"Four? This way, sir."

A shapely woman in high heels snaked her way through the busy tables right through to a corner table at the back. Mannix hadn't realized his admiration was quite so obvious until he caught his wife's bemused expression.

"What?" he asked innocently.

"You know what," she said tartly.

"I'll take this chair . . ." said Mannix, making for the chair with its back to the room. He knew that Kate would enjoy a bird's-eye view.

"I'd like your chair, Dad," Fergus piped up. "I'd like to see the photographs."

On closer inspection, the exposed brick wall hosted black-and-white movie stills. *Breakfast at Tiffany's, Roman Holiday,* and, of course, the original *King Kong* movie. What could be better? Everyone was happy. And to crown it all, the menu was reasonably priced.

Mannix looked around at the clusters of people, eating and chatting much as he imagined they might do in their own homes and kitchens. They were informally dressed, the men with rolled-up shirtsleeves and casual jeans, younger women in weekend sweaters with little makeup, as if the decision to eat out were last minute and casually made. As if dining out in this neighborhood café was a regular occurrence, no ceremony required.

The one exception to this was a table of elderly well-groomed ladies. Their hair and bones looked stiff.

"Nice to see," remarked Kate.

"The old ladies?" said Mannix.

"Yes. It's nice that they feel safe to come out at nighttime. To enjoy themselves in company. Not be invisible."

"Wow, look at all that jewelry . . ." Izzy tried to whisper, joining in the conversation.

"Ssshhh . . ." said Kate, as their shapely waitress arrived with Cokes.

"Class!" said Fergus. Usually he had to beg and cajole for a Coke, but to have one arrive without any groveling was a pleasure indeed.

Kate took out her camera and snapped a happy Fergus and his Coke.

"Mum, stop!" hissed Izzy. "You're making us look like dorks."

"You'd better get used to it, Izzy," said Kate. "I'll be taking tons of photos on this holiday."

As they waited for their calzones they discussed their schedule for the next few days.

"Empire State tomorrow, pleeease?"

Fergus coughed as bubbles went up his nose.

"The guidebooks say that Sunday can be the best—the queues are shorter," said Kate. "Do you think you could wait until then?"

Fergus crossed his arms and thought. "Mmmm . . . I suppose if the queues are shorter and it means we get to the top quicker . . . Yeah, okay, we'll wait till Sunday."

"Good call, Soldier." Mannix patted him on the back.

"The planetarium at the Natural History Museum tomorrow?" Izzy asked. "If that's okay with everyone? There's supposed to be a really cool show—I read about it on the Web. A big bang simulation and stuff about black holes."

Kate looked at Mannix.

"I don't see why not. That's okay with me. How about you, Mannix?"

"Sounds like a plan!"

Mannix's list of must-sees was modest: Greenwich Village, the Dakota, Strawberry Fields. Kate's included the Museum of Modern Art and the Guggenheim. A thought struck Mannix.

"Hey, Ferg, give me the map a minute—something I want to check," said Mannix. "Thought so!"

"What?" said Kate.

"The Dakota—it's just across the street. We have to take a look-see when we finish here. That's where John Lennon lived just before he was shot." He looked from Izzy to Fergus.

"Yeah, Dad—we know." Izzy rolled her eyes.

"Hey, Izzy—how many eleven-year-olds can say they've seen where Lennon lived?"

"How many would care?" Izzy retorted.

"Are you sure we tipped enough?" asked Kate when they left the restaurant after a pleasant meal. Outside the air was biting, but it was a dry bracing wind, unlike the bone-drenching wetness of the west of Ireland.

"Well, it's a bit late now if we didn't," said Mannix. "Now, one slight detour, guys. It'd be a pity not to take a look. We're so close . . ." And he marched them across the street and around the corner.

"That's Central Park, isn't it, across the road?" said Izzy, as they stood admiring the Dakota.

"Sure is," said Mannix. "We're in a great location. We've lucked out with the apartment, all right. Haven't we, Kate?"

"We sure have," Kate agreed.

"It's odd, though, don't you think?" Mannix said. "The Harveys doing a house swap? They can't be short of money."

"I know. It *is* odd." Kate looked thoughtful. "But you know, there are some people who just don't like staying in hotels . . ."

"That's just as well, then," Izzy piped up. "Because our house is no hotel!"

Back on Riverside Drive, the doorman had changed. A fresh-faced guy in his early twenties. He looked like a college student.

"Hi, I'm Henderson, the night porter. You folks must be the O'Briens. Du Bois filled me in. Did you all have a nice evening?"

"Lovely, thanks," said Kate. "It's so pretty, everywhere decorated for Halloween."

"You guys going to the Halloween Parade in Greenwich Village Monday?" He looked at the kids.

"Can we, Dad?" Fergus tugged his arm.

"That's a definite maybe," Mannix replied, smiling. Their schedule was shaping up nicely.

Back in the apartment, Kate went to settle the kids into their bedrooms. Fergus was asking probing questions about time zones, which could become complicated. Mannix went into the kitchen to sort out a nightcap. His body was telling him he was stupid with fatigue but his mind wouldn't rest. His head had gone into overdrive. He kidded himself that a drink would knock him out.

There were a couple of bottles of wine chilling in the fridge, together with bottles of orange juice, eggs, and ready-to-heat Danish pastries. Mannix wondered if Kate had left a similarly stocked fridge at home. Best not to ask.

His mobile vibrated again as he stood there staring into the cold white light of the fridge. He'd ignored it in the restaurant. Maybe it *was* work this time. He scrolled through the messages.

"I see you," came a whisper from behind.

He jumped. He tried to slip the mobile into his pocket.

"It's Spike, isn't it?" said Kate. "You never look this worried about work. Come on, Mannix, I know it's Spike. I know there's something going on."

He was trapped. He'd have to give her something to chew, at least. And that something might as well be Spike. He'd intended to tell her, but not like this—not at the end of their very first day in New York.

"Can't it wait, Kate?" He handed her a glass.

"I think I've waited long enough, don't you? I never asked why Spike stayed, not the real reason. I never asked what was going on—I didn't want to know. I went along with your cock-and-bull story. I don't want whatever it is to spoil our holiday but you're on that thing all the time. You're obviously uptight. God knows, it's not that I want to know what Spike's been up to, but this can't go on, Mannix."

Kate sat down. Waiting. Looking at him patiently. God, he hated when she spoke to him like that. Like he was a kid. Like he was going to disappoint her again. Which he was.

But it was a question of where to start and where to call a halt. Where was the beginning of this thing and where was the end? He could just about remember how it started but it wasn't over yet. He might as well start with Spike.

"Look, you're right, Kate. Spike's in a spot of bother. With the Bolgers."

As soon as he said it, he realized how ridiculous that must sound. Being in a spot of bother with the Bolgers was rather like saying he'd had a brush with the Taliban or a minor skirmish with al-Qaida. The Bolgers didn't do spots of bother. They did mayhem. Revenge beatings, drive-by shootings, and in the last few months scalped a guy they felt had slighted them. The Bolgers were hard-core psychotic criminals.

"What kind of *bother*?" Kate asked. Her eyes were wide, searching.

"The Bolgers want Spike to let their guy into the club. A dealer. Hard stuff—not weed or E or any of that stuff. Serious stuff."

"Like heroin?"

"I dunno exactly. Yeah, heroin, I guess. Crack cocaine, crystal meth . . ."

Kate looked stunned. *Shit—he'd miscalculated!* Maybe this was too much. He should have kept his mouth shut.

"I take it he's refused?" said Kate.

"So far."

"Out of conscience?" She sounded derisory now.

"Jesus, Kate. Of course out of conscience. What do you think he is?"

"He wouldn't just turn a blind eye?"

"I really don't think that's an option, Kate. He turns a blind eye to the softer stuff. But heroin—he could lose his license. Be put away himself."

"Tell me *why*, Mannix. Tell me *why* the Bolgers are asking Spike to do this. There are other nightclubs in town. Why pick on *Spike's*?"

He'd hoped she wouldn't ask him that. He really had. A forlorn hope. His wife always asked the incisive questions. The questions other people missed. He'd thought he was prepared for this. Sitting on the plane, he'd played the scene out in his head. It was one secret less if he told her. The last few months, all the secrets had made him feel isolated and lonely. But there was a price to pay for everything.

"They're calling in a debt," he said.

Her blue eyes looked almost black in the half-light.

"At least that's the way the Bolgers see it," he said. "They think they did Spike a favor, you see . . ." He looked away, unable to hold her gaze. "They helped him find a buyer for some stuff, helped him shift it. Put it through the right channels."

"What stuff?"

"PCBs—printed circuit boards—you know, computer circuitry."

"I don't get any of this, Mannix. What would Spike be doing with printed circuit boards?"

Here it was. The moment of truth. It was here. He dug his nails into his fist.

"Spike was doing it for me, Kate. For us. This was a good while ago. Two years ago. In my last place. You remember . . . before we sold the beach house. Before you went back to Art College. The bank was hassling me, phoning me all the time. It was that time we got the enormous bill for Fergus's assessment and they threatened to cut off our electricity supply . . . remember that?"

Kate sat in stunned silence. She opened her mouth to say something but nothing came out. She leaned back against the chair instead. Mannix looked out through the big windows to the twinkling lights of the skyscrapers across the river.

"Other guys had done it. I knew that. Some of the whackos on the manufacturing floor had tried it. Some got caught. Some didn't, and made a bit of money. But I figured out a way. A way not to get caught. The other chancers—you see, they all involved someone else. I didn't.

Kept my mouth shut." He remembered how smugly guilty he'd felt at the time. Sealing the boards in watertight ziplock freezer bags and stashing them two at a time over in the quieter toilet cubicles in Zone F. It was stealing. Of course it was. But as a plan, it was neat and simple.

His throat was dry. He didn't dare look at her but could hear her breathing softly a few feet away.

"There were a few of us randomly chosen from QA to do spot checks on the lines. The night shift—everyone's a bit more relaxed, less cautious. I only took two or three at a time. Hid them in the cistern of a toilet at work. No CCTV in the cubicles—obviously." He stole a glance in her direction. She was listening intently, her fingers stroking the stem of the wineglass.

"So, then I . . ."

"You stole PCBs from your last job?" Kate interrupted. She sat forward now, her eyes wide and probing.

"Yes. I guess I did."

"So, Mannix. Just let me get this straight. You stole valuable equipment from your employer which you then off-loaded to Spike who used the Bolgers to sell it on? Through their *channels*. Through their *contacts*."

Her anger was controlled and quiet. He felt nervous.

"Yes."

"You—Mannix O'Brien, with a decent job, a wife and family— invited the Bolgers into our lives? The Bolgers—a gang who'd eat their own young? What the hell is the matter with you?" She spoke as if she were afraid she might explode into rage.

And there it was again. That look of disappointment.

His heart sank. It had seemed like a way out at the time. An opportunity presented itself and he had taken it. He'd had no way of knowing the Bolgers would end up in the mix. There had never been any mention of them. The contacts that Spike had dealt with initially never mentioned any involvement with the Bolgers. He supposed he was naïve. And Spike too, for all his street smarts. He too had been taken by surprise. But it was a small city. Of course the Bolgers were going to want a slice of anything that was going on.

"But we had—have so many debts. I know my job was decent. But it wasn't enough. All the mortgages . . . the bills . . ."

Mannix suddenly began to experience a feeling of disassociation. He started to feel light-headed. As if he were dreaming this confession. Imagining himself telling her about how he got into this mess at some point in the future.

"You know what, Mannix? And I thought I'd never hear myself say this. But for the first time in my life I almost feel sorry for Spike. He's the one in the firing line here."

It was true. What Mannix had done had put his brother in jeopardy. But he didn't want to think about that now.

"That's why he was staying with us—because of the Bolgers?"

"He just wants to lie low for a while. Juggle his routine a bit."

"They're threatening him, I take it."

Mannix wasn't going to tell her they'd threatened to burn him out.

"It's all talk. Posturing. Being the big man. Spike is sorting it out."

"Posturing?"

Okay, a poor choice of words. The Bolgers didn't posture. They followed through.

There was silence for a moment or two. The sound of snoring was coming from one of the bedrooms. One of them was asleep, at least. Mannix had a deep and sudden craving to lie down and curl up in a ball. Instead he kept his eyes fixed on the lights twinkling in the distance.

"At least I know we're out of harm's way for the week at least," Kate said eventually.

"Oh, Kate, don't worry. There's no way any of this is linked to *us*."

"Don't be stupid, Mannix. Everyone knows you and Spike are as thick as thieves." Kate laughed at the irony. "One more thing, just so we're clear on this . . ." She sat bolt upright.

He held his breath. He hoped that the holiday could be salvaged somehow.

"You did NOT do this in our name. Not for me or for the kids. You did not do this for us. You never asked me if I wanted to be involved. You did this all on your own. For the thrill of it. Because you thought you could get away with it. I know you, Mannix O'Brien, so don't lay that one on me."

She was right, of course. But still, Mannix couldn't help but feel hard done by. He'd been up the walls. Everyone was screaming for money. Everyone wanted a piece of him. He adopted his best hangdog expression. This was going slightly better than he might have imagined. Only slightly.

Kate leaned forward as if to get up. Almost immediately she sat back down again, as if something had occurred to her.

"This was about the time you were made redundant?"

"About that time."

"Tell me the truth." She stared at him hard. "Were you made redundant? Or were you fired?"

That was a tricky one to answer. It depended on what way you looked at it, he guessed. In the weeks and months that followed his departure, he'd wrestled with that question. Looked at it from every angle. There had been downsizing rumors for months but he'd always thought himself safe. Then about that time his name was gradually dropped from the lists of invitees to planning meetings, strategy meetings, even the quarterly review. He'd turn up at conference rooms and suddenly everyone would look embarrassed until he'd realized his mistake—he wasn't invited. And yet there was no way anyone could have known about the PCBs. He'd made sure of that.

"I was made redundant, Kate. I got a redundancy package, didn't I?"

And so he had, paltry though it was.

She got up this time and smoothed her hands over her thighs.

"I'm going to leave it to you, Mannix. As far as I'm concerned, we're in New York. This is a once-in-a-lifetime holiday I want the kids to remember. This is about Fergus and Izzy. And nothing is going to stand in the way of that. So what I propose is that you do not allow what's going on with Spike to affect this holiday. This is about us as a family. For this week, at least, I'd like not to think about this whole disgusting episode."

He couldn't believe his ears.

"I'm with you on that. Absolutely no problem with that. Agreed."

He couldn't believe he was about to get off this lightly. But was there a sting in the tail?

"Can you turn off the lights here?" Kate looked at him. "I'm dead on my feet."

"Sure, of course. You head off to bed."

He let out his breath. The bollocking he'd expected was not forthcoming.

"Jesus, Mannix . . ." She stopped in the doorway, shaking her head, maybe he wasn't safe yet. "Really, what were you thinking of? Don't you think we had enough on our plates with Frankie Flynn? Wasn't hassle from one criminal family not enough for you? Of all people—*the Bolgers* . . ."

"I know . . ." He shrugged.

He couldn't tell her. He couldn't tell her that. Could he? How could he tell her that the Flynns and the Bolgers were related? She was ready to put things on ice at least for a week. No. No, he decided. Kate didn't need to know that the two criminal families were connected. She didn't need to know that Martin Flynn and Gerard Bolger were first cousins. Best to keep his mouth shut.

A few minutes later he followed Kate to bed. Already she was burrowed under the duvet, way over on her side of the bed—asleep or at least pretending to be. He hoped that sleep would come to him too, in any guise. Deep, fitful, or uneasy. He'd take whatever came. He was weary to the bone.

Hazel

"Sorry about the choice of wine, sir. Your hot meal will be along immediately after the drinks service." The stewardess was flushed now, harangued by Oscar's precise line of questioning. "I'm not sure about low-fat options and I'll certainly check at the back if we have any dry white wine. I suspect all we have on board tonight is a German Riesling."

With lacquered nails, she handed him a half-full plastic tumbler and a small bottle of Riesling.

"See what you can do, I'd appreciate that," Oscar said, nodding earnestly, crystal-blue eyes commanding a follow-up.

"And the children, sir?" The stewardess was double-checking now, realizing the importance of getting it absolutely right. "What was it you said, Coke or Seven-Up?"

"Diet soda. It must be diet. Whatever you got." Oscar sniffed the offending wine as if to reinforce his displeasure, and with a sigh went back to his magazine, dismissing the stewardess.

"The woman is doing her best, Oscar." Hazel forced her eyes open, no longer pretending to snooze. She didn't bother to look at him but stared unseeing at the headrest in front.

"It's her job, Hazel. You know, hon, you don't always have to make excuses for everyone." He rubbed her hand and then squeezed it. A little too hard.

"Oscar," said Hazel as gently as she could. "We're on holiday, couldn't you let the diet stuff slide . . ."

His look was cold. Icy cold. She was warned. She was the one who should let it go.

"Those two seem to be getting on okay." Oscar jerked his head in the kids' direction.

Hazel craned her neck to catch sight of Jess and Elliot three rows back. Her neck felt the strain and she raised a hand to soothe the ache. Weeks later, it was still sore.

"It seems so, for now. I guess this way Jess can pretend she's not with us at all. In fact, I think the seating arrangement suits her just fine. Poor Elliot." Hazel shook her head.

Jess could really crank up the temperature when she wanted, deliberately flicking her long brown hair straight into Elliot's face. Hazel had been dismayed at first to learn that they weren't all sitting together. But she'd been so distracted booking the flights that she'd paid scant attention to the seating plan. In fact, with the way she'd been feeling, she could scarcely believe that she'd managed to organize this trip at all.

Strapped in at 30,000 feet between Oscar and the padded lining of the cabin, she had another sudden rush of panic. Instead of abating, the attacks were becoming more frequent. She wondered what she was doing here. What was this journey all about, really? She'd positioned it as that long promised trip to Ireland for the kids—to show them where she had grown up, the country that had formed her. Why was she really doing it? She wasn't sure. But she had a suspicion that if she could go back to where she'd set out from, maybe she could find her way again. Retrace her steps. Reinforce those values that she knew in her heart to be good and true. It had felt like the right thing to do, to book this trip. She wasn't running away from any of her problems, away from the bogeyman, for they were coming on this journey with her too.

The last month or so, she'd spent hours at a time in the dog run on Riverside Drive. It wasn't that she wanted a dog, even though the kids nagged and whined for one. Oscar certainly didn't want one. She wasn't even sure that he really liked them. What she wanted was to be in company but not in company that could tax her, demand anything of her. She wanted the comfort of people around her but not to feel obliged in any way to engage with them.

Each day she alternated the park bench she sat on, lest she become part of someone else's routine and be forced into conversation. She brought a periodical with her—*Time* or the *Economist*. She found herself unable to devote long spans of attention to a novel. Her mind would not stay the course. In the park, she felt seen and safely alone in the company of strangers.

Helen was more excited than anyone about the trip to Ireland. Hazel suspected she'd jump at the chance to be invited along. Single and lonely, she was a third parent to Jess and Elliot. Hazel had made a habit of including her in as much of their lives as possible. But Oscar could stomach his sister only in small doses. Anything beyond their weekly dinner together was likely to provoke a sullen tension and often unkind and pointed jibes—these jibes normally directed at Helen's weight.

On their last family meal at an expensive restaurant near Columbus Circle, which Helen insisted on paying for, it was Hazel who'd been niggly and argumentative. Normally she let things slide, but from memory it was Elliot's T-shirt that had done it that night. For some reason she just saw red. She put it down to the pent-up fear and tension.

Hazel had been the last to arrive at the restaurant. "Mission accomplished?" Helen had asked as Hazel slid the J.Crew shopping bags under the table. Helen loved to shop with Hazel, to ask her advice in a sisterly fashion. But no matter what Helen tried on, she somehow managed to look matronly.

Hazel had been keeping up the pretense of teaching, both to Helen and to the kids, for now. Her principal had been understanding. She was signed off for another month. Then she'd have to make a decision. A permanent decision.

"You've lost weight, Hazel." Helen was looking at her enviously. "You'll have to share the secret."

"Secret? It's not rocket science, Helen. Keeping your mouth shut should work." Oscar said, perusing the menu.

Elliot sniggered. Helen looked hurt. And once again Hazel let it go. This had gone on for years.

"Let's just order, shall we, Oscar?" said Hazel, wearily.

Like Oscar, Helen had grown up in the dispassionate and clinical Harvey home. Hazel suspected that it had been a home of few hugs and little outward display of affection. A Vassar graduate, Helen was currently funded on a research project to investigate the increasing levels of sarcoidosis in New York since 9/11.

"So, you guys are all off next week." Helen rubbed her hands. "I must say, I'm feeling jealous. I don't know if I ever told you kids but I had an Irish boyfriend once—here in the city on an internship with Merrill Lynch."

Jess had raised her eyebrows and Elliot was sniggering again. Both obviously finding it hard to imagine their large aunt Helen ever having a boyfriend. Just as Hazel was about to reprimand them both, she was distracted.

"Elliot!" she said sharply.

"Mom!" He jumped to attention, mocking her.

"Where did that T-shirt come from?"

"This? I borrowed it. Mine got wet with the water pistols . . ."

"Whose is it?"

"It's Luke's. I was at Luke's today, remember? His mom gave it me." Elliot was looking puzzled.

"What's up, Hazel?" asked Oscar.

"I don't care, Oscar. I'm not having it. I'm not having that propaganda. Look at what the T-shirt says."

"'Legalize Freedom.' Yeah, so?" drawled Jess. "What's up with that? You can't seriously have any objection to that, Mom."

"'Legalize Freedom' is a slogan for the libertarian movement, Jess, for the Tea Party movement!"

"Oh, please. Spare us the politics today, Hazel." Oscar sat back in his chair and threw his eyes to heaven. "It's only a T-shirt, for Christ's sake."

"Don't you see what they're trying to do? They're trying to hoodwink ordinary people with all their talk of civil freedoms and free markets and less government. What these oligarchs at the top of all these huge corporations want is the freedom to do as they will and pay no taxes all at the expense of the little man. My child is not going to be a puppet in their hands!"

"Our child," said Oscar calmly. "Are you really going to do this now?"

The kids had gone quiet and Helen looked uncomfortable, embarrassed. Oscar was right, of course, but this thing was just too important to let go. For too long Hazel had sensed the creeping insidious acceptance of some of the more abhorrent values of capitalist politics. It plain stuck in her craw.

"You're right." She tried to mute the frustration in her voice. "But I cannot have Elliot wearing a T-shirt that advocates the virtues of individualism over collectivism. An ideology that derides the notion of health care for all, that heaps scorn on the very notion of social security."

"Gee, Mom. It says all that? I can only see two little words," said Elliot, chin down, examining the writing.

Oscar guffawed with laughter.

Reluctantly, she'd decided to let it go. She wished it didn't matter. She really did.

"My clever little wife has just read Ayn Rand"—Oscar had looked at Helen—"and has now taken it upon herself to be a one-woman propaganda machine against the libertarian movement."

"Ayn Rand?" Helen raised an eyebrow.

"That's right—*Atlas Shrugged*," Hazel explained, "acts as a type of handbook for the Libertarians."

"Heavy-duty shit," said Elliot, making a paper plane of the menu.

"Hard-core shit," agreed Jess, looking bored to tears.

Hazel really was going to have to take her kids to task. She'd let too many things go this year. Exhausted by the demanding days at school, her own parenting skills had been put on the back burner.

As she recalled, the rest of the meal went by without incident. Almost like the weekly meals before all of this had happened. They'd chatted about the impending trip.

"Where exactly are you going?" Helen had asked.

"Limerick. The house is next to the Curragower Falls in Limerick. Just over the bridge from where I grew up."

"This is another home exchange, right? Like North Carolina?" asked Helen.

"That's right," Hazel said.

"I like the idea," said Helen. "I should do that. Stay in someone's home. Makes the experience much more real, I'm sure."

"It's that, all right . . ." muttered Oscar.

What Helen didn't understand or even know was that the home exchange had materialized out of necessity. In the past, there'd been the five-star Marriott resorts, the luxury condos with daily maid service and cook. Oscar's choice, not hers, but she'd fallen in with his holiday plans. All of that was before Susan. The settlement with Susan had put paid to all of that. But Helen knew nothing of Susan. They'd kept it between the three of them—four of them if you included the lawyer. Harry's friend. Reputation was everything. Hazel understood that. Especially in Oscar's profession. Who was going to attend a dentist accused of sexual harassment?

Susan had been Oscar's partner in the practice. Susan was a flirt—there'd been no denying that. But because the flirting was conducted in the open, for everyone's supposed amusement, Hazel had never worried. If she'd worried about anything when Oscar took Susan on, it was Susan's competence as a dentist. She seemed skittish, with big doe eyes and stiletto heels. Still, Hazel told herself, appearances could be deceptive. Just because she embraced her femininity didn't mean she couldn't do the job. Hazel didn't subscribe to the notion that a woman should look genderless to be taken seriously. And yet when the day arrived that Oscar told her Susan had accused him of forcing her onto the reclining chair and groping her breasts, could Hazel say that she was all that surprised?

Hazel stayed out of it, confident that Oscar's network of old school buddies would magic up some arrangement. But it cost considerably more than she thought it would. What really galled her was that the lawyer got nearly as much as Susan. He certainly knew the value of preserving a reputation.

They'd put the grubby episode behind them. Oscar couldn't afford to take on a new dentist and had decided to go it alone for a few years. Hazel too had severed all ties with Susan, swapping the dance class that she and Elizabeth had attended with Susan in favor of the dance studio closer to home on Broadway.

"Thank you for dinner, Helen. You're too generous." Hazel had thanked Helen in the washroom.

"Oh, honey, you're so welcome. You know I'd do anything for you, Oscar, and the kids." Helen looked at her with a sincerity that made Hazel want to go back out to the restaurant and have a go at Oscar for all his nasty jibes.

"I'm sorry about Oscar," Hazel had apologized. "He's sharp sometimes . . ."

"I don't take notice of all those silly comments. It's hard for Oscar today. You do know what day it is, don't you, Hazel?"

And with a start, Hazel realized that this was the very first time she'd forgotten. She always made sure that she trod more gently at this time of year.

"The anniversary, right?"

Helen nodded.

Birgitte. Oscar's first wife. Today was the anniversary of her death.

"The saddest funeral ever—only four of us. We never thought Oscar would take the plunge again. Until you came along . . . He adores you, you know." Helen squeezed her arm affectionately as they'd struggled through the doorway together.

"You know what? Even after all this time, it feels the same." Hazel braced against the rear seat belt to talk to their driver up front. "Like an old pair of slippers . . ."

"I dunno about that, Hazel. Wait till you see," their driver replied. "There's been a lot of change in the last fifteen years." He flashed a smile at Oscar, who sat up front next to him.

Hazel was in the back with the kids. It felt odd to be looking at the driver on the right-hand side of the car. He was certainly friendly enough, this guy Spike. Perhaps a touch overfriendly. He'd scanned her up and down in the arrivals hall. Hazel was surprised to see him wearing what looked like motorbike leathers. He seemed somewhat unkempt, with an unshaven face and tousled hair. But he and Oscar had hit it off straightaway.

"You should go to the game tomorrow. At Thomond Park, the new rugby stadium." Spike checked the rearview mirror. "Yeah—yourself and the young fella. You like rugby? Munster are playing tomorrow."

"I guess we could take in a game, what do you say, Elliot?"

"Cool," said Elliot.

"Elliot and I go to the Giants at home."

"The Giants, eh? Now, there's a thing. They were my team when I worked in the Bronx in the nineties. Put it like this—Munster's the Giants without the padding and the headgear, you get me? And without the paycheck too of course . . ." Spike chuckled.

The ride in the back of the VW saloon was smooth, something Hazel was thankful for, as she was not a good backseat passenger. Spike whizzed along, checking his mirror at regular intervals. Hazel noticed they were breaking the limit on the speed signs. As the road descended over a plain of green fields cut through by the Shannon River, she watched black and white cows grazing in the early morning damp.

The cars that sped by seemed newer, shinier, and in better condition than the cars she remembered from fifteen years ago. Many of them had 2007 registration plates. The year that the boom had peaked. The zenith of the Celtic Tiger years. By the looks of things many had shared in the spoils. In the country she had left, cars were an expensive commodity, and a brand-new car was a sure sign that someone was a real success.

As they neared the city limits, the skyline had changed. A split in the road signaled an arching overpass on its way to a toll road burrowing its way under the river.

"That's the tunnel," Spike confirmed.

Hazel was surprised. Economic intensity must have demanded greater access across the river. She didn't know whether to be pleased or disappointed. In her mind's eye she had a picture of what she'd left. Would it be so changed that it no longer felt like home? For that is what she wanted, craved. She needed sanctuary.

Tall glass buildings glinted on the horizon.

"Those buildings over there, they're new?" Hazel pointed.

"The one with the curved rooftop, that's a hotel. And the taller one to the left, that's an office block. It's a shame, really. Most of the units are empty. The recession, you know. Well, actually that's not quite right . . ." Spike looked in the rearview mirror again and Hazel felt the car surge forward in a burst of acceleration. The guy was jittery. "Yeah," he continued, "things went buck apeshit here for a few years. The banks throwing money at everyone. Guys working in car washes were getting mortgages. Everyone was a developer, a property speculator. Lads with perfectly average jobs were driving Mercs and BMWs. Every auctioneer in town thought they were Donald Trump. And kaboom. Suddenly the banks were found out. I reckon it all started with you guys across the pond—Lehman Brothers, wasn't it? Or that crowd with the funny names like the Flintstones—Fannie Mac and Freddie Mae!" He snorted at his own joke.

"That's right, buddy, blame the U.S. Sooner or later everyone always lays the blame at our door," said Oscar. Spike's banter had struck a nerve.

"Aw, no, pal, I'm only ball hopping. We certainly didn't need any help from anyone else. Sure, the banks here partied until they dropped. The rest of us are left to carry the can while the fat cats who robbed us blind have ridden off into the sunset with their big fat-cat pensions."

"No jail time for anyone?" asked Hazel from the back.

"Jail time! You kidding me? These guys are still swanning about going to their swanky villas in Spain and Portugal. It makes me stone mad if I think about it too much. So hey, you know what? I try not to think about it. Like the man says, we must accept the things we cannot change."

And there it was again, albeit here at the other side of the Atlantic—yet another instance of apathy in the face of misconduct. Hazel was disappointed by Spike's remarks but it was unreasonable to infer that his attitude was representative of the country as a whole. Yet the Ireland she had left had been slow to anger. Ambassador Jean Kennedy Smith had been right all those years ago when she remarked how Ireland was a great country but the Irish simply didn't do outrage.

"You'll get a good view of the Riverpoint building if we come in the Condell Road. We can come up O'Callaghan Strand then and Clancy Strand that way," said Spike.

"That's where you lived, isn't it, Mom?" Elliot asked groggily. "O'Callaghan Strand?"

"Yes, sweetie, that's where I grew up."

"I thought you were farther up—on Clancy Strand?" said Spike. "I thought that's what Kate said."

"No. I was in a house just up from the boat club."

"St. Mick's? That's where my brother, Mannix, rows—whenever Kate lets him out!" He chuckled again.

And suddenly Hazel felt uncomfortable, as if she were peering into someone else's life. She didn't want to know intimate details about her exchange partner's life. She didn't want to know about the state of their marriage. And she didn't want to violate anyone else's privacy.

Minutes later they turned off onto the North Circular Road heading toward the old toffee factory and to the bend in the road with the boat club. Up until now the suburbs had had a slow Saturday morning feel. They'd spotted one or two joggers on a walking trail but it was early yet, 6:45 according to Hazel's watch. And yet as they slowed to take the bend in the road, she spotted blue-and-yellow-clad crews hoisting and shouldering rowboats down the slipway onto the high tide.

"Oh, slow down a minute," said Hazel. "Doesn't that look fun?"

"Yeah, nice morning for a spin on the river," said Spike, slowing to a crawl.

"Looks fun . . ." drawled Jess, alert now, scanning the square-shouldered boys with admiration. Hazel smiled to herself. How many times had she and her friend Lizzie ogled the crews from the top-floor window of her house when they were teenagers? She wondered where Lizzie was now.

"And there's my old house, over there on the left . . . Can you go a bit slower, please?"

As they inched their way up the strand, Hazel sensed a reluctance from Spike, as if he were impatient somehow, itching to be somewhere else.

"There! There it is. The one with the green door . . ." Hazel squeezed Elliot's knee. Oscar had turned around and was smiling at her indulgently. Remarkably, the house still looked the same. The same green door. The same long lawn at the front. The huge magnolia in front of the sitting-room window. Memories of the undertaker trundling her mother's coffin down the crazy-paved pathway to the hearse on the road.

On the other side of the road, the city had put in a fancy riverside walk, and the old wooden benches where she'd sat enjoying fledgling romances had been replaced with weatherproof seating. Autumn had not yet torn all the damp leaves from the great sycamore trees that dotted the walk. Across the water of the full tide were functional looking buildings or apartment blocks. They neither added nor detracted from the view, they were just there. Hazel wondered just how many buildings had been born and died in her absence.

As they traveled slowly up the strand, Hazel noted the twin landmarks of Shannon and Limerick rowing clubhouses were still the same. However, the modest hotel that had stood on the site close to Sarsfield Bridge was now replaced with a large swollen building dominating that corner.

"All new around here," said Spike, drumming his fingers on the steering wheel. The lights at the bridge were red and they'd been forced to stop. "Great views of the river and the city from the hotel terrace. Pretty swanky bedrooms too. With so many hotels going to the wall this one seems to be holding its own, for now at least . . ."

Spike continued to drum his fingers on the wheel, pressing his foot on the pedal, causing the engine to race. "During the boom, every time you turned a corner there was a new development going up. Not any old crap either, might I add. Four- and five-star establishments, all with spas. Oh, you couldn't be seen frequenting a hotel that didn't at least have a spa!"

"Really?" Hazel was amazed.

"That's the truth of it. Of course they're nearly all in NAMA now."

"NAMA?" asked Oscar, analyzing his surroundings.

"Yeah—the crowd that takes over when everything goes belly-up. It's a government agency—supposed to get the most out of any assets left over. But who knows what's really going on there. I wouldn't believe daylight out of them myself. Christ Almighty, what is going on with the feckin' lights this morning. That's nearly a full four minutes we've been here!"

Hazel felt Elliot shudder with laughter by her side, but the next thing she knew, all three lurched forward as Spike accelerated through the cross-hatch over the hump in the road to Clancy Strand. There was no more small talk as Spike sped down the strand past the late Victorian and Edwardian houses toward the old barracks building. Within seconds he had screeched to a halt outside a row of red-bricked houses. He carefully reversed through the low gates into the gravel driveway that curled around the side of the building.

"Curragower Falls—here we are!" Spike turned around and surveyed them all, grinning widely. The guy really did look as if he'd been up all night.

"Thank you so much for all your kindness," said Hazel. "We're in great shape here—if you need to be off," she said, feeling that they'd imposed too much already. Oscar and the kids were already taking their luggage out of the trunk.

"No worries. Here, give me that suitcase, you'll have your little shoulder out." Spike took the suitcase out of Hazel's hand, his fingers brushing hers. Equally swiftly, Oscar relieved Spike of the same suitcase, slighted at the implication that he wasn't looking after his wife.

Inside, Hazel was delighted to find that the house was true to the charm suggested on the Web site. The walls of the main living area were covered with abstract artwork in the primitive style that she knew Oscar was partial to. A display of multibranched gold-painted twigs sat in a ceramic pot in the big picture window overlooking the river. Decorated with miniature black and gold Halloween paper lanterns, a string of fairy lights snaked its way through the branches.

"Cool beans," said Elliot, fingering the lanterns as he looked out the window. "So where are the falls?" he turned around and asked Spike.

"Sorry, pal, the tide's too high just now. But as the tide goes out you'll see the rocks and the river racing over them. In a few hours' time. But I guess you guys will want to get a snooze in first."

"Some shut-eye sounds good to me," said Oscar.

Jess had already collapsed in a heap in one of the downstairs bedrooms. Spike guided them through the central heating controls, the hot water, and the refuse before leaving the car and house keys with them along with a cell phone contact number should they need him.

"I'll love you and leave you, then," said Spike. Zipped into the biker jacket, he leaned forward and pressed his lips against Hazel's cheek before putting on the crash helmet that had been resting on the breakfast counter. He looked like a gladiator. Again Oscar bristled.

Seconds later Hazel heard the engine roar and watched from the window as the black-clad figure disappeared on the motorbike up the strand and around the bend toward the Treaty Stone, out of view.

"Bit of a weird dude, wouldn't you say?" said Oscar, who'd gone down to wave him off.

"You think?" Hazel was cautious.

"For sure. There was something going on with him. Jittery as hell."

"He did look like he'd been partying all night . . ."

"He was looking around that backyard like there was someone

lying in wait for him. Looked up and down the street a good two or three times before he took off."

"Really?"

"And he has the hots for you," said Oscar in a lower voice.

"You're tired, Oscar. We're all tired." She couldn't do this now.

"That's true. Some shut-eye before we regroup."

"You go on," said Hazel. "Just give me a few moments to myself. A few moments to let it all sink in. Home, after all this time."

"Sure." He squeezed her shoulders tightly, then wrapped his arms around her, silently but firmly exerting ownership rights.

Alone at last, Hazel reflected on the last few hours. Sluice gates of nostalgia, fear, and affection had all creaked open, their jumbled contents sloshing about her head. She needed her journal. To jot it down on paper, to make something concrete of her thoughts. Writing always gave her a sense of calm. Putting her feelings on paper made her feel in control of them, not a slave to them.

Almost instantly, she was struck by something else. Panic. *Oh, God. Where was her journal? When was the last time she had it? She hadn't packed it, had she?* In the daze of simply existing, she had no memory of packing her precious diary. Her beautiful Japanese lacquered diary containing her most intimate thoughts, feelings, and reflections. Her heart was pounding. Think. Think. Back to when you last had it, you crazy woman . . . think . . . think.

She steadied herself a moment and then it came to her. It must be at home in her bedside drawer. It had been at least a week since she'd written in it. And even if she'd left it in the park somewhere or even on the subway, what was there really to link it to her? Her name was not on it. It just looked like a pretty journal. She tried to think back. There were no names. Events were described. Conversations, fears, and plans for the future. *But there wasn't anything that could link it to him, was there? She hadn't mentioned his name, had she?*

"Coming, Hazel?" Oscar had come to check on her.

"Yes," she said. She should try to sleep. Getting up from the cane chair, she noticed a hooded figure in the park across the road staring up at the window straight at her. Startled, Hazel jumped back.

"Come on, then," Oscar said impatiently.

"Coming," she said, a coldness gripping her. This holiday was supposed to heal, but as Hazel went wearily down the stairs she felt overwhelmed by something else.

A profound sense of foreboding.

Oscar

"Sorry, boss, watch yourself there now, boss!"

A wiry youth scuffled past Oscar in a pocket of people walking over the bridge into the town of Limerick. The wind had picked up and as Oscar looked upriver he could still catch sight of the quirky terrace house that was to be their base for the next few days. Across the river was the castle. Head down against the wind, Oscar thought about the scant comforts that would have been offered within its dank walls. Good old King John—whoever the poor dude was— must have had his nuts frozen off in that place.

Oscar knew little of Irish history. Nor was he much inclined to inform himself. Such research would inevitably lead to the sorts of political discussions with Hazel that he found too draining. In the early days, he'd found such discourse enlightening, invigorating even, but not now. He would surely end up suckered into some discussion that could perpetuate itself for days.

He had no particular purpose in mind as he walked briskly. A jet-lag sufferer, he'd been unable to sleep and had crept out of the house while Hazel was snoring gently. As he walked past empty shop fronts interspersed with older buildings, he ruminated about how he could ill afford such a long vacation in Ireland. But he had to do this for Hazel. He had to accept his share of the blame. To try to make things right. He did feel guilty. If only she had listened to him, taken his advice. He had warned her. She couldn't say he hadn't warned her. But Hazel was stubborn. It hurt him that she ignored him like that. It was disrespectful and it stung.

He walked past red-brick Georgian buildings, some that had been elegantly refurbished, some with brass plates, others that needed care and attention. Every few blocks of this town had a different character. He hung a left and then another. A series of pleasant cafés greeted him, some with outdoor seating, people sitting outside smoking and drinking coffee. He followed this street until it narrowed into a lane with delis and butchers and bakeries. The sugary smell of baking made his mouth water. He suppressed the urge to go inside.

He came to a junction with another street. Left or right? He turned to the right. Abruptly the atmosphere changed. Buses screeched and shuddered to a halt. It was busy, noisy. The smell of fried food and the acrid smell of vinegar. The smell of poverty. Women with deeply lined faces and large gold earrings looked at him suspiciously as he passed them at a bus stop. A hunched-over man stared at him. There was a glint in his eye. Oscar felt as if he'd stumbled on this street, uninvited.

As he hurried past charity shops and shops advertising goods for under a euro, an altercation was taking place up the street. As he drew closer, he spotted a woman in a cotton-candy pink leisure suit with a pram. She was hollering abuse at a woman also with a pram and toddlers on the opposite side of the street. It was late October. It was cold. Yet the children were in T-shirts. Both women had orange permatans and their leisure suits separated in the middle, exposing Jell-O–like stomachs. Oscar shivered with revulsion. Passersby made a wide arc as they scuttled by, heads down. It occurred to Oscar that these women could do worse than heed Michelle Obama's advice on weight. They were obese.

Passing through another narrow lane, he found himself under the giant canopy of an outdoor market. The smell of curry mixed with the rich aromas of coffee and baked goods. Oscar's mouth watered again.

But he was not giving in. He meandered his way around stalls laden with cheese and olives, fresh pasta, and pesto. Some kid was playing the flamenco guitar with an older man. A woman with curly hair displayed handcrafted jewelry. A thought occurred to Oscar. Hazel wore blue well, so he got the woman to package a pair of blue earrings beaded with pewter. It was only a token—but it was an effort to reach out to her.

A sudden whoosh of air whipped about his legs.

"Come back here, you little scut!"

A burst of dark blue energy whizzed by him. A policeman in pursuit. Jostled into a fish stall, Oscar stumbled and almost fell.

What the . . . ?

"You all right, sir?" the vendor enquired. "Young fellas with illegal fireworks. The guards are cracking down this Halloween."

It was time to make his way back to the house at Curragower Falls. Time to whip his family into action for the day. He hoped Hazel was ready to enjoy her vacation. He knew he sure as hell was putting in as much damned effort as he could.

Twenty minutes later Oscar found himself back at the house. As he made his way up the narrow staircase and into the kitchen, he was relieved to see Hazel dressed and with a mug of coffee as she sat in the swing chair.

"You went without me?"

"I couldn't sleep. Going east—happens every time," he apologized.

"I was looking forward to showing you around. I thought it was something we could do together."

Christ, he couldn't win.

"Hon, we've got all week. I can't have seen everything. Anyway, it was only a breath of fresh air."

"I suppose . . ." She looked away.

"You slept? You were snoring when I went out."

"For a bit, yeah. But I was woken up. The doorbell went."

"Spike?"

"No. Someone to read the gas meter."

Hazel still sounded despondent. Time for a peace offering.

"I got you something."

"You did?" She looked up from her mug.

"I thought they were pretty."

She did him the courtesy of looking curious as he handed her the small box.

"You're right, Oscar. They are pretty. Really pretty. I love them. Thank you."

Was it just words or did she really mean it? It didn't matter. The important thing was that she was trying. Just like him. She really was.

It was cold. A wet kind of cold. No matter how much he stamped his feet, they still felt numb. His brain told him he was flexing and wriggling his toes, but he experienced no physical confirmation that this was actually happening.

They were squashed together in the seething red mass swarming about the rugby stadium. It was small by Giants' standards but the energy inside felt huge. It was tribal, raw, and primitive. The kids were enjoying it too. And so was Hazel. She seemed relaxed now, unlike earlier in the day. She'd been on edge going to get the groceries. He'd put it down to using a stick shift after driving an automatic. They'd already decided that Hazel would do the driving, as she was more familiar than he was with a stick shift. But she'd been even more unsettled when she returned. She seemed to think that someone had been following her in the grocery store. He told her she was imagining it.

"Take him down! Buckle him! Bury him!!"

Next to them, a crazed fan with distended eyes roared at a player. His fired-up bulk jumped up and down in his seat, obscuring the view in front. The legend on his red sweater read "Irish by birth, Munster by the grace of God." As he jumped up with his big bald head, he pumped the air with his fist. Oscar couldn't tell if there was a behavior disorder in the mix as well.

When another huddle took place in the center of the grounds, a now familiar ripple started up on the other side of the stadium.

"Why are they singing about prison ships?" Oscar asked. It seemed an odd choice to sing at a game.

"It's a ballad about the famine, about people being deported for stealing," Hazel shouted.

"What's the connection with rugby?"

"Beats me." Hazel said, shrugging. "Somehow 'Low Lie the Fields of Athenry' became a Munster rugby anthem." And with sudden gusto she joined in.

After repeated renditions Oscar was able to decipher most of the chorus and he sang along too. Oscar liked this game.

He thought that if he lived in Limerick, it was easily a sport he might follow. He liked that fusion of brawn and passion.

A few seconds later the whole stadium erupted as the red-shirted fans roared their approval at a hulking player who made it over the line with the ball.

"Beautiful. Absolutely fucking beautiful," said the man to his left to no one in particular.

"Want one?" The guy turned to Oscar and pulled a squashed-up bag of jellies from his pocket. In the process a used cloth handkerchief appeared as well.

"No, thanks. Watching my weight. But thanks anyway."

"Suit yourself."

Oscar turned to look at Hazel. He raised his eyebrows and threw his eyes to heaven.

"Nut job," she mouthed. "Look over there, that woman's got the right idea . . ." Hazel indicated a woman farther along the stands. She was wearing a black and red braided bandana around her forehead and was rearranging a rubber hot-water bottle under her sweater.

"I can't feel my feet," said Oscar.

"Me neither," said Hazel, "but this is fun, though, isn't it?"

"Sure is," Oscar agreed, trying to remember the last time his wife had said that anything was fun.

She looked animated and pretty tonight and he was reminded of the first time he met her in Verona. She'd been alone and he remembered thinking her beautiful. Gripped by a curiosity he hadn't felt since Birgitte, he'd found himself shuffling past the other tourists to get to her. From the very first instant, he'd felt the intensity of their connection. Unlike tonight, it had been hot in the amphitheater. He remembered the pinpricks of light from tiny candles lighting up the stone terraces. As she'd held her candle, he'd observed her in the flickering light. He'd studied that long blue vein that climbed from the hollow between her clavicle bones and up the slender column of her neck. She was slight. He liked that. Her features neat and symmetric. Not one extra ounce of flesh clung to her frame. Her skin was spare and taut. The way it should be.

He'd noticed how her chin jutted out subconsciously. How many times had he seen that since? She did it when she was being stubborn. Birgitte too had been stubborn. But Oscar had been caught off guard. Once again he'd been seduced by that delicious cocktail of beauty and vulnerability.

He remembered the sex. Staring into her eyes as he made love to her. He enjoyed the communion that allowed him to feel complete and utter ownership of her, the feeling of being one. That kind of intensity couldn't last. As their relationship inevitably slipped into something habitual, he found it easier. He was more in control. He'd felt addicted to her and it made him afraid.

In those early days he had her all to himself. As time went by, Hazel had needed more. She needed to save people. She needed to save them from themselves or circumstance. Oscar had grown resentful. Resentful of all these people and all their fucking causes. Why couldn't the bloodsuckers latch on to someone else? Hazel was *his* wife. Couldn't he be enough for her?

When the rugby match was over the four of them hung on to one another's coats so as not to be become separated in the melee of departing Munster fans. Their immediate company was happy, Munster having won. They were carried up the street in a swell of fans, their number dwindling every time they passed a pub.

"Bit of a rough diamond, isn't it, Limerick?" Oscar thought aloud.

"Dad!" Elliot was disapproving. He knew the affection his mother had for her hometown.

"It's okay, Elliot," said Hazel. "It's an honest place. What you see is what you get. Rich and poor. Side by side. The posh china with the chipped cups and saucers. Everyone's lives are knitted together here. There's a lot to be said for it. Why should certain sections of society be shut away as if they didn't exist . . . ?"

"Oh, please, not another lecture!" drawled Jess.

Jess had little patience and less diplomacy. But unlike Oscar she could vent her feelings with more impunity.

"Do you think we could try surfing tomorrow, Mom?" Elliot sounded doubtful. He pulled his scarf around his neck. Hazel had some madcap idea about going to the coast to revisit her old holiday haunts. Oscar was already resigned to humoring her.

"I don't see why not, sweetie."

"It's November soon. Seems a crazy idea to me," said Jess, flicking her hair.

"We can do crazy on vacation, right, Elliot?" Hazel put her arm around her son's shoulders.

They marched along, past betting shops, a chip shop, a liquor store. Small terraced houses spewed smoke into the night sky. Some draped huge Munster flags out top-floor windows. Raucous banter was tossed back and forth across the street. They arrived at the church and the Treaty Stone, their signal to turn right onto Clancy Strand. It was busy. Cars were parked nose to tail, and as they approached the Curragower Bar, crowds of people milled outside, drinking from plastic glasses. Laughter and the smell of tobacco filled the air. The covered terrace was thronged.

"Miller time?" Oscar took Hazel's hand and squeezed it.

She considered it a moment.

"I'll give it a swerve." She squeezed his hand in return. "Don't let me stop you, though. You stop for a drink. I've got the keys. It's only around the corner."

He was grateful to take her up on her offer. He had a whole six days more to go and already he felt the beginnings of cabin fever. Some head space was called for. Inside the bar, the atmosphere was fevered and it was difficult to get to the counter. It was elbows, big-bellied men, sweaty heads, and some of the widest necks Oscar had ever seen. He suddenly thought the better of ordering a glass of wine. A beer would do just fine.

"Some match, wasn't it?" shouted a woman into his ear. Her cheeks were scored with black and red face paint.

"My first," Oscar shouted back. "I'm only visiting."

"On your own?"

"At the moment, yeah," Oscar replied, smiling.

"Come on, join me and my friends out the front."

And so he did. Beer in hand, he went and joined the woman, her Munster rugby jersey straining across her chest. He told Majella and her friends where he was staying and what he planned to do over the next few days. They insisted on buying him a pint of Guinness, and although the bitter taste was not to his liking, he made approving noises and managed to consume some of it before quietly ditching the rest in an outdoor plant next to a patio heater.

When next he checked his Rolex, he saw it was nearly eleven. Time to get back. He thanked Majella and her friends for their kindness. He squeezed past two guys who looked hammered, smoking in the doorway.

"Up Munster," said the men as he left.

"Up Munster," he replied.

As he made the short walk back to the house, a violent crackling disturbed the night. Oscar flinched. A shot rang out and then another. Alarmed, he looked across the river to what looked like project housing in the distance. And then it dawned on him. Small puddles of color blemished the sky. It wasn't shots that he was hearing. It was fireworks. He'd forgotten it was nearly Halloween.

"Kids in bed?" he whispered as Hazel opened the door.

Hazel didn't answer. She looked over his shoulder into the street. She too must have heard the fireworks.

"Kids in bed?" he asked again.

"Did you see?" she asked nervously.

"See what?"

"You didn't notice?"

"I heard some fireworks, that's all. What's up?"

"Ssshhh. Upstairs." She quickly locked the door, sliding the chain into position across.

The kitchen was in darkness except for a small halogen light coming from the cooker hood. The drapes were drawn across the large window. Slowly, Hazel padded across to the window, gingerly peeling the edges of the drapes apart. She peered through the gap.

"Sure you didn't notice anything?" she asked again.

"What's wrong, Hazel?"

"Out there," she whispered. "Across the street. Someone staring at the house."

"Really? Show me . . ."

The little park with its benches was deserted. He stayed watching for a few moments. But there was no one there. A cab screeched to a halt a few feet away and sounded the horn. Seconds later, a party of high-heeled women, barely clothed, fell laughing and shouting from a nearby house. They piled into the cab and drove off. But there was no one in the park. Hazel's breath was short and rasping as she stood behind him.

"There's no one there, Hazel."

He let the drapes fall back in position.

He looked at her. "It's a public-seating area, Hazel. I don't see what the problem is."

"I know that, Oscar, but there was someone sitting there in a hoodie, just *staring* at the house, *staring* up at this window. That's why I closed the drapes. I was sitting here in the wicker seat looking at the falls and the lights on the river when suddenly I saw this hooded face staring up at me."

"There's no law against that, Hazel."

"I know that. But whoever it was, was taking photographs, I'm pretty sure. I saw the glow of a cell phone . . ."

Thud!

Thud! Thud!

Hazel let out a small yelp and stared at Oscar, eyes wide with alarm. *The sound of running feet.*

"What the hell?" She grabbed Oscar's arm.

Startled, Oscar hurried to the window again. Three or four figures in sweatpants were sprinting up the street. Senses on alert, he hurried down the stairs. Jess was outside her bedroom door, groggy but curious.

"What's going on, Dad?"

"I'm about to find out," said Oscar.

Releasing the chain and opening the door with caution, he immediately spotted the reason for the commotion. A soggy mess was sliding down the door frame. Oscar craned his neck and could see that the two downstairs windows had also been hit. He wasn't going to deal with this now. They could deal with it in the morning.

"Well?" said Jess, shivering in the stairwell.

"Eggs. There's egg smashed all over the front door and the bedroom windows."

"Eggs?"

"A prank, I guess. A Halloween prank. Who knows? Anyway, back to bed. Mom wants to get an early start for this trip to the coast tomorrow."

Hazel was waiting, white-faced, at the top of the stairs.

"Eggs," said Oscar. "That's all. Kids playing a prank."

Hazel looked done in. Oscar was beginning to wonder about the value of this vacation to Ireland. As he lay next to her in an unfamiliar bed in an unfamiliar house he wondered what to do. It was taking Hazel a long time to get back to her old self this time. Her behavior was becoming increasingly difficult.

As he turned on his side and snuggled in next to her he wondered if a few slaps could really have had such an effect on her?

Oscar hadn't expected much from the trip to the coast on a fresh October day. For one thing, Hazel's driving made him edgy. He'd already decided to keep his mouth shut and he'd been very patient so far. Taking in the sights of County Clare proved to be just what Hazel needed. She didn't mention the strange events of the previous night, telling them instead of her teenage exploits in the seaside towns of Kilkee and Lahinch.

When they reached the surfing beach at Lahinch, Elliot managed to persuade his sister to join him in the water. The O'Briens had left out wet suits for the kids. Their fellow surfers seemed oblivious to the cold as they pulled on wet suits over their mottled skin. Oscar found it funny. They could just as easily have been taking in waves in California. The weather didn't deter them any.

As the kids mucked about in the surf, Oscar sat on the seawall nursing a take-out Americano. Hazel wouldn't sit with him, concerned she was too far away from the kids. She walked across the beach to where the sand was wet. And for a few moments he felt a stupid, irrational pang of jealousy toward his own children.

It was dark when they pulled back into the driveway at Curragower Falls. The weir was visible and the sound of spilling water came from the falls. A line of cars parked the whole way down the street and a somber line of people was making its way up the street past the house. As they gathered the soggy wet suits from the trunk, the church bells tolled.

"A funeral," said Hazel, the Sunday papers under one arm and a wet suit in the other. "You guys, shower. Elliot first—then you, Jess."

This was another drawback of a home-exchange holiday, thought Oscar. Sometimes the facilities were not what they had at home. They each had their own shower in Riverside Drive.

"Please, Mom, I want to go first," said Jess.

"No, Jess. Elliot's quick, at least. And when you've finished, I'm going to soak in the tub after all that driving. Then I'll Skype the O'Briens to find out if everything's okay with them."

Oscar went upstairs to the kitchen. It struck him then that he didn't really know what to do with himself. He missed his routine. He was missing the gym. He was missing his run in the park and his game of squash. He paced up and down the kitchen, going to the window and back. Outside, mourners were still making their way up the street. He heard the electric hum of the shower as he flicked through the CDs on the kitchen counter. The Doors, Fleetwood Mac's *Rumours*, Pink Floyd—*The Wall*—not his favorite, some Donna Summer. Some stuff there he approved of. There was a vinyl collection upstairs in the study. He should take a look. He wondered if the hotel on the bridge had leisure facilities. A swim might do the trick.

Wallop! Crash!!!

What the hell?

Heart pounding, Oscar went to investigate.

It had sounded like breaking glass.

"You stupid kid!"

"It's *all your* fault. You're a stupid freakin' psycho!" Elliot was shouting at the open doorway of his sister's bedroom.

"Hey, you guys!" Hazel appeared, wrapped in a towel.

"What is going on here?" said Oscar.

"It's all her fault, Dad. She's a bitch!"

"Whoa there, Elliot. You can cut that out for a start—what exactly did Jess do?" Oscar remained calm.

"I set up all the soldiers in my room and she just came in and walked right through them, knocking them all over. *Deliberately.*"

Oscar wondered how long it would be before something like this happened. Cooped up with Elliot, Jess was going to lash out sooner or later. It looked like he wasn't the only one with cabin fever. There were tanks and soldiers everywhere.

"It was *not* deliberate," said Jess, hands on her hips. "Mom, you wanna see what the little twerp did just now . . . he threw a freakin' jeep at me and missed . . . and that really cool cast of the arm that was on the chest of drawers? The stupid twerp hit that instead."

Hazel was already at the other side of Jess's bed. Oscar followed her.

"What the . . . ?" said Hazel as she bent over the shattered plaster. *"What on earth is this?"*

The cast was indeed broken, shattered into white chunks all over the wooden floor. But that wasn't what concerned Hazel. There, in what remained of the plaster mold, was a hammer. A hammer wrapped in a flowery pillowcase. And the flowery pillowcase was covered in what looked like blood.

Oscar tried to play the incident down. He told Hazel that staying in other folks' homes you occasionally stumbled on stuff that seemed weird. As a very unsettled Hazel went off to get dressed, Oscar set to, collecting the broken plaster from the floor.

Later that night, in bed, Hazel whispered to him in the dark, "I know you think I'm making it up, Oscar. But there's something strange going on in this house."

"You're imagining things, Hazel," he said, turning over. He went to sleep to the sound of fireworks, wailing sirens, and a sound he hadn't heard for many years. The sound of an animal screaming in pain.

Kate

"Well, blow me . . ." Mannix let out a low whistle. "Come and get a load of this, Kate."

"What?" She swung her legs out of the bed. She'd just woken up.

"Oh, man, you've got to see this dude . . . I could tell he was a prick from his owner profile." Mannix was standing in front of an open wardrobe door.

"How do you mean?" Kate hadn't noticed anything untoward on the home-exchange Web site.

"That photo of him posing in those tight bicycle shorts and that spray-on Lycra top."

"Well, you go round in tight rowing gear . . ."

"I don't have a fucking wardrobe like this guy—look at it!"

Kate shuffled over the soft carpet, hugging her T-shirt tight. Behind the dark louvered door was an extensive rack of crisply ironed shirts. It was no hotchpotch arrangement. Like colors hung together in their individual colorways. Above that were neatly folded, soft-colored sweaters and T-shirts. But what had really caught Mannix's eye was the collection of shoes. The sheer number of shoes was staggering. There must have been at least eighty to a hundred pairs, all neatly housed in pigeonholes.

Kate picked up a pointy brown-laced pair. She turned them over. Italian. She guessed as much. There were all kinds of sports shoes, runners, and golfing studs. The formal shoes were all pristine and shining.

"Christ alive!" Mannix said, laughing. "This dude's got it all!"

Kate thought back to the ten or so well-worn shirts hanging in their shared wardrobe at home. Tidy, but probably unironed. And as for shoes—Mannix had a few pairs under the bed. They'd all been heeled and soled in the last year.

"Some of these have never even been worn . . ." He hunkered down and pulled a cardboard box out of its cubbyhole.

"Leave it, Mannix."

It was one thing going through clothing on display, but rummaging about in boxes, even if they were only shoe boxes—that didn't feel right. But Mannix had already taken off the lid.

"Nope," said Mannix. "This one ain't shoes . . ."

He stood up, cardboard box in hand, the lid half-perched on top.

Kate stepped closer to Mannix, about to lean her palm against the scar across his back. She pulled back quickly without touching, remembering she was still half angry with him.

"Fuck me! Look at that kid, Kate. The lad's a bit of a porker, isn't he?" Mannix held up a fading black-and-white photograph.

"Can I see?"

In the photo, two kids stood in front of a very large tree, a Christmas tree. The chubby little girl was dressed in a nurse's uniform. She clutched a first-aid box to her chest. A boy stood next to her in a cowboy hat, a gun slotted into his holster, his dark waistcoat about to pop, straining at the buttons. He was extremely overweight, obese, in fact. The little nurse was smiling. The cowboy sullen. Kate turned the photo over. Someone had written OSCAR AND HELEN, CHRISTMAS in capital letters on the back.

"This one's worse," said Mannix, picking another photo from the pile. "At least poor fatty had his clothes on in the other one . . ."

It was a color photo this time, showing the same two children.

This time they were sitting on the steps of a porch outside a pale-blue clapboard house. The little boy was in bathing togs, clutching a plastic bucket on his knees. The bucket hid some of the rolls of belly fat. The little girl wore a polka-dot sundress. Her arm was draped around her brother. The inscription on the back was in the same hand. OSCAR AND HELEN, SAG HARBOR, SUMMER VACATION.

"Come on, Mannix, that's enough. Put them back," said Kate.

There was something sad about both photos.

Whoopi Goldberg's voice came over all warm and earthy in the darkened planetarium. Kate glanced along the row to see if the kids were enjoying the show. They were enthralled. Kate felt proud of Fergus, delighted at his patience about the delayed visit to the Empire State. A wave of tenderness washed over her as she watched his little upturned face, his mouth open, brilliant galactic explosions reflected in his glasses. Then, for a second or two, her eyes came to rest on Mannix. Kate sighed and looked away, trying to concentrate on the show.

What did I tell you? What did I tell you about those O'Briens? All those O'Briens are the same. Like their father before them. Like all their uncles. Every whole one of them the same, to a man. Oh, shut up, Mam, she said to the voice in her head.

She'd decided last night as she pretended to sleep. Kate wasn't going to think about Mannix's disturbing confession. Not on holiday. There was a welcome otherworldliness about being in New York, so far away from home. As if the real world didn't matter. They were safe here, far across the ocean. Safe from bullies. Safe from the Flynns and the Bolgers. Safe from mortgage worries and phone calls from the bank. Safe from Spike and all the mayhem that followed him.

For the rest of this week, at least, she was going to bury her head in the sand and live for the moment. She might even let Mannix make love to her. Last night, he hadn't dared to slide as much as a hairy leg anywhere near her. Pity that. She'd been looking forward to some intimacy, but the stupid idiot had gone and spoiled it all.

Withholding sex was risky. She'd learned that to her cost. She remembered back to the beginning of the year and yet another argument about money. Things were tight and she'd pleaded with Mannix to get Spike to return the money they'd lent him five years ago.

Predictably, when that didn't work out, she tried giving Mannix the cold shoulder. But matters soon escalated, and before she knew it, five months had slipped away without so much as a cuddle. Reluctantly, she came to understand what her single friend Rosie in the Art School meant by not minding being left on the shelf, as long as she was taken down and given a good dusting every now and then.

Kate had become fearful then that a rift had opened up that might not heal. Yet somehow they'd arrived where they were now, with ground to make up, but happier. It was their common bond with Fergus that had pulled them back together. So for the next few days she was going to pretend that all was well. She was going to ignore what Mannix told her last night. And she was going to pretend the guy she'd married was just a regular guy.

She stole another look at Mannix. What was he up to now? And then she realized. The electronic glow was a giveaway. He was texting. She wouldn't get annoyed. But she felt unnerved. Mannix was usually a laid-back guy. When he was uneasy, it made Kate uneasy too. He looked up and, realizing he was being watched, let his hand fall to the side. He smiled innocently, teeth pearl-white in the dim light of the planetarium. She found herself smiling back. Oh, he was smooth, this man of hers.

The kids pronounced the show as "awesome," and they were all in for a big surprise as they left the museum.

Snow!

It was snowing outside. It wasn't even November and fat flakes of snow filled the sky. Foamy white flurries fell on the trees in Central Park—trees still thick with leaves. Pedestrians caught by surprise hailed cabs and scurried for cover.

"This is so cool," said Fergus.

"I don't know about that," said Kate. They'd planned on having lunch somewhere in Central Park and Kate had wanted to see the Boathouse restaurant. The snow had changed all that.

"How about we get a cab to the Museum of Modern Art? We could get some lunch there . . ."

Her suggestion was met with blank faces.

"How about Abercrombie on Fifth Avenue?" said Izzy, not expecting her suggestion to fly.

"You know what? Let's go for it!" said Kate.

Hell, the child had put in a rough year. So what if Kate thought it a criminal use of time? It would make Izzy happy.

Back out on Fifth Avenue after a torturous hour in Abercrombie, Kate was glad of the bracing air and the smell of toasting chestnuts. There was something disturbing about the physically perfect shop assistants in there. She'd allowed the kids to buy a T-shirt and a sweatshirt each. The snow had stopped falling and what lay on the street was wet and slushy. Mannix marched ahead with the kids, who were merrily swinging their shopping bags.

They were headed for Times Square and the Hard Rock Café. The plan was to eat early, and hopefully by the time they got back to the apartment, Du Bois would have managed to get them tickets for *War Horse* at Lincoln Center. Fergus had read the novel with his special needs teacher and it had struck a chord with him. When Hazel Harvey mentioned to Kate that Du Bois had a contact for discounted theater tickets, she had been delighted. They certainly couldn't afford to pay full price.

"Hang on, Mannix . . . You guys!" Kate called to them to come back.

They were unaware that they'd walked past a famous landmark from their favorite *Home Alone* movie. They'd passed by an opening to Rockefeller Center. Kate had noticed the row of flags in front of a skyscraper and thought it looked familiar. On first glance there was little evidence of skaters, but as they drew closer to the central square, they spotted the pockets of hardy skaters on the rectangle of ice. How deceiving television could be, thought Kate. The ice rink had a cozy, almost intimate feel and was not at all on the scale she had imagined.

"So, guys, this is where young Kevin found his mother," Kate declared.

"This is it?" said Izzy.

"Sure is. Look, over there is where the huge Christmas tree was. We're too early in the season for the Christmas tree. Just one second, stay there," said Kate, and she quickly snapped the three of them.

Twenty minutes later they found themselves outside the Hard Rock Café in the gaudy quarter that was Times Square. It seemed strangely lifeless in the daylight. Like fireworks on an inky sky, it needed night to kick it into life.

"I'm bloody starving," announced Mannix. "I'd eat the arse off a Christian brother."

"Mannix!" said Kate.

Fergus and Izzy giggled.

They all tucked into burgers, Fergus removing only some of the "alien" gherkins and tomatoes from his burger bun. By the time they finished their meal and got outside again, darkness had fallen. Harsh and garish lights exploded from every angle.

"Feck it anyway," said Mannix looking up at a flashing alert.

"What is it?" asked Kate, alarmed.

"Shares are down today . . ."

"What shares?"

"Exactly . . ." He laughed ruefully.

Kate smiled and slipped her hand in his. The kids walked ahead, looking for a subway sign.

Out of nowhere, a guy with a long overcoat approached the kids, doing a grapevine dance routine alongside. Mannix tensed. The guy forced a CD into Izzy's palm and dark spots of embarrassment stained her cheeks.

"Only five dollars to you, sweet cheeks! It's got some cool beats. What do you say now? C'mon. It's wholly Justin Bieber approved . . ." He shoved his face closer to Izzy's.

"Lay off!" Mannix shouted at the guy. "She's only a kid. Fuck off, pick on someone else . . ."

"Hey, chill, no panic, bro . . ."

And just as quickly he pranced off, swooping on someone else.

"That was a little aggressive, you don't know what he could have done," ventured Kate.

"That stuff really annoys me, Kate. Don't worry, I can handle myself." He looked at Fergus. "I could take a guy like that anytime, isn't that right, Soldier?"

Fergus looked up at his hero. Kate had no doubt that Mannix could do just that.

Half an hour later they climbed the steps at the Verdi Square subway station. Kate had wondered just how safe the subway was. From what she'd read, Ed Koch's zero tolerance policy had worked a treat on cleaning up the transport system. She was happy to find it was a surprisingly easy journey, from buying the MetroCard at the vending booth to finding the right platform and train.

"You get caught up in this crazy snowstorm?" asked Du Bois.

"We were indoors mainly," said Kate, "but we could certainly do with a change of footwear."

"I've got news for you," he said, grinning. "My buddy's got four tickets for the Lincoln. Four good seats as well." Du Bois handed them a thick white envelope.

"Thanks a million," said Mannix. "Now, what does that come in at, Mr. Du Bois? I'd like to fix up with you." Mannix reached for his wallet.

"Nothing at all, sir. Lenny owes me a favor. Just you go and make sure you all enjoy yourselves."

"Are you sure?" said Kate.

"Sure." Du Bois smiled again. "Oh, before I forget . . ." Suddenly his face clouded over. "This arrived for Mrs. Harvey."

He placed a small paper carrier bag on the marble counter.

"It's a personal item that Mrs. Harvey left behind at a local diner. My sister is a waitress there and she dropped by with it earlier."

The paper bag had Duane Reade lettering. Duane Reade was a chain of drugstores, wasn't it? Du Bois pushed the bag toward Kate. "Maybe you can take it up to the apartment? Or I can hold on to it here until Mrs. Harvey returns, if you prefer?" He pulled the bag back toward him as if unsure.

"It's no problem at all." Kate took the bag.

Once inside the lift she took a look. Du Bois had made her curious but it was only a book with a note stuck on the front:

> Mrs. Harvey,
>> *You left this in Viand last Thursday.*
>> *Thought you might like it returned.*
>> Anita

Back in the apartment, Kate offered to make a pot of tea. They had only an hour to spare before heading out again. Mannix had collapsed onto the sofa without even taking off his coat, hat, or scarf. He was surfing the TV channels with the remote. Every channel was carrying the same news story.

"Snow, snow, snow. Yeah, we get it, guys," he muttered.

Kate listened to him muttering as she walked across the kitchen floor enjoying the cool feel of the marble floor on her bare and swollen feet. She put on the kettle to make tea.

As she waited for the kettle, her eyes fell again on the Duane Reade bag. What did Hazel Harvey read? What kind of a person was she? Hazel Harvey had come across as personable but reserved in her e-mails and on Skype. It was difficult to tell what she was like, not having met her face-to-face. What did feel peculiar to Kate was that every time Hazel Harvey's name came up, Du Bois bristled protectively. This woman was in Kate's house in Ireland. Curiosity aroused, she took the book out of the bag and looked at it again.

Oh, shit!

She did a double take at first. She felt as if she'd been slapped. Shocked, she dropped the book onto the work surface, letting the cover slam shut. *There had been nothing on the spine or the front cover to indicate what it was.* Nothing to indicate its contents. Japanese lacquerwork. A gold ribbon acting as a placeholder. Nothing more. Tentatively, she picked it up again. She knew she shouldn't. But she couldn't help herself. Had she really read those words? She quickly fanned through the pages again. There it was. At the bottom of the page. She read the diary entry for a second time.

September 4—I can still hear it. The hissing in my ear. The smell of garlic on his breath. You're a cunt he hisses. A prize cunt. I find it hard to write. To see those words on paper. But I need to keep a record. Over and over he repeats it. His face contorted with rage. I am afraid.

Kate felt herself go cold. This was not a conventional diary. No preprinted dates. It was more like a notebook with a mishmash of diary entries and scribblings. Her heart in her mouth, Kate turned the page.

September 5—Met Elizabeth today. She agrees that it's a good idea to record everything. She is angry with me too. All of a sudden it's like everyone's angry with me. Oscar, Elizabeth, even the kids.

The writing was neat, written in blue pen. She read on.

September 11—Getting flashbacks. It's over a week ago now but I'm still trying to make sense of it. How it happened. I need to get it clear in my head. This time he accused me of showing him disrespect, that I do not value his opinion. I find myself wondering if I have been unfair in any way. I know I cannot let myself condone this behavior. Yet I'm trying to rationalize his response. Sometimes I think it's my fault, I shouldn't have laughed. He thought I was laughing at him, not laughing with him. I know things haven't been easy for

him. I'm confused. I feel powerless, like he's the one con-
trolling everything.

September 12—Think he suspects I've been talking. He said if
I told anyone, he wouldn't stand for it. Told me it would be
over. I try not to show my fear. As long as I stay composed and
look like I'm in control, there is hope. I have been here before
I say to myself. I can find a way through this.

The writing became bigger, more uneven, no longer sticking to
the confines of the pale-blue lines. As if the entries were made in haste.
Kate wondered now if, like she was doing, Du Bois too had scanned
through the pages. Could that explain his hesitation?

September 13—We are going to Ireland. I can find a way
through this. I could leave, I know that. But I cannot admit
failure. I have invested too much.

September 17—Flashbacks getting worse. I cannot sleep. Afraid
to go to bed. I toy with the idea of telling Helen. And then I
think the better of it. She knows we are going to Ireland but
she doesn't know why.

"What happened to that tea?" called Mannix from the sofa.
"Just coming!" Kate shouted back, her stomach feeling sick.
She quickly leafed through a few more pages. Some entries weren't
even dated. Lopsided scrawls that were hard to read. She tilted the
journal, trying to decipher the letters. And then there was another
spate of dated entries.

October 10—Feel like I'm going mad.

October 11—Went to the dog run today and pretended to read.

October 13—Went to the dog run again. I think about going back to work.

October 14—Had palpitations last night. Work not a good idea.

"I'm dying of thirst in here," Mannix shouted again.

Snapping the cover shut, she dropped the journal on the table as if it had bitten her.

"You okay?" Mannix took the mug from her. "You look a bit pale."

"No, I'm fine," she replied, still in shock from what she'd read.

"We don't have to go out, you know. We don't have to go to this show—I mean, if you're withered from all the walking . . ."

"God, no." She couldn't miss the show for Fergus. "Of course we're going. I'm just a bit tired, that's all. It'd be a sin to miss it. I just need to get off my feet a minute."

"Here, get them up next to me." He patted the sofa. "Rest your weary little feet."

Leaving her mug of tea on the coffee table, she did as he said. She lay with her head against the armrest as Mannix rubbed her feet and calves. The gentle pressure of his fingers did little to stop the alarm bells ringing in her head.

In terms of a spectacle, *War Horse* lived up to expectations. The puppetry was on a scale Kate hadn't seen before. Fergus was enchanted, and for long stretches at a time he even forgot about the foot tapping that usually beset him in the cinema or at a show. Izzy too drank it all in with her big dark eyes.

Kate didn't tell Mannix about the disturbing diary. She didn't want to spoil their holiday. Hazel Harvey's life was none of their business and Kate had inadvertently violated the woman's privacy to no good end. There was nothing to be done, Kate told herself.

Surprisingly, she slept well that night and woke to find Mannix in front of the television. The news was full of stories of the freak October snowstorm and power outages across the state and in New

Jersey. Parts of Central Park were closed, as branches still in leaf and heavy with snow were breaking and falling to the ground. The Con Ed electricity company was working around the clock to restore power. Halloween trick-or-treating was in danger of being canceled.

"We *are* still going to the Empire State, though, aren't we?" Fergus was dressed and ready to go. Kate could almost see cartoon dust wheels spinning from his little heels.

Barely an hour later, they were standing outside on Thirty-fourth Street. "So, Soldier, this is it!" Kate declared to Fergus as they shuffled in the roped-off queues. He trembled with excitement. As they exited the first lift, Kate could feel the subtle vibrations of the building as it swayed. Fergus surveyed the *King Kong* posters on the walls as they waited a full five minutes for the next lift up to the observation deck.

As the lift doors opened and Kate walked toward the outdoor terrace, she experienced a momentary sensation of dizziness as her eyes adjusted to the scale of the panorama outside. "Hang on, just a minute, Soldier." Mannix put a hand on Fergus's shoulder, restraining him a moment. The wraparound terrace was wedged with tourists jostling for a viewing space. Mannix cut a path through the crowd and managed to corral the four of them into a corner next to a viewfinder. And for the next twenty minutes, Fergus remained frozen to the spot, with the lens of the viewfinder welded to his face.

Kate looked out west to New Jersey and then downtown to the tower blocks of the Financial District. She thought how vulnerable they looked, there on the very tip of the flat island. The iconic buildings, bastions of capitalism, screamed out to be noticed. She thought back to the events of 9/11 and imagined how surreal it must have been to see those planes as they fireballed into the World Trade Center. She shivered and said a quiet prayer for all the lost souls.

Mannix kept shifting position to shield them from the icy blasts. How cozy and safe he made them feel. What a tight family unit they must look, thought Kate. But looks could be deceiving. Her thoughts slipped back to Hazel's diary. What exactly was going on inside the Harveys' marriage? *What was happening in Kate's house at Curragower Falls?*

Later that morning, they walked about with no particular purpose in mind, past the New York Public Library and on until they reached an entrance to Central Park at Columbus Circle. As they entered the park, some paths were cordoned off with tape. Tree surgeons were busy dealing with branches that had split under the weight of snow. Fergus began to complain of hunger. Until now he had been happily silent, savoring the morning's experience. Rounding the crest of a small hillock, they found themselves at a pagoda-style coffee shop, Le Pain Quotidien. Izzy was struggling to say it correctly.

"What do you think about this Halloween Parade tomorrow?" asked Kate over lunch.

"Sounds great. It's in Greenwich Village, yeah? I definitely want to go there."

Kate knew they'd lose him for at least a couple of hours to the secondhand music stores.

"Okay, so we'll do that Circle Line cruise in the morning—the one that goes from Forty-second Street around the bottom of Manhattan and then head to Greenwich Village afterward?"

"You're the boss," said Mannix.

"I think I'll Skype the Harveys."

Back at Riverside Drive, Kate could no longer contain her unease.

"Isn't that a bit like checking up on them?" said Mannix. "They'd contact us if there was a problem."

"You know what? It's six P.M. there now. I'll Skype, and if they're in, they're in, and if they're not, they're not."

Kate set herself up at the screen on the pull-out console table in the kitchen. The call was answered within seconds.

"Oh, hi there, Kate! How wonderful to see you in our home . . ." A jittery Hazel Harvey zoomed into view.

It felt surreal to see Hazel in their study back at Curragower Falls. Kate went through some chitchat and apologized for borrowing a pair of Hazel's shoes when her own had been soaked in the snow. Interpreting Hazel's face and body language was difficult with the jerky video delay, but Kate felt her instincts had been right. Hazel Harvey looked upset.

"I'm going to cut to the chase here, Kate. I'm afraid there's been an accident."

Kate prickled with alarm. So she had been right.

"Can you hold on just a minute?" said Hazel. "I just want to get something."

"Sure."

Hazel disappeared from view and Kate had the bizarre experience of staring at her own bookshelves from thousands of miles away. *Where were Oscar Harvey and the children?* A full minute or so went by before Hazel returned. She was holding on to something.

"The kids were fooling around, Kate . . ." She looked nervous, apologetic. "And I'm very sorry but they broke this. I don't know if it can be mended . . ."

For a moment Kate couldn't make out what it was. She tilted her head from side to side. It looked like tubing. And then it came to her. Hazel was holding on to Izzy's cast. It was the cast of Izzy's arm that Izzy and Kate had made on Take Your Child to Work Day, and it was broken.

Relief washed over Kate. "Oh, Hazel, don't you worry about that. We can always make another one. Izzy will understand." She'd been expecting worse.

"That's so good of you, Kate. There's just one other thing, though . . ."

"Yes?"

"Something a little weird, I guess. This is what we found inside . . ."

Kate was stunned. Stuck for words, she felt her stomach lurch.

Hazel looked awkward. "I'm not sure what I should do with these? I'm not sure, Kate, but I think that could be blood."

In one hand, Hazel Harvey held a hammer. In the other, a bloodied pillowcase. A chill ran up Kate's spine. It was the same flowery pillowcase that Mannix had the night he took Izzy to Girl Guides. *The night that Frankie Flynn was injured. The night that Frankie ended up in hospital.*

Kate felt the blood drain from her face. "Oh, that's all just part of

Izzy's project," she improvised. "Honestly, Hazel, don't worry at all. Just put the whole lot in a plastic bag in one of Izzy's drawers."

"If you're sure . . ."

Kate inquired about the Harveys' holiday. Did they do the cliff walk in Kilkee? What did they think of the café at the Diamond Rocks? She thought she sounded okay but felt a telltale rash spreading up her neck.

"Everything good in the house?" she asked, anxious now to end the call.

"You have a lovely home, Kate. Spike showed us where everything was. Oh, yes, and someone dropped by yesterday morning to read the gas meter."

"You mean the electricity meter?"

"No, I think it was the gas, Kate. No, in fact I'm sure. It was the gas."

Kate's stomach lurched again. The rash was spreading down her arms. She felt herself go clammy.

Agreeing to touch base later in the week, she cut the conversation short.

Kate was truly shaken. *But what could she have said? How could she tell Hazel Harvey the house at Curragower Falls had never been fitted with a gas supply? That they'd never been connected?* But she couldn't dwell on that just now. There was something even more urgent Kate had to see to first.

She stood up and walked into the living room.

"Look at me, Mannix."

He didn't move.

"Turn around and bloody well look at me!" she shouted.

"Jesus, Kate, what is it?" He swung around.

"What the hell did you do to Frankie Flynn?"

"What are you talking about, Kate?"

"Frankie Flynn! I can't bloody well believe that you could be so bloody stupid, Mannix! It *was* you, wasn't it? It was you who attacked him and landed him in hospital. You're the one who attacked him with a hammer!"

"Kate, this is ridiculous. Where did you get all this?"

"The Harveys found the evidence. Today. Hidden inside the cast in Izzy's room! The missing hammer wrapped in the bloodied pillowcase. The same one you left the house with. I saw it, Mannix. Don't deny it. I'm sick to death of all the lies!"

"*Stop! Stop it now,* please, Mum!"

Kate spun around. Christ, they'd woken the kids. How much had Izzy heard?

"Please stop shouting at Dad."

Poor Izzy. Always rushing to her father's defense.

"Go back to bed, Izzy," Kate said wearily.

"No, Mum. I heard what you were talking about. And there's something I must tell you." Izzy paused.

"What is it, Izzy?"

"You see, Mum, it wasn't Dad that went for Frankie Flynn."

"And how do you know that, Izzy?"

"I know that, Mum, because it was me."

Mannix

It was a windy day in March when Mannix boarded the plane as a condemned man hikes the steps to the gallows. He'd been unhappy out of work. Loath though he was to admit it, he found himself more unhappy in it. Shackled to his mortgage arrears, he had little choice.

If only his new boss weren't such a pimply teenage prick. The bigger tragedy was that Mannix was sure that he and Spike would make an excellent team at the nightclub, but Kate was having none of that. So it was back to the suits and ties. Back to the strategy meetings and the leadership conferences and the vision statements and the career planning and all that bullshit.

There were few plus sides to this trip, but if he finished early some evening, he might catch up with some rowing buddies from his early twenties. Danno and Mental George had gone to Boston after college and never returned. He doubted they ever would. As illegals they couldn't afford the risk.

Mannix secured his bottle of Jameson in the overhead locker and settled himself into the window seat over the wing. Gone were the days of traveling business class. He'd have to earn his stripes again. Wedging his novel into the sleeve in front, he put on headphones, hoping to doze off. He hoped to Christ some pain in the arse didn't sit next to him wanting to talk.

"What the . . . !"

"I'm so very sorry! I can't believe I did that."

Scalded awake, he grabbed his stinging arm. The hot caramel liquid seeped into the pale blue shirtsleeve that Kate had ironed earlier.

"No problem, I'll live," he muttered as graciously as he could.

The woman beside him tried to dab his arm, to soak up the already absorbed coffee. Her nails were shiny red.

"Thank you. I'm fine," he said.

She smiled apologetically.

Mannix looked at his watch. He must have been asleep for more than an hour. Streaks of rain were lashing against the tiny window and the wingtips shivered in the sky. It was bumpy.

"I guess I missed the drinks trolley, then?" He tried to smooth over the embarrassment.

"The steward didn't want to wake you." The woman paused. "You were snoring . . ."

There was a hint of mischief in her voice. It was Mannix's turn to be embarrassed.

"Mannix O'Brien." He held out his hand.

"Joanne Collins."

Her hand felt small and smooth. She wore no rings.

"And this is Grace."

She leaned back in her seat to introduce the child beside her.

"Hello, Grace," he said.

"Hi," said the child, looking up from her crossword. She was a miniature version of her mother. Small chin, dark eyebrows.

"Any empties?" interrupted a steward.

Mannix watched as Joanne Collins daintily handed the steward her empty tray. She fastened the tabletop and, leaning back, rested her hands on her lap. She didn't speak again and he was grateful for that.

Resting his head against the window, he stared out at the shuddering wingtip. How had he ended up here? he wondered. In this life?

In this job? He was lucky to have the job, he supposed. His hometown had become a wasteland, tumbleweeds rolling through the industrial parks. No one seemed to care. Politicians, government agencies, local agencies. There was nothing doing. They cared about the other cities in the country. But no one seemed to care about his. Mannix woke up most mornings with a feeling of despondency, queasily making his way through the day. He was forty-three on his next birthday at the end of August, in six months' time. Christ! Forty-three already.

As a teenager, he'd imagined a different life. He'd work a few months of the year and travel the rest. He'd work as an illustrator or as a photographer for *National Geographic*. He might teach diving in the Red Sea. Or he might even go into the casinos with his dad. He'd never thought about a wife and kids.

Mannix sighed. Things were equally miserable on the home front. Some space apart might not hurt. He was doing his best, squeezing and contorting himself into the rigid box that was now his life. Still, it wasn't enough for Kate. He'd seen her disappointed many times, but the anger, that cold brittle anger—that was new. In the last few months, Mannix found it hard to recognize the scorched and barren landscape of their marriage. Kate harbored vast reserves of resentment, of that he was sure. For the most part Mannix kept out of her way. And for Kate's part, she raised no objection.

"Have you figured out who did it yet?"

"I'm sorry?"

Pulling his book from the sleeve in front, Mannix had settled himself for a read. He was flattening out the dog-ear.

"Was it the spurned wife or the guy in the wheelchair?"

Joanne Collins held up a copy of the exact same thriller.

"Neither." Mannix laughed at the coincidence. "My money's on the daughter. With this guy, trust me, it's always the least likely character."

"It's pretty formulaic, all right," she agreed.

Joanne Collins was a tidy woman. Snug jeans, snug cotton sweater, shiny hair tied back in a ponytail. Her clothes smelled of fabric freshener. The kind that was supposed to make you think of the sea.

"Tell me," she said, looking straight at him, "have you ever yet read a detective series where the detective didn't have a drink problem?"

"Well, now, let me see . . . that depends," Mannix considered. "Do you mean a drunk or an alcoholic?"

"Either, I guess." She looked surprised. "What's the difference?"

"That's easy," said Mannix. "The drunk doesn't have to do the meetings."

Her head fell back as she laughed. It was a nice sound. He noticed how perfect her teeth were. Unlike his, none of them was filled.

"I'm really sorry about your shirt," she said again.

"Oh, don't worry about it." Mannix brushed it off.

"Work or pleasure?" he found himself asking.

"Oh, pleasure, definitely. On a stopover on our way to Disney, isn't that right, Grace?" Joanne rubbed the child's hand. "Grace has been such a brave girl in hospital, so this is her treat. We're taking some time off school. Naughty, I know . . ."

"School can wait, you'll have a super time," Mannix said to the child. She seemed like a nice kid.

"And you?" Joanne asked. "Work or pleasure?"

"Work for me." He pulled a face.

Joanne laughed.

"What is it that you do?" she asked.

"Fuck knows," he said quietly. "I'm trying to figure it out . . ."

"Let me guess," she said, "you're an investment analyst or an accountant maybe?"

"Jesus, no." An accountant? He knew it. He knew the suits and ties would do that to him someday. Flipping open his wallet, he fished through the wads of plastic and business cards. He found the newly printed business cards. *Mannix O'Brien, IT Business Strategy and Project Support Analyst.*

"Hold on to that," he said to her sarcastically. "You never know when you might just need a business strategist or a project support analyst."

She put a thinking finger up to her chin. "Come to think of it . . ."

"Is that your family?" Joanne Collins was looking at the laminated wallet photo of the four of them taken before last Christmas. Just before the cracks appeared. In it, they looked happy. Kate particularly so, her blond hair draping over Mannix's shoulder where she rested her chin.

Mannix had surprised himself. Almost without his knowing, he'd struck up a rapport with this woman.

"She seems a good kid," said Mannix, looking at her daughter. The child was watching a cartoon.

"She's great," said Joanne. "Just great. She's had a tough time." She sighed. "It can be pretty rough when you're a single parent."

"I'll bet," said Mannix.

Out of nowhere, the plane shuddered violently. The conversation dried up instantly and his companion went silent, gripping the armrest. An announcement advised that they were entering a spot of turbulence.

"Oh, that's just great, just what I need," Joanne muttered, eyes squeezed shut.

"Mummy doesn't like airplanes," said Grace in a strange sort of role reversal. The child patted her mother's hand. Suddenly, the plane lurched forward and then dropped, making his stomach flutter.

"Ooops, that's a bit of a drop . . ." Seeing the look on Joanne's face, he let his hand rest on hers for comfort.

"Planes—they're designed to take these conditions, you know." Mannix tried to sound reassuring, feeling none too reassured himself. A bolt of lightning cracked across the sky.

"Oh, Jesus!"

Joanne's hand fluttered to the pearl sitting in the hollow of her neck. Her other hand trembled underneath his palm.

"This is what's supposed to happen, Mummy." But Mummy was too petrified to reply.

For the next fifteen minutes, as the plane bounced through air pocket after air pocket, dodging lightning forks, both Mannix and the little girl tried to distract her mother. He and Grace chattered across Joanne about all manner of ridiculous things—anything to make light of the turbulence.

"Cabin crew, return to your seats."

Grace's eyes connected with his and she stared at her stricken mother. The announcement had made Joanne go more rigid. Mannix felt her stiffen.

"Uh-oh," mouthed Mannix silently to Grace.

At the next violent jolt, all three leaned back, gluing their backs into the imaginary security of their upright chairs.

"What's that smell?" whispered Joanne in his ear. "I smell burning." Her head was resting against Mannix's arm. He couldn't smell anything except her fabric conditioner and the smell of her hair. Her breath was warm on his ear.

"It's nothing. You're imagining it. There's no smoke."

The plane juddered again. Squeezing his hand, Joanne opened her eyes and looked up at him. "God, what am I like? Pathetic or what? I thought that I could do this flight thing. For Grace . . ."

"You're doing just great." Mannix squeezed her hand. "And you know what? I think the worst is over."

"God, I could murder a whiskey," she said.

"If it wasn't so bumpy, I'd get my Jameson from the locker."

"Thwarted at every turn." She managed a laugh.

"You're good with kids," Joanne said shakily when the flight eventually resumed an even path.

Realizing she was feeling safer, he withdrew his hand before it became awkward.

"Practice," he replied. "I've had plenty of practice."

Was she attractive, Mannix wondered? He wasn't sure. But she looked clever.

"Want one?" Grace was leaning across her mother with a tube of fruit pastilles.

"Any black ones in there?" he said.

"They're my favorites as well," said Grace. "Hang on . . ."

As Grace tried to extricate the lone black jelly, the tube fell apart, the jellies spraying into her mother's lap. Embarrassed that his request had led to this mishap, Mannix reached to tidy the sweets in Joanne's lap. Joanne looked at him with an amused expression, sensing his embarrassment. "Really, it's okay . . ." she said in an odd replay of the coffee incident earlier.

When the trolley service arrived with dinner, they swapped food between the three of them, and in the companionable silence that followed, Mannix dozed off and came in to land the same way he had taken off, asleep. It was seven P.M. local time.

"How I wish I could be as relaxed as you," said Joanne Collins. "I do hope the flight to Orlando tomorrow is okay. You don't fancy coming and keeping us company?" There was a twinkle in her eye.

"I wish," he replied. He leaned over to Grace. "Give my best to Minnie Mouse."

"I will. I just can't wait."

The child had packed up her crosswords and her coloring. And in that moment, he couldn't help but contrast the excitement that surrounded this child with the lot of his own children. Fergus's struggles were all too obvious. And Izzy—well, on more occasions than he liked, his eldest child appeared detached and strangely joyless.

"Thanks for the hand to hold," said Joanne as they were making their way out of the aircraft. She was ahead of him with Grace.

"One should never be without a hand to hold," said Mannix.

"Isn't there a song about that?" asked Joanne. "Yes—I have it, 'May You Never' by John Martyn."

"The very man," Mannix confirmed.

It was a song he used to sing to Kate in the early days.

Mannix hated staying in hotels. The blandness of this chain hotel did little to change his mind. The air in the room felt recycled and dried the inside of his nose. Just off the highway and close to the airport, it didn't lend itself to exploration. He could see the continuous ribbon of car lights from his soundproofed window. With a little more imagination the admin staff could have put him somewhere more accessible. A car was coming for him in the morning to take him to the training course. But for now, he was trapped.

The room was big. He supposed it was a suite. One of the queen-size beds was out of sight in the short leg of the L-shaped room and the bathroom was enormous. Mannix didn't want to go to bed just yet. There was nothing on TV but a succession of presenters with white teeth and big hair, so he changed into a fresh shirt and headed downstairs to the bar. He ordered a Miller and sat at the counter. The lounge chairs and sofas were occupied by suits with laptops.

The Hispanic bartender was extremely courteous. It occurred to Mannix that some of Spike's staff could do with brushing up their hospitality skills. On second thought—with Spike's clientele, that effort could be wasted.

What exactly was eating Spike, he wondered? On a few occasions lately, Mannix felt that Spike was going to let him in on what was bugging him. Mannix knocked back his beer. Sometimes ignorance and deniability were safer options. But Spike was his younger brother and Mannix felt a responsibility to look out for him, though only within reason.

Spike and Mannix had grown up in the smoky backrooms of their dad's casino watching punters on the slot machines. And Spike could smell the victims and the vultures. The bloodsuckers waiting for those without a criminal record, like a teacher or a tradesman gambling it all, then stepping neatly in. Debts paid off for favors in return. A simple car journey to Dublin in clean number plates, an apartment to stash some gear in, a request to courier goods from one city to another. Spike had seen it all. He knew whom to talk to and whom to avoid. Spike was big and bold enough to sort things out for himself.

If only Mannix could sort out his own life. He had sent Kate a quick text when the plane touched down in Logan. *"Landed."* She came back with a curt *"Ok."* Though he knew she'd be in bed, he'd intended to send a lengthier message when he got to his hotel. But the brevity of her reply had left him feeling flat. He wouldn't bother.

"Another?" asked the barman as Mannix finished the second Miller.

"No, thanks."

Back on the fourth floor, he stopped at the vending machine. He was sure he'd wake up thirsty during the night. Gatorade would do the trick. Like a disgruntled teenager he shuffled down the corridor toward his room. Discarded room-service trays and shoe-shine machines were lined up against the walls. Looking for the key card in his wallet, he suddenly noticed his brown loafers. They were scuffed and dusty. They had seen better times. Or had they? They were his funeral shoes, his interview shoes, his work shoes. Better times? Maybe not. But they could certainly do with a shine.

Mannix went back to the nearest shoe-shine machine. He swigged his Gatorade as he watched the brushes whir over his three-year-old shoes. The corridor was empty. Again he thought on how soulless the place was.

A door clicked open behind him and he turned around. Someone in a bathrobe and towel turban bent to dispose of a tray. He turned back and took another swig.

"Mannix?"

Startled, he swung around. He stared for a second or two.

"Joanne?"

It was her, wasn't it? The woman from the plane. In bare feet she looked smaller, more girlish. But the clever eyes, the small chin, those he recognized.

"So this is where you're staying?" Joanne looked equally surprised. She tried to secure the turban, which was in danger of toppling over. Wet hair escaped underneath.

"Three or four doors up." He pointed with the bottle.

"Good Lord, what a coincidence!"

"Yup!" He found himself grinning.

They looked at each other a moment without saying anything, marveling at the strange turn of events.

"Is that Gatorade? You like that stuff?" She turned her nose up.

"Love it," Mannix replied. Next thing, he heard himself say, "Hey, you don't fancy that whiskey, do you? The one you wanted to murder on the plane? I have some Jameson."

"Oh, I don't know . . . Grace, you know?" Joanne paused and indicated the open bedroom door. "Unless, of course, you want to come inside? Grace is sleeping. You'll have to be quiet."

"Yeah, sure. Why not?"

"All right, then." She smiled. "I'll just pull on a sweater. You get the whiskey."

If he had thought it through, he might have done things differently. But he didn't. He didn't think it through at all. He just reacted.

"Got the goods," he whispered minutes later, rounding the door to room 4166.

Her room was exactly the same as his. He spotted Grace asleep in the second bed around the corner, the outline of her small body visible under the covers.

"I'll just rinse these."

Joanne held two tumblers, cloudy with the remains of milk. Her hair was loose but she was still in her bathrobe, and he was surprised to see she hadn't changed into a sweater. He should have given her more time.

Unscrewing the bottle, he followed her into the bathroom.

"Just a small one for me, we've got an early start."

"A small one it is," he replied.

He watched as she wiped the tumbler with a paper napkin and handed it to him. Then, turning to the sink again, she leaned over to wash the second tumbler. He wasn't sure exactly how it happened but he became aware that he was staring. He stood transfixed as he watched the folds of her bathrobe slowly part. The toweling fabric gently slid over her shoulders to where it was tied at the waist.

Wordless, he held on to the bottle and the tumbler. Joanne herself did not move but stared at him now in the mirror. At ease with her naked body, she made no attempt to cover herself. There was no hint of embarrassment.

"Well?" she said.

And he took it in the only way it could be meant—an invitation.

Slowly and deliberately he put down the bottle and the tumbler on the glass shelf behind the bath.

"What about Grace?" he asked softly, his breath now catching in his throat.

"Grace is asleep."

As Joanne made to go through to the bedroom, he gently tugged at her toweling belt.

"Wait," he said, not wanting to be in the same room as her child.

Firmly, he shut the bathroom door. Completely naked now, she turned to him and suddenly he realized how much he wanted her. It had been months and months. He could wait no more. The guilt could come later. He pulled his shirt over his head while she swiftly unbuckled his belt.

Bending down to kiss her, he caught his fingers in her still damp hair. The feeling of flesh on flesh excited him. She was enjoying it too. She wanted him just as much. In the mirror, he saw her red fingernails dig into the skin of his back as he slipped himself inside her. And when he came, it was sudden. It was sudden and furious and forbidden.

"Mummy, Mummy, where are you?" came a cry from the bedroom.

"Jesus, she's awake . . ." said Mannix.

"Just a minute," Joanne called out.

"I'd better go," said Mannix, his lust sated and feeling ridiculous with his pants around his ankles.

"I think that would be best," said Joanne.

Covered again, she reached up on her toes to kiss him. "Thank you," she whispered.

What was he supposed to say? "You're welcome"? He wasn't sure what one said in this situation. He tried to think what Spike might say. Thinking about it, it struck him that's exactly what Spike might say.

"Enjoy your holiday," he said lamely, feeling the situation had now become surreal.

"I will. Now."

She smiled.

"Good night." She shielded him at the doorway so Grace couldn't see him leave, and Mannix went back to his room with the unopened bottle of Jameson, wondering just exactly what he'd done.

Back in the office in Ireland, Mannix did his best to immerse himself in his job. He tried coming in early. He tried staying late. All to create a good impression. But he soon realized that no matter how early or late he managed, there was always some sickener there before or after him. Some younger blood with an MBA and/or a PhD under his belt.

He tried not to be cynical. He tried not to sneer. In fact, lately he found himself worrying about the bitterness now seeping into his life. Yet there was something in the eagerness of his colleagues, their zealousness to please, that he found unseemly.

"Hey, Mannix. How's tricks?"

It was his line manager. He plonked his pimply chin over the cubicle wall.

"Yeah, good, thanks. You?"

"You got those PowerPoints for the budget planning this afternoon?"

"Let me see . . ." Mannix checked his out-box. "You should have them already, Brendan. In fact, I actually sent them to you at seven last night."

"You did? Marvelous. Marvelous stuff. Sure, you can't keep a good man down," he quipped.

Praise from someone he didn't rate did nothing but grate on his nerves.

He smiled. "Now you said it, Brendan. Now you said it."

Maybe it was him. Maybe Mannix himself was the problem. Brendan was only doing his job. It was Mannix who didn't fit. He looked around the cubicle walls. He'd found himself unable to personalize it in any way. He didn't want to lend it any air of permanence. Thinking of himself as transient went some distance to preserving his sanity. As he sat tapping at the keyboard he wondered if this was how salmon felt in cages in a salmon farm.

"For you, O'Brien!"

Jim, the building maintenance intern, handed him a card.

"Less of the O'Brien, thanks, I'm old enough to be your dad." He stood up from his desk to take the card.

What on earth . . . ?

He stared at the card. His tongue went dry and his heart skipped a beat. It was Mickey and Minnie Mouse—holding hands. He turned it over. *"Hello from Mickey Mouse,"* it read in a neat but childish hand. It was signed, *"Grace."* He looked at the date stamp. It had been posted from Orlando more than a week ago. Two days before he got back.

Feeling a stab of guilt, Mannix scanned the open office floor. *Had anyone seen the card delivered? Anyone who would know him?* Get a grip, he told himself, narrowly missing the swivel chair as he sat down again. Colleagues got holiday postcards all the time.

But how had she known where to send it? And then he remembered. Of course, she had his business card with all his details. He'd made her take one as he joked about his job. Shaken now, he looked again at the postcard, wondering exactly what to do with it. Tear it up? Put it in a drawer? He opted for the latter.

Alarm bells were jangling in his head. Surely this contravened the rules of a one-night stand? What was in Joanne Collins's head when she allowed or possibly even encouraged her child to send that postcard? He felt nervous.

Mannix had been doing his best to forget that night. The guilt was compounded by the fact that Kate was making more of an effort ever since he'd arrived back from Boston. Maybe the old adage was true—absence makes the heart grow fonder. Conjugal relations were still at an impasse, however. He wasn't sure, but he thought she'd spooned her body into his in bed last night. Half asleep, he'd turned around to face her, wondering if she was up for more. But she'd quickly turned away and shimmied over to her side of the bed.

Mannix had gone for a pint in the Curragower Bar with Spike after the rugby match at the weekend. He had been tempted to tell Spike then, but it felt even more of a disservice to Kate to do so. He'd decided to keep his mouth shut. But now this? What on earth did this mean?

Picking up his "teamwork" mug, he made his way to the tiny office kitchen. He needed coffee. Splashing the instant granules into the mug, it occurred to him that the mug really needed a good scrub. A caffeine scum had stained the white insides.

Shit. He really felt unsettled now. It's only a postcard, he said to himself. *What harm can a postcard do?* Making his way back to his desk, he left a trail of splash marks all over the floor. He had ten minutes before the budgets meeting. Ten minutes for something mind numbing and calming. He'd clear out his e-mail.

Junking unopened e-mail into the trash felt great. There were lots of e-mails he should respond to but he couldn't bring himself to care. He kept repeating the same mouse actions over and over again. And suddenly he stopped and looked again. Was he seeing things now?

Mug in hand, he missed his mouth. Coffee splattered all over his trousers. Jesus! What was going on? There, in his junk mail, was a name that struck fear in his heart. Not in his in-box, but shunted off to his junk mail somehow. *"Subject: Hi there! From: Joanne Collins."* Received three days ago. Heart pounding, he opened the e-mail. He could hear his heart thumping in his ears.

She wanted to meet him. Christ! The woman wanted to meet him. Why? For God's sake, why? Why would she want to meet him? She knew that he was married. Mannix tried to think it through. Fearful of what might happen if he ignored the e-mail, or just said no, he found himself nervously typing a quick response. He'd have to head her off at the pass. Before she could do any damage. There was nothing else for it.

He was going to have to meet her.

Joanne Collins greeted him at the door wearing tights and leg warmers. Mannix left the car at the rowing club after training. He wasn't taking any chances. The walk to the red-brick Georgian buildings in Pery Square took only ten minutes and it was dark. Joanne's directions were accurate. He spotted the solicitor's brass nameplate and took the steps to the basement flat underneath.

"You found us, then," she said airily. "Come in. I'm a bit behind—the class ran late. I'm just in myself."

"A dance class, I presume?" he asked, trying to sound casual—as if they were old friends.

The floorboards squeaked and his voice echoed down the long hallway. A colored Chinese paper lantern lit the hall. A school bag leaned against a rubber plant.

"That's right. Contemporary dance out at the university. I teach there on a Wednesday night."

Like a slap it struck him how bizarre this situation was. This woman he'd had sex with, he'd never even asked her what she'd worked at. He felt uncomfortable.

"I'm making a grilled cheese sandwich, if you fancy it?"

Mannix followed her into the kitchen.

"No, thanks, I've eaten." He didn't want to stay any longer than was necessary.

"Sure? I can just as easily make two . . ."

"You look after yourself," he said.

"You'll have a coffee, then?"

"Coffee's fine."

He might as well be civil.

It was an old-fashioned kitchen, with a stripped oak table and a black French stove recessed into the back wall. It was surprisingly cozy for a high-ceilinged basement flat. Underwear hung on a clotheshorse next to the stove. Mannix looked away but Joanne had already spotted him looking.

"I'm not much of a housekeeper."

She set the cafetière on the table. In her dance tunic she looked shapely, curves in all the right places. With flashbacks to their brief encounter, he tried to ignore the images whizzing through his head.

"You wanted to see me?"

Mannix felt sick with trepidation.

"Yeah, yeah, I did. I found your business card when I was clearing out my purse. I thought it might be nice to meet."

Mannix wondered where this was leading. He trod carefully.

"You do know I'm married, Joanne?"

"Of course I do."

She cut her grilled cheese sandwich into neat triangles. She offered him one. He shook his head.

"You have two kids and a pretty blond wife. I saw the picture, remember." She tore a triangle in two and popped it into her mouth. Her nails were still red and perfectly polished.

"I don't understand," Mannix said.

She poured herself a coffee.

"What's to understand? You're married with kids. I get it. I have Grace. You get it. I just thought it might be nice to meet again . . ."

As he struggled with her logic, a second door slowly opened into the kitchen. He held his breath.

"Oh, hi . . ."

It was Grace in her pajamas.

"Hello, Grace," he replied.

"You got my postcard? I sent you one from Disney on the last day."

"I did. Thank you."

What else could he say to the kid?

"You had a good time, then?"

"Absolutely awesome. You should have seen the rides but I was too small to go on the good ones. Maybe next time."

"Off to bed now, Gracie, you know what the doctor said. You need your rest."

"Good night, Mum." Grace hugged her mother tight.

"'Night, 'night, Gracie," said Joanne as Grace shut the door behind her.

"She looks a lot brighter," said Mannix.

"She's definitely on the mend," said Joanne.

"I think I'd better get going," said Mannix, looking at his watch. It was getting late. He needed to get out of here and he didn't want Kate accusing him of sloping off for a drink with Spike again.

"Oh, if you're sure . . ." She looked disappointed. "It's not that late."

She looked around at the clock above the stove. He noticed where tendrils of hair had escaped her ponytail and curled into the nape of her neck.

"I'm sure."

Mannix got up to leave. He was heading for the door.

"Your collar, it's crooked," she said. "Let me . . ." As she reached up to straighten the collar of his waterproof anorak he smelled the closeness of her and his skin began to tingle. She smiled and looked at him, a question in her eyes. Without thinking, he leaned down and kissed her full on the mouth.

This time they made it as far as a darkened bedroom. Not as furtive or as furious as before, they took their time. And this time there were no interruptions from Grace.

"It's okay, you know," she said afterward, wrapped in a sheet. She was gathering together the tights and leotard and tunic scattered over the floor. She came back to the bed and ran a red fingernail down the hairline on his stomach. "Just now and again it might be nice to meet. Nothing regular. Just if we feel like it. I think we click, if you know what I mean."

"I do," said Mannix, his arms behind his head. She was easy company.

It was definitely late now. No matter what time Mannix returned, he was going to get a frosty reception. So he might as well be hung for a sheep as a lamb. Mannix felt relaxed for the first time in ages. He'd stay awhile longer. And half an hour later, as if to cement their arrangement, they had sex again.

Later that night, Mannix walked back over the Condell bridge with a spring in his step. I can do this, he said to himself. As long as we're both straight up with each other, there shouldn't be a problem. No worries, I can definitely do this. No strings, no attachments. No one gets hurt.

Easy.

I've got it all under control.

It was the last day of October. Halloween. At Pier 83, Mannix, Kate, and the kids queued for their Circle Line boat trip around lower

Manhattan. Conversation was strained. Fergus had borrowed Kate's camera and was snapping photos of the *Intrepid* on the adjacent pier. A relic from World War II, it had been an aircraft carrier. It reminded Mannix of the Airfix models he used to paint as a kid. Fergus was the only happy camper this afternoon. He'd mentioned his visit to the Empire State at least ten times today already. Mannix envied him, having already fulfilled a life's ambition at the tender age of eight. The child was happily oblivious to last night's disturbing revelations about his sister and Frankie Flynn. As they shuffled in the queue, Mannix saw Kate snatching the odd glance at Izzy. She had so surprised them both, this child whom Kate later claimed in private not to recognize. This child they had somehow failed.

"Something's wrong," Kate had said on waking. "And it's not just Izzy. It's more than that." She was leaning on the crook of her elbow now. Staring at him. That piercing stare. She was drilling into him. "There's something else. I feel it. Don't ask me how. I feel it—a sense of impending doom."

"For God's sake," he groaned. "We're on holiday! Don't do this . . ."

"I can't help it, Mannix," she said softly. "Like my mother says— when you feel it in your bones . . ."

This time he didn't bother replying. There was little point. Up against his mother-in-law, he didn't stand a chance. Alice Kennedy had never liked him. And without putting it into words, when they had moved to the house at Curragower Falls, he made it plain that she wasn't welcome in his home if she was going to look down on him. From time to time, Kate would remark how it would be nice for the kids to see more of their granny. Instead, the woman wisely chose to stay away. That suited Mannix fine.

Once aboard the Circle Line cruise, the O'Briens opted for a bench outside in the sunshine, even though it was chilly. The boat chugged out into the Hudson and the commentary began. The voice was deep and rich and made Mannix think of an old cowboy. Moments later, their narrator came into view. Mannix smiled. He hadn't been wide of the mark. As the boat rocked and chugged against the tide, their narrator pointed out the air-conditioning ducts for the Lincoln Tunnel between New York and New Jersey. He pointed out the bizarre driving range in lower Manhattan with its giant nets to catch the golf balls. And as they drew closer to the site of the Twin Towers, he recounted his harrowing experiences on 9/11.

Mannix became aware of a vibration in his pocket. He waited until they came closer to Ellis Island before he pulled the phone from his pocket again. It was from the same number. This time, he didn't even read the text. Instead, he made the decision he should have made at the start of the trip. He powered the mobile off.

"We are now heading into the East River," said their tour guide. "Of course, the East River is not a river at all," he added. "It's actually the Atlantic . . ."

"So now you know," Mannix said, smiling at Kate.

She looked pretty in her burnt-orange coat, with a rosy glow in her cheeks. The sun was going down behind her. She smiled back and was about to say something but the wind took her breath. Mannix looked at Izzy and Fergus. Their cheeks were equally rosy. Life wasn't perfect, he knew that, and they had their problems. But looking at his family, Mannix felt a deep pang of guilt at what he'd jeopardized.

"And here we have the heliport for the United Nations." The white-haired tour guide passed by them. "This is where the U.S. president comes in to address the UN."

"It looks different on the telly." Kate laid her head on his shoulder.

But things were rarely as you imagine them to be. Mannix thought back over the last few months. He'd been so smug. So in control. Or so he'd thought. He could have his family and a bit on the side as well. He'd succeed where other men unraveled. On the face of it, things had been going smoothly all summer. He'd had the server problems at work as cover. There had been a few snatched hours here and there most weeks. Even when Kate had gone to Kilkee with the kids, he'd come back to Limerick to the flat in Pery Square. He and Joanne would sit out in the small cobbled garden at the rear of the Georgian basement and drink cold beers. Gracie had sat with them too, painting stones, or getting them to taste the multicolored ice pops she'd made.

But then his birthday came. That much dreaded forty-third birthday at the end of August. A shiver ran up his spine as he remembered it.

The day of his birthday, he'd promised to drop in to Joanne before going home after work. He'd left work early and made it to the Pery Square flat before six.

"*You came!*" said Joanne, opening the basement door in a long white cotton shirt and flip-flops.

"I said I would!" He planted a kiss on her cheek.

Gracie was standing in the doorway to the kitchen, smiling. Looking over her shoulder, Joanne caught sight of Grace. "Come out to the garden," Joanne said, taking Mannix by the arm. "I know you can't stay long. But we have a surprise for you, don't we, Gracie?" She was looking at Grace conspiratorially.

"We sure do . . ." The child was beaming.

He'd followed them out into the tiny garden, hidden from view of office block windows by a covered trellis. Mannix had always felt safe and unseen here. The small round table was set with a flowery cloth. A fat matching teapot sat in the middle.

What he saw next struck fear deep in his heart. He stared hard at the table, trying to cope with the shock. He couldn't bring himself to look at Grace but looked at her mother instead. Joanne was smiling. Seeing the look on his face, she raised an eyebrow, the smile glued into place.

"What's the matter, Mannix? Don't you like it?"

He didn't reply. He couldn't.

Turning on his heel, he'd made his way through the flat, exiting the hall door and climbing the stone steps hurriedly out onto the street outside. Something had to be done, and quickly. He knew that now. Things had gone too far. Way too far.

He only hoped it wasn't too late.

Oscar

"Hey, guys, you up for this trip to Bunratty?"

Oscar was scanning Kate O'Brien's suggestion list and tourist leaflets.

"What's Bunratty?" asked Jess, swinging in the cane chair in the window recess.

"Remember the castle we passed on the highway near the airport? That's Bunratty." As well as the medieval castle there was a reconstructed medieval village. "According to this brochure, there's a Halloween event today. Visits to a creepy crypt, séances, and fire eating."

"Count me in," Elliot shot up from the sofa.

"Okay, then," said Oscar. "Jess, you go organize Mom. She can't still be in the shower."

Hazel was still fretting over yesterday's incident with the hammer. And twice now, she'd mentioned someone in the park watching the house. Oscar didn't want to think about it, but every now and then four shadowy consonants flashed before his eyes. PTSD. Post-traumatic stress disorder.

"It's okay, I'm here," said Hazel, making an appearance. She looked strained under her makeup.

"It looks like everyone's on board for Bunratty," Oscar said.

"Great," said Hazel. "I'll just go check if my sunglasses are in the car."

"Sunglasses, Mom? It looks like rain," said Jess innocently. Hazel was being overly sensitive, you'd have to look pretty hard to see the remains of any bruises.

On Hazel's return, Oscar sensed that something was wrong.

"What's up, hon?" He saw that she had found the glasses.

"Out there," she mouthed, pointing to the window.

Not again. This was getting tiresome.

He strolled to the window. There was no one in the park. It was deserted. He waited. A woman with a stroller walked by. He looked at the river. The tide was out, leaving the boulders of the falls exposed. But there was nothing else remarkable. Or unremarkable, for that matter. Certainly nothing sinister. He turned to Hazel and shrugged.

Hazel walked slowly to the window to check for herself. "I could have sworn . . ." she said softly.

An hour later they were wandering around the reconstructed nineteenth-century village. Oscar was feeling pretty virtuous about himself, he was doing this Ireland thing for Hazel. It was more than he'd ever done for Birgitte—he'd never even gotten around to visiting Sweden. But there had never been any compelling reason to visit, there was no family there. Like Hazel, Birgitte too had been an only child. Her parents had died before Oscar had a chance to meet them.

In Bunratty, the Harveys spent the afternoon going from one thatched cottage to another, listening to ghost stories around peat fires. On October 31, the Celtic festival of Samhain, they learned that the division between this world and the next is at its thinnest, the thin division allowing the spirits to pass through on Halloween. After the storytelling, they made their way to the crypt in the castle. Entering the castle through the portcullis door, Oscar could feel the cold reach out to touch him. It seemed colder inside than out.

Elliot was on a high after leaving the dungeons. The live tarantula in the glass box had really caught his imagination. In the car on the way back, he ran his fingers up and down Jess's arm, pretending to be a spider.

"Enough already," hissed Jess.

"Come on, you guys. We had a super afternoon. Don't go and spoil it," said Hazel.

"Can we rent a scary movie for tonight, Mom?" asked Elliot.

Every year, back home in the States, Hazel made a big deal of Halloween. She invited the kids' friends. She lit pumpkins and put glow-in-the-dark witches out on the balcony of their Riverside Drive apartment.

"I'll see what I can do about a scary movie." And then casually, "We could get in just a few little goodies . . ." She paused. "What do you think, Oscar?"

"A few goodies . . ." he repeated.

"Oh, come on, Dad. Chillax for once!" said Jess.

Oscar said nothing.

They went ahead and made their plans. Hazel would drop Oscar and the kids back to the house before heading off to source a scary movie and all the accompanying junk deemed necessary to celebrate the night. Oscar had real difficulty watching his kids eat junk. Hazel thought him too Draconian. But Oscar knew only too well where such sloppiness could lead. Over the years, he'd seen how his sister, Helen, had steadily turned her food into flesh.

It was dark and murky as they reached the Limerick suburbs. Drizzle fell on clusters of kids in garish bloody masks, pointy hats, and witches' broomsticks. But there was a real menace to the strutting herds of teenagers dressed in all-white track suits. They drove past youths gathering in packs on a supermarket forecourt, marking territory like a raggle-taggle militia, torsos taut with aggression. Their sense of purpose did not feel wholesome. Oscar was glad he was inside the car.

Back in the house, Oscar put on some music. The kids were downstairs in their rooms. They wanted to change into pajamas for a lazy evening's viewing. After a while Oscar got up to close the drapes. Outside, the river looked full and angry, tumbling over the rocks, sluicing along the sides. Above the muffled roar of the water, he heard a sharp crack. A lone red light zigzagged and flared into the sky. And then another. More fireworks. The street outside had become busy. Oscar stood watching. A black-cloaked child wielding a plastic ax walked by, led by an elderly woman. In the park, a group had formed on the grass, their backs to him. Wearing leisure suits, they were smoking and drinking from cans. He pulled the drapes now, conscious that he could be seen, should they turn around.

Oscar looked at his watch. Hazel should be back soon. As he arranged the cuff of his sweater, he noticed that his fingernails were dirty. He'd been handling the sods of peat in Bunratty earlier. Perhaps it was his profession, but clean nails were something he was particular about. Scrubbing his hands at the kitchen sink, Oscar remembered how he used to enjoy regular manicures before the Susan thing. Before that bitch screwed things up for them. The weekly manicure was only one of many cutbacks. He stood there at the sink brooding, scrubbing his nails, one at a time.

He dried his hands carefully. Hazel should be back by now. She'd been gone at least an hour. What was she doing? He'd found it difficult to gauge her many shifts in mood today. Hearing the crunch of gravel outside, he looked out the little window over the sink to the side entrance below. Yes, that was Hazel in the VW sedan. He stood and watched her from the window as she got out of the car. She walked to the back of the car and opened the trunk. He could see that Hazel wasn't happy about something. She was shaking her head in annoyance. Oscar leaned farther over the sink for a better view. That was better. He could see the problem. Some groceries had broken free of their plastic shopping bags. Hands on hips, Hazel shook her head. Then, swiftly stooping under the hood, she set about repacking the purchases.

Then he saw what she had bought. Among the packets, tubs, and jars—an outsize pack of potato chips, two massive tubs of what looked like chocolate ice cream, and a supersized bottle of full-calorie Coke. Junk. Junk. All junk. The whole lot of it. She'd bought nothing but junk.

Wait! What was that? What the hell . . . ? He could hardly believe his eyes. And in an instant everything changed. Like a forgotten circuit crackling into life, a switch tripped, and Oscar found himself hurtling down the stairs. It had taken only a moment to register and he could scarcely process what he had seen. He was reacting purely on instinct now, head screaming, a pounding in his ears. He raced outside.

The next few moments were a crazy blur. And after that, for the briefest of moments, time stood still. Oscar tried to understand it, tried to make some sense of the sudden unexpected violence, but an explanation wouldn't come to him. His mind was separating from his body, protecting itself, retreating like a tortoise into a shell.

The numbness passed, and then it came. He could feel it coming, standing there in the drizzle. He knew that feeling. That sickening empty feeling. That feeling of impotence. After all the adrenaline and fear had flushed through him, the memories came flooding back. One after another they replayed in his head. Those memories he'd tried so long to suppress. He was shaking uncontrollably. Shivering like an animal.

Under the harsh outside light on the wall, he watched the blood seeping through her hair. Hazel was slumped over the lip of the trunk, where the blow had felled her. Her head was twisted awkwardly to one side, an open eye staring straight ahead. She looked surprised. Fragments of bone had shattered and splattered into her red-blond hair where the back of her skull was smashed. Oscar pressed two fingers onto his wife's neck to feel for a pulse. He kept them in place for what felt like a long time. Nothing. He bent down, leaning next to her mouth, listening for a breath. Nothing. He stood up and looked again. She was so very still. The blow was catastrophic. Final.

There was no time. There was no time. He had to move. The kids. Gripped by panic, he bent down and grabbed her lifeless legs. He tried to do it gently. He heaved. It was harder than he thought. He heaved again, a still warm arm draping itself around his shoulder, the fingers brushing his cheek as if to caress him. Stricken now, he let out a sob.

He had to hide her. *The kids couldn't see their mother like this.* Whatever happened after this, this could not be their last memory of their mother. He would spare them this. They were only kids, their whole lives ahead of them. Oscar knew such pictures stayed in the mind forever.

Swallowing back the bile that burned his throat, Oscar heaved as hard as he could. He gagged, suddenly fearing that he might throw up. He arranged her so that she almost looked like she was sleeping. Curled up, facing him. Gently, he leaned in and closed her eyelids. And one last time, he checked again for a pulse. Reluctantly, he closed the hood, and leaning on it a moment, he felt himself go dizzy.

He lay against the hood for a minute, maybe two, maybe ten. He couldn't tell. Out of the corner of his eye, he spotted the scattered groceries lying in the rain. He didn't know what it was that he should do next. As if in a trance, he could hardly move. Gradually, he became aware the kids were standing there. Elliot looked around, puzzled, remarking how Oscar had been gone for ages. Jess knew something bad had happened. Alarm flashed across her face. She asked Oscar something but he could barely hear her over the roar of the water. He watched the way her lips were moving.

"What did you say?" he shouted.

"Where's Mom?" she shouted back.

"Come inside, Jess." He willed himself to move.

"Where's Mom?" she asked again.

"Inside, Jess. *Now.*"

He had no idea what he was going to tell them. Elliot too was standing on the path, afraid to move. But Jess ignored Oscar's instruction. Already she was walking around the back of the car, eyes wide, taking in the smashed jars, the exploded bags of popcorn and potato chips.

"What's going on, Dad?"

He followed Jess's eyes as she took it all in, until her eyes came to rest. Jess was staring hard at something over his shoulder, something he couldn't see. With a jolt and without turning around, he realized what it was that made her look like that. Confused, she opened her mouth to form another question. No words came out.

"Come, Jess." He took her by the arm.

The spade!

He should have hidden it. Slid it under the car. But there had been no time. Lying abandoned among the debris, with its frosting of flesh and hair, he'd left it where it was.

Oscar stopped and bent over to pick up three bananas that had escaped intact. He felt a stupid stab of guilt. It didn't matter now, but it hadn't all been junk. And the giant bottle of Coke was Diet Coke. He'd been mistaken. Hazel had been listening to him after all.

"What happened? Where's Mom?" asked Elliot, still standing in the doorway.

"Upstairs now, Elliot," said Oscar.

But Elliot was rooted to the spot, staring at something on the ground.

"My feet, Dad," said Jess.

"Look at my feet. There's blood on my feet."

The kids sat on the sofa warily, hesitantly, almost willing Oscar not to say anything. They wanted to know. But they didn't really want to know. Elliot was chewing his fingernails, unable to drag his horrified gaze from Jess's feet. Her mother's blood was on the white ribbon of her pajama bottoms. In the distance, fireworks went off. The HAPPY HALLOWEEN banners they'd received in this afternoon's goody bags at Bunratty hung from the ceiling.

"There's been an accident."

Somehow the words came out of Oscar's mouth. The fidgeting stopped.

"Mom's been in accident and . . ." But the words got stuck, his throat constricting, choking the sounds. Oscar tried to continue, digging his nails into his fists.

"Mom's not . . . is she? She's not . . ." Elliot couldn't say the words.

How could he look his children in the eyes and tell them *this*?

But there was no way out. "I'm afraid so, Elliot."

It was as if someone else were speaking with his voice.

"I'm so, so sorry. So very sorry. But Mom is . . . Mom is . . . Mom won't be coming back."

It felt like a boulder was pressing down on him. Inside, Oscar felt hollow. In the way a small child takes a few suspended seconds to register a pain, there fell an eerie quiet.

"NO!! NO!!!"

Jess screamed into the horrified silence. "Take it back! You *cannot* say that—take it back, Dad, take it back!" Jess launched herself at Oscar, pummeling his chest.

He tried to grab her flailing hands. "It's okay. It's okay, Jess. Stop. Stop it, please. It's okay."

Jess fell against him, shuddering, wailing. The wailing like the animal in the dark a few nights earlier. Elliot stared at his older sister. He was shaking violently now, his face deathly pale.

"Dad, you're not really telling us that Mom is dead?"

Fear and disbelief flickered in his eyes. "Not DEAD?"

With his free arm, Oscar tried to reach out to his son, but Elliot recoiled.

"Come here, son . . ." Oscar begged him gently.

Livid blotches erupted across Elliot's cheeks. He stared hard at Oscar.

"You're sick, Dad. This is one sick Halloween prank. It's not funny at all and I don't FUCKING believe you! I'm going outside to get her. I'm going outside to get my mom!!" Elliot sprang up from the sofa and made a break for the door.

"No! Stop, Elliot!"

Oscar made it across the room, pushing Jess aside and grabbing Elliot, winching him into his chest. The two of them clung on to each other as they rocked to and fro. The room filled with pain, Jess wailing, Elliot joining her now, howling like wolves in the snow.

It was a full two hours later before a lull came. "What are we going to do, Dad? What are we going to do now?" Jess asked Oscar.

That was his dilemma. What should he do now? Whom should

he call? Whom could he call? He knew he should call somebody now. The kids would need support. Not only was Oscar in a foreign country but he felt he was in a foreign body.

Bad things had happened before and he'd managed. But this was different. This was the worst by far. It occurred to Oscar then that if he sat here quietly for ten minutes or so, resting his eyes, all of this would go away. It never happened. He sat back on the sofa and took Elliot's hand in his. For a minute or so, he did nothing but listen to his own breathing. And then Oscar opened his eyes. The sound of Jess's howling was coming through the floorboards. He knew then what he must do. Whom he'd call. A plan was forming in his head. There were at least three phone calls. He'd find the energy somehow. He had to do this for his kids.

"Spike. It's Oscar Harvey."

"Hello there, Oscar. How's it going?"

"Not good. I wonder if you could come over."

"Oh, I'm sorry to hear that. Look, that's no problem, buddy. I'm a bit tied up at the moment but I'll be over in an hour or so."

Oscar could hear Bob Marley in the background and the sound of a woman's voice. He needed Spike now but he had to be careful how he proceeded. Elliot was still sitting on the sofa, staring at the wall. Oscar was very worried about him. He almost looked catatonic.

"There's been an accident, Spike. I think it would be best if you came now."

There was a sudden muting of Bob Marley.

"An accident?"

A muffled conversation was going on in the background. But there was no further hesitation. "No worries, hang on. I'm on my way."

The line went dead.

That was the first phone call done. He could move on to the next. Oscar had a choice for the next. But he grappled with whom that should be. He tried to think straight, to stay focused.

"You okay? Where are you off to, Elliot?" Elliot stood up robotlike from the sofa.

"To the bathroom, I don't feel so good."

He was moving and talking mechanically.

"When you're done, come back and get a drink of water."

"Okay."

It was an innocuous exchange and it struck Oscar how bizarre this was—that they should be having this mundane conversation, with the child's mother growing cold in the trunk among the tins of soup and melon.

"Stay focused. Stay focused," he repeated aloud. Returning to the business of the second phone call, he tried to think logically. Whom had he always gone to in times of crisis? Who was the one person who was always there for him, no matter what he'd done? Who understood him and his weaknesses? Who understood what drove him? Who would support him and help him with the children? And, as always in these situations, he found the answer was his sister. It was Helen whom he should call. Helen should be the recipient of the second phone call.

The day had lost its pattern and its rhythm but Oscar had to think. He had to factor in the time difference. It was 8:10 P.M. here, so it must be 3:10 in the afternoon in New York. Helen would be at her desk downtown. He was finding it difficult to put a coherent shape on anything, to make even the simplest of calculations, as if the motor in his brain were stuck in quicksand.

On the rare occasions he'd allowed himself some introspection, he felt unworthy of Helen. He'd even felt self-loathing for the way in which he treated her, more often than not dismissing her. For it was Helen who had stuck with him through thick and thin. In the cold competitive home of Jack and Estelle Harvey, it was to Helen that he turned for comfort. Helen had seen him through that first major trauma with Ike, his crazy cocker spaniel. That giddy, senseless, writhing mass of fun and energy. The best friend a six-year-old boy could ever have.

He remembered it all so clearly. It had been a hot August day in Sag Harbor. Jack and Estelle Harvey had gone sailing, leaving their children behind with the housekeeper. Ike was good at playing catch. In the torpor of the afternoon, Helen sat on the porch eating strawberry ice cream and reading a book. Oscar was throwing a bouncy blue ball for Ike to catch and lay at his feet, panting, yapping, dancing forward and back, eager to go again. And again. His tongue lolling at the side of his mouth, dripping saliva everywhere. It was hot under the afternoon sun.

It happened in slow motion. More than thirty years later, like a reel from an old cine-camera, it still played out in his head. Ike barking, insisting on another throw, eyes bright, nudging the ball with his nose, dancing backward and forward. Oscar sees something rounding the corner and pulling into their drive, but Ike is barking, louder now, going crazy. Oscar lifts the ball, raising it above his head. Aiming for the long reeds that separate the lawn from the dunes, he follows the path of the ball, but as it reaches the top of the arc, the brown of a truck comes into view. He didn't see Ike disappear underneath. He only heard the thud, crunch, and screech of tires. Nothing for a moment, then a pitiful moaning like he'd never heard before.

The driver was there before him, looking under the truck. He had swerved but still managed to hit him. There was nothing to be done. Oscar pushed the man away, screaming at him to get lost. Hunkering down, he stayed for what seemed like an age, smoothing Ike's golden head until the whimpering became less and less. He'd seen the rip in his body but he couldn't look again—Ike's tummy open, twitching like a mass of earthworms.

"There, boy. It's okay. You did good. It was going to be a good catch. Your best one ever. There, boy . . ."

"Oscar, he's dead . . ." Helen was standing behind him. "Oscar, come with me . . ." she said. But it took Helen and the housekeeper and the driver, all three, to tear him away. The driver kept apologizing but what good were apologies? He and the housekeeper got Ike and put him into an old sack from the woodshed. They left Ike out back, there by the woodshed, for his dad to decide where to bury him.

Oscar stayed for a long time looking at the lifeless sack. When he came back around to the porch again, he noticed that the deliveryman had left a box on the front step. It was addressed to Mrs. Estelle Harvey.

Helen was sitting on the step, eating more ice cream.

"I got two spoons," she said. They both sat there, solemnly eating the bowl of pink ice cream, scraping the bowl clean. Oscar remembered its velvet sugary comfort, the salve of something sweet. They were still on the porch when his mother and father got home, ruddy faced and laughing. It was getting dark. Helen filled them in on the catastrophic events of the afternoon.

"I'm not surprised," his mother said. "That silly animal didn't have a modicum of sense. I suppose we should look out for something sensible next time . . . Poor Oscar." She touched his cheek. Then, bending down, she looked at the box on the step. "About time," she said. "I wondered when that Panama hat would arrive." She pulled open the screen door and went inside carrying the box.

Later that evening, his father went to dispose of the body. His father would not entertain the idea of burying Ike in the garden. He drove off somewhere in the car with Ike in the trunk. Oscar was not allowed to go. The next day, when their parents went sailing once more, Oscar went to his parents' room and found the Panama hat.

He remembered it smoldered at first but after a few moments it took hold. He remembered the housekeeper trying to put out the flames, but it was too far gone. She never told his mother what had happened to the hat. And for the rest of that summer he spent a lot of time with Helen. Eating ice cream.

He had just finished the call to Helen when the doorbell went. He heard a key turn in the lock downstairs. Spike.

"Up here," he called from the hallway outside the kitchen door.

Spike was taking the steps three at a time.

"Jesus Christ, what went on out there?" The drizzle glistened on his motorbike leathers. "There's stuff everywhere. Some maggot up to Halloween high jinks?"

"Didn't you see the car?"

Maybe the rain had washed the blood away.

"Yeah, I saw it in the drive. Is the windscreen smashed?"

"Come with me," said Oscar, steeling himself for what he had to do.

"Curiouser and curiouser . . ." said Spike.

Oscar had to warn him.

"I told you there had been an accident. This is serious."

"Yeah, serious. I get you," Spike replied.

Outside now, the roaring water hadn't abated. Oscar noticed that the group in the park was still there, drinking. And yet they hadn't raised the alarm. It seemed unlikely, but it was possible that they hadn't noticed anything.

"Take the car keys." He handed them to Spike. He pointed at the trunk.

"What's this about, Oscar? Why don't you just tell me?" Spike was looking at Oscar as he released the catch of the trunk with the key. The door of the trunk sprang open and slowly hinged up.

Spike recoiled.

"Fuck! Oh Jesus, oh fuck!"

He stepped back in horror.

"Jesus, is that . . . ? Is that . . . ? That's your wife, isn't it?"

Oscar felt Spike's shock. Standing at a distance, he was unable to see into the trunk. But he could see it through Spike's eyes. Spike was the first outsider to see and Oscar wanted to gauge his reaction. He knew he'd have to go through this many times.

"Oscar, Oscar!"

His mind had wandered but Spike spoke sharply now, wanting his attention.

"Yes?"

Oscar felt a sense of detachment, as if it didn't matter if he were there or not, if he answered Spike or not.

"It *is* your wife, isn't it, Oscar? Please answer me," he said softly now.

"Yes," he said. "That's Hazel. My wife. She's dead."

"I see that, Oscar. She's very dead," said Spike, staring back into the trunk.

"What are we going to do?" asked Oscar.

Oscar wanted someone to tell him what to do. Helen couldn't be here before tomorrow, but in the meantime, he wanted someone to tell him what to do. And then he saw the spade again. Still lying on the ground among the spoiled groceries. He should really move that spade.

"Christ, is that a spade?" asked Spike as Oscar bent to move it out of sight.

"Yes," said Oscar.

"You know what, Oscar? I really think we should leave all this. Just leave it where it is, okay?"

With the heels of his arms Spike pushed down the hood again, careful not to touch it with his hands.

"Have you phoned the guards?" he asked.

"Phoned the guards?" repeated Oscar. The cops. *Of course, that was the third phone call.* He knew there were three.

"Okay, Oscar. Look, come inside. Not my favorite people in the world—but for this, we really need to phone the guards."

"I know that. I just hadn't got around to it."

"Of course not. You're in shock. I can see that," said Spike.

"What happened, exactly? If you can tell me . . ." Spike said once they were back in the kitchen.

"It's a bit confusing. I remember standing here at the window . . ." Oscar tried to start at the beginning.

"The kids?" interrupted Spike suddenly. "Where are the kids?" He looked suddenly panicked.

"In their rooms. Jess and Elliot are in their rooms," said Oscar.

"Do they know?"

"They know."

Spike relaxed. "So, can you tell me how this . . . how this . . . accident happened?" He looked pale against the black leather.

"Well, the thing about it is . . ." Oscar hesitated. A lump swelled up in his throat. He swallowed. "As you'll see, the thing about it is . . . it wasn't an accident at all . . ."

As best he could, Oscar tried to methodically describe the chain of events. Whatever Oscar said, he had little doubt he'd have to repeat

it, he'd have to regurgitate it over and over again. He tried to remember exactly how it all unfolded, what had happened in the dark,
the frenzied blow with the spade as Hazel was leaning over to repack
the shopping. The flailing limbs. The precise sequence of what had
happened lost in the frenzy. It was difficult to describe.

"We have to tell the guards, obviously," said Spike when Oscar
finished talking. "What we have here is a crime scene."

"I know that," said Oscar, quietly. "Will you tell them for me or
at least call them?"

"I'm making a 999 call now, but you'll have to tell them all of this
again when they come, Oscar. Do you think that you can manage that?"

"I'll try," said Oscar, really wishing that Helen were here.

He had a sudden flashback to Annabel Klein. Annabel Klein,
whom he had punched in the stomach in fourth grade. It was Helen
who had sorted all that out. He remembered the teacher screaming at
him, Annabel screaming at him, the school principal shouting at him
accusingly. Jack and Estelle Harvey looking at him in disgust.

But none of them thought to ask. No one asked why. No one but
Helen, that is. It was self-defense. Neither the teacher nor the school principal nor his parents knew about Annabel Klein and what *she* did. Jabbing
him with her fountain pen. *Jab, jab, jabbing him as he sat beside her.* Under
his school sweater, his side was blue with ink and red with blood.

He'd told Helen. She was the only one who ever listened. He
knew that she'd believe him. Helen wrote a formal letter to the school
principal—Helen was good at letters—and then she marched him into
her office with the letter. She made Oscar verify everything she'd
written down. She made him pull up his navy sweater to show the
puncture marks. Then she suggested that the school should take
Oscar for a tetanus shot because they were the ones responsible. But
Oscar balked at that. He wasn't sure if salvaging his reputation was
worth a needle.

But Helen's ploy worked. The school principal backed down in
her threat to expel him. In a letter to Jack and Estelle Harvey, she said
there had been "unforeseen mitigating factors." Helen always looked

out for him. He remembered celebrating his clean slate with her. They'd had a whole drum of fried chicken together. He learned again that food could be used to celebrate as well as to comfort.

"Dad?" Jess had come into the kitchen. Spike was making tea.

"Yes?" said Oscar.

"I think the police are here. I can see flashing cars outside." She was trembling, her eyes swollen from crying. But at least she was talking more than Elliot. He wondered if they needed a doctor. He wondered if they should be given a sedative.

"It's okay. I'll go," said Spike, looking with concern at Jess.

"Come here, honey." Oscar patted the sofa. Obediently, Jess sat down. He put an arm around her.

"This is horrible. Unbelievable. The most horrible thing that has ever happened to you. But you are going to get through this, Jess. You'll get through this. I'm here. I'll make sure of that."

"Oh God, Dad . . ." She looked at him with dead eyes.

He felt her shoulders shake. Once again, she was convulsed by tears and anguished sobbing.

"Shhh, honey. Shhh, the police are here. I'll need to talk to them."

On autopilot, he found the strength to stand up and greet the officers. There were three of them but he had a feeling that there were more outside.

"Detective James O'Rourke," said the middle policeman, holding out a hand.

"Oscar Harvey," he said, offering his own. "And this is my daughter, Jess."

"There are two children, is that right, sir?"

"Yes," said Oscar. "My son is downstairs."

"I'm here, Dad," came a small voice around the doorway.

"Ah, Elliot, my son . . ." Oscar said, gesturing.

"They've put a tent up over the car, I can see out the bedroom window," Elliot said, his eyes glazed. "There are police everywhere," he added, moving to stand next to Jess.

Oscar felt a tightness at his collar. There were too many people in the room, too many people looking awkwardly at one another. He was starting to feel claustrophobic, hunted.

"Maybe we can get started, sir," said the detective. "Detective Gary Burke here is going to assist me. The sooner we get started, well . . ." He didn't finish his sentence.

"The kids?" asked Oscar. "Not in front of my kids. Not yet . . ." He couldn't bear that. To see the looks on their faces. He'd spare them that as long as possible.

"That's what Garda Dolan is here for," said the detective. "Garda Dolan is our on-call junior liaison officer. Maybe the kids could go downstairs with him for now . . ."

"Come on, Elliot," said Jess, taking her brother by the hand, glancing back at Oscar.

"Don't worry, Jess," said the detective in a kindly voice. "It shouldn't be for long. Garda Dolan will take care of you for now."

"Spike, can I ask you to step outside a moment also?"

So the detective knew Spike. Oscar thought he'd seen a flash of recognition pass between the two of them.

Seconds later, there were only three of them in the room. Oscar, Detective O'Rourke, and Detective Burke. They sat around the small kitchen table underneath the HAPPY HALLOWEEN banner.

"In your own time now," said James O'Rourke. "Just take a run at it and tell us as best you can . . ."

Digging his nails into his palms, Oscar recounted again what he'd told Spike. He imagined it was almost word for word. Not a detail more, not a detail less. The two men opposite nodded and wrote and nodded again. In a way it felt cathartic, telling it again. The suddenness of it, the fury, the finality.

When he'd finished, the two men looked at each other as if satisfied.

"Now, Mr. Harvey," said James O'Rourke, "you do realize you'll have to come with us to Henry Street Garda station?"

"Yes, I thought as much," he replied. He knew nothing of the Irish judicial system but he'd reckoned on this at least. He knew he'd have to make a formal statement.

"Do you have anyone in Ireland? Any relatives? Anyone who can look after the children?"

"I'm afraid not. Hazel, you see . . . well, Hazel was an only child, adopted."

"Pity." The detective nodded.

"But my sister," he said hurriedly now. "My sister, Helen. She's on her way from the States. Can't it wait until tomorrow, till she arrives?" he asked. "My kids love Helen."

"I'll need to check," said James O'Rourke. "In the meantime, would you like us to contact the U.S. embassy in Dublin? Would you like some consular assistance?"

"Yes. Do that, please. That would be good."

Oscar knew that he would need all the help he could get.

Much later that night he'd lain on the bed, fully clothed in the dark. Jess and Elliot had sought the comfort of each other, both collapsed in the same room in a wretched slumber. Through a half-sleep Oscar gradually became aware of an awful sound. It was something deep and sorrowful and mournful and it frightened him. More lucid now, he listened again, and then slowly, horribly, it came to him. He knew where the noise was coming from—it was coming from himself. From deep within himself. His body was convulsed with pain. His face wet with tears. Oh, his poor, poor children. What were they to do? The chambers of his heart had emptied and the sound escaping from his body was the sound of his own heart breaking.

Kate

_____

The sun had gone down completely when they stepped off the cruise ship again at West Forty-second Street. Kate had been glad to spend the afternoon outdoors. Sleep had not come easily to her last night and it must have been after four when she finally succumbed. Mannix lay beside her, having drifted off hours earlier, mid-conversation.

All day, her heart felt heavy. The world felt like a different place today. She was struggling with Izzy's confession of the previous night, trying to understand her drastic actions. What had driven solid, reasonable, cautious Izzy to such a violent attack? Disbelieving at first, the cold reality of what she'd done, with all its possible repercussions, had started to set in.

"But why, Izzy? Why did you do it?" Kate had asked.

"Are you really asking me that, Mum? Seriously?"

Izzy's tone frightened Kate. Izzy's eyes seemed darker than ever. Was there something obvious that Kate had missed?

"Yes, Izzy. Your father and I would really like to know."

"I can't believe I really have to explain this." Izzy shook her head. Kate was completely unnerved.

"I kept telling both of you," said Izzy. "I kept telling you what they were doing to Fergus. But you wouldn't listen, either of you. Dad was too busy. And you, Mum, well, I tried. And every single time you said you'd look after it. You told me not to worry. But you never did a thing, Mum. You never did a single thing."

Her dark eyes seared into Kate. Accusing her. Blaming her.

"Who else was going to sort it out for Fergus?" Izzy challenged.

Kate was reeling. She looked to Mannix for support. But Mannix didn't open his mouth. He was listening carefully.

"But we didn't bring you up like that, Izzy," Kate protested. "We didn't bring you up to take the law into your own hands, *to act like a savage.*"

"No, you didn't, Mum. But you made us go to school with them."

Kate slumped back on the sofa, winded.

She never expected this. To be so judged by her eleven-year-old daughter. She'd seriously miscalculated. Had she really failed her children that badly? Kate felt sick. Sick at the thought that she'd failed in the most fundamental of all parental duties—to make her children feel safe. Had she failed so abysmally in providing a duty of care to Izzy and Fergus that eleven-year-old Izzy had been forced to take matters into her own hands?

Kate's head was a mess. She'd always thought of herself as a good mother and Mannix as a good father, for all his faults.

"Come here and sit down, Izzy," Mannix said quietly. "Now, this is important. I want you to tell us exactly what happened that night. Every last detail. You may not think so, but this is really important."

Mannix, ever practical, was thinking ahead. He seemed calm, seemed unscathed by the criticism, but in truth, the worst of it had been directed at Kate.

"You already know what happened," Izzy said petulantly.

"Tell us, step by step, Izzy." Mannix was firm.

Sitting down, Izzy stared at her feet, curling her toes. "Well, I took the hammer, for starters—okay, so you know that already. I took it out of the toolbox in the hall at home. I knew that night that Frankie would be at home on his own. He was always boasting, Frankie, you see, about how when his mother was working he'd have a can of cider from the fridge and watch a load of horror movies. He'd been talking all day about this horror movie he got from his uncle. He showed everyone in the yard a video clip on his phone of his uncle biting off a guy's ear."

Good God. Kate winced. It was all coming out now. The *scale* of the intimidation. The pedigree of their classmates. Kate looked at Mannix, shaking her head. Her stomach churned. Mannix was listening intently.

They'd had no idea. Choosing the school had been a joint decision. It had a good social mix. There were middle-class kids and kids from disadvantaged areas. And as Mannix often argued, in life, the children would meet all sorts. They needed not to be judgmental and to negotiate the social divide. But at no point had either Mannix or Kate realized the rawness of that divide.

"I had the hammer in my Girl Guides bag along with the pillowcase that Dad got for me. You dropped me off at Guides that night, Dad, remember?" Izzy looked at her father.

"Not really, but carry on . . ." Mannix stared at his daughter with a blend of shock tinged with respect.

"Well, you did. *I* remember."

Izzy was adamant.

"And the Flynns' house is around the corner from the community center. So when Dad dropped me off, I waited until he'd driven away and then I went around the corner to the Flynns'." Izzy paused to draw breath. "I knew the house. Everyone knows the house. There's a shopping trolley in the front and there's a car with no tires on it set up on bricks. There's a big bush at the front door that nearly covers the door completely. It's all overgrown and everything."

Mannix nodded as if he too knew where the house was. Kate had never seen it.

"It was dark," Izzy continued, "but I could see that Frankie was inside the sitting room watching TV. He was eating crisps and drinking from a can. I rang the bell and waited. I waited behind the bushes in the dark. But I don't think he heard me. The TV was really loud, so I rang the doorbell again. He came to the door this time and I ran back behind the bushes. There was something not right with him—the way he was walking. I think he really had been drinking cider. Frankie started shouting 'Who's there?' but I stayed where I was behind the bushes. Then Frankie turned around to go back in. That's when I got him . . ."

"You got him?" Kate repeated, her throat getting tight. She was finding it hard to listen to this.

"Yes," said Izzy.

"I threw the pillowcase over Frankie's head so he couldn't see and then I hit him with the hammer. I hit him hard. He fell. I kept hitting him on the arm. I wanted him to pay for everything he did to Fergus. Frankie was roaring his head off. Roaring and screaming, going crazy. You should have heard him cursing lying there on the ground. He ripped the pillowcase off and threw it out on the footpath. I hid behind the bush again but when he pulled the pillowcase off, I ran. I picked up the pillowcase and I ran as quick as I could, back to the community center.

"Oh my God, Izzy. Oh my God." Kate went numb. *What had her child done? What had she let her child in for?*

"I know you're saying 'Oh my God,' Mum. Like you're really disappointed and stuff. But I'm not sorry. That's God's honest truth. I'm not one bit sorry for what I did. If I had to, I'd do it all over again."

Kate stared at Izzy, seeing her anew. She felt a sudden spasm of panic.

"Do you realize what you've done, Izzy? What the Flynns would do to us all if they ever found out?" Her own voice was shrill in her ears.

"That's not helping, Kate," Mannix said calmly. "Izzy has told us what happened. Like we asked her to. Now we have to deal with it."

How could Mannix be so calm?

Izzy looked her straight in the eye. "Well, Mum, the Flynns haven't found out anything so far and they're not going to either. Frankie has no idea who did it. Like I said, he was drunk." Izzy looked from Mannix to Kate. "Can I go back to bed now?"

It was as if she'd told them nothing more unusual than an account of a book she'd just finished or a movie she'd watched.

"Yes, Izzy, off you go." Mannix was equally casual. Ridiculously unperturbed. Was Kate the only one who was totally petrified and bewildered by all of this?

"Is that all you're going to say to her?" Kate exploded.

"Take it easy, Kate. Let the child go. You and I need to talk."

Reluctantly, Kate signaled that Izzy should follow her father's advice. Kate was shaking. Her confidence as an able parent shattered. Her view of Izzy forever altered.

"Oh my God, Mannix, what are we going to do about this? I feel so guilty. So very, very guilty . . ." Kate stared at Mannix, expecting him to follow suit. But he was lost in thought. Mulling it all over. For a while, they both sat in silence, gathering their thoughts, absorbing a side to their daughter they never knew she had.

Kate thought back over the last few months. She had spent so much time concentrating on Fergus, she'd never noticed the effects on Izzy. All this time, Izzy had been brooding, harboring a vengeful hate for Frankie Flynn, and a sneering disdain for Mannix and Kate.

It was frightening. Kate tried to think back to her own childhood. Would she have been capable of such a thing? In spite of her youth, Izzy had managed to concoct a plot that had inflicted serious injury. Izzy had coolly analyzed the situation, and with a focused determination had carried out her plan.

But none of this was Izzy's fault. Kate was the one who'd let her down. She'd let the situation slide and fester. In her role as Izzy's protector, Kate had surely failed. She'd exposed her children to danger, putting them in harm's way. And by her own desperate actions, Izzy had brought her childhood to an abrupt and bloody end.

"We don't have to talk about it all again, do we?" Izzy said, arriving into their bedroom that morning. Despite her insistence on going back to bed the night before, she looked like she hadn't slept a wink.

"What's that, Izzy?" Mannix had said, propping himself up on his pillow.

"You know, the stuff we spoke about last night? I don't want it to ruin the holiday. Fergus's holiday. We were having a really nice time. I'd just like to go back to having a nice time."

"Okay, Izzy," Mannix said. "If that's what you want. We won't talk about it for the rest of the holiday. I don't want to spoil a nice time either. But when we get home, we'll have to talk about it again. It's not over."

Izzy seemed relieved with this.

"Okay, Dad." Her mouth turned up at the sides, but the smile stopped short of her eyes. "Until we're home." She turned on her heel and left the room.

Kate looked at Mannix and held her tongue. Typical Mannix. Why do today what you could put off until tomorrow? Kate knew she couldn't let this slide. Somehow Izzy would have to realize the gravity of what she'd done. She couldn't behave like that and get away with it. It would be far too dangerous to let her think she could behave with such impunity. And, as always in these matters, it would be up to Kate to nudge their child back on track. Other things would stuff their way into Mannix's headspace, and what seemed urgent today would fade into inconsequence. Kate sighed. It was true, they had been having such a wonderful time. Maybe Mannix's advice was the best they could do for now. She'd deal with Izzy once they got back home.

They were sitting in a coffee shop in Greenwich Village. "This is a very different Halloween," said Fergus, entirely unaware of just how right he was. They were finished with the cruise and tired of trawling around the secondhand shops in search of some great vinyl find for Mannix. They'd abandoned him and his "old-folks' music" to the shadows and mustiness of the one-roomed shops down the street.

The coffee shop was busy and they'd decided to have a sandwich before the parade kicked off in about an hour. Even though Fergus's sandwich was minus the crusts, as requested, Izzy threw her eyes to heaven as he still insisted on slicing off the edges and making a neat tower at the side of his plate.

As Kate sat sipping her coffee, a familiar face peered in at them through the fogged-up window. It was Mannix—brandishing a square-shaped plastic bag and a wide smile. At least the quest for that elusive album was over.

"Mission accomplished," he said, beaming. Kate was always amazed at his powers of recuperation. At his ability to pigeonhole the distressing things in life.

By the time they entered the street again a Mardi Gras atmosphere was building. Street artists with ghetto blasters were putting on performances. They passed at least three Michael Jackson look-alikes doing versions of "Thriller." As they made their way to Broadway, police were ushering the crowds back from the roadside with the gravitas of bomb disposal experts.

Mannix found them a spot next to a basketball park where he reckoned they'd have a view. Their corner was thronged with Chinese tourists taking photographs of themselves taking photographs. The noise and excitement was growing and people kept looking to the left, wondering when the parade would start.

"Here they come!" screeched a bystander from the other side of the road. This time, the urgency in the voice had the ring of truth. Fergus was hopping up and down, trying to see over the heads in front. Minutes later, carnival sounds were followed by a giant paper dragon that weaved and shimmied, manned by a line of puppeteers pumping poles like pistons in an engine.

"Is the whole of the New York Police Department on duty down here?" Mannix asked.

There seemed to be as many police officers manning the barricades as there were street performers.

"Oh, wow . . ." gasped Fergus as a sea of floating eyeballs lit the sky.

"Now, that's impressive," Mannix remarked.

The eyeballs were fashioned from white helium balloons festooned with ribbon nerve endings. The naked eyes without their sockets were macabre against the dark night sky. An excited woman in front shifted and stood on Kate's foot. "It's getting a little crowded, don't you think?" Kate was starting to feel uneasy. The crowds had become more dense and packed more tightly. "I think we should make a move," she shouted at Mannix above the din of the music. But Mannix hadn't heard. He was busy pointing out the display of skeletons coming up the road. The skeletons danced and leaped far above the crowd, jaws dropping and closing, limbs flailing, skulls lolling.

"Ow!" A couple jostled into Fergus. There was the sound of scuffling as if there were some aggravation behind. All of a sudden, there was tension. People were being pushed about.

"Come on, kids," said Mannix. "It's a bit too busy just here . . ."

"*Aww, Dad.* Can't we see the rest of the skeletons?"

"Maybe farther on. Come on, Soldier," he said firmly and took the lead. "We'll catch some more a few blocks up."

With a start Kate realized her mobile was ringing. She rummaged about her nylon bag and located the lit-up phone. *Spike. What on earth did Spike want? And why was he phoning her?* Pinpricks of alarm went off inside her head. It must be after two in the morning back in Ireland.

"Spike? Is everything okay?"

They had stopped dead on the pavement. Mannix was looking at her curiously now, with a very strange expression.

"Hi, Spike, can you hear me?" said Kate. The line was crackling.

"I can, I can hear you perfectly. Kate, I've got some dreadful news."

Her heart sank like a stone. This was going to be bad.

"What is it, Kate?" mouthed Mannix.

Kate looked away, concentrating on the call.

"What's happened, Spike?" she asked with dread.

"Hazel Harvey is dead."

Kate went weak.

"Dead?" she said.

"Dead?" echoed Mannix, sharply.

"I'm afraid so, Kate. Look, I hate to be the one to tell you this, but

Mannix—I couldn't get him. His phone is off. The thing is, Kate, well, you see, the thing is, it very much looks like she was assaulted. In fact, she *was* assaulted."

"What happened, Spike?"

But in her heart she knew already. *She'd had that feeling. That really bad feeling.*

There was a delay of a second or two and she heard her own voice echo back at her.

"You're not there on your own there, are you, Kate? Manny's there with you?"

"Yeah. He's here. Standing next to me."

Mannix put out his hand to ask for the phone. She shook her head.

"The guards are here, Kate. It looks like Hazel was assaulted in the driveway outside."

Assaulted? Jesus. She turned her back on the kids and managed to walk a few steps away. Her legs felt strange.

"What do you mean, assaulted?"

"Her skull was bashed in with a garden spade."

"Oh, my God . . ."

Kate made no protest as Mannix prized the mobile from her grip.

"Spike? Spike? What's going on there, man?"

Kate could see that the kids were becoming alarmed and she led them away to some steps outside a shop.

"What's happened, Mum?" asked Izzy. Already Izzy knew that it was serious.

But Kate was unable to answer. She sat on the step shaking her head. Oh, God. How could this have happened? In the driveway of her home, a woman had been murdered. Her skull smashed in. Kate was finding it hard to take it all in. This was unthinkable. They were an ordinary family. Why was this horror being visited on them? And yet in her heart she felt she knew exactly what had happened.

Mannix spent the next few minutes speaking in hushed tones as he scuffed imaginary stones in the street.

"Let's get back to the apartment. *Now*," he said to Kate.

Fergus and Izzy didn't say a word.

"I know who did it," Kate said quietly, as soon as the kids were out of earshot.

"You do?" said Mannix, looking at her strangely. "I really don't see how . . ."

"Oh, I know who did it, all right," she said. "And so do you."

Mannix

It was past ten o'clock when they got back to upper Manhattan. Mannix knew that Kate was dreading that Du Bois might be on duty and was relieved to see he wasn't. She couldn't face him, knowing what they knew. In the cab, Kate had told the kids that there had been an accident at home, that they would be heading back to Ireland ahead of plan, just as soon as they could change their tickets.

"Is it the lady who's staying in our house?" asked Fergus.

"Yes, Fergus. It is. She's had an accident. A dreadful accident."

Without asking any more questions, the children seemed to know that she was dead.

"I'd better go and pack my things," said Izzy, making for her room.

"Me too," said Fergus, sadly. He fiddled with the shoulder straps of his backpack. Mannix knew that Fergus would spend the next hour or so packing and repacking his suitcase, until it was just to his liking. Red T-shirts could not be packed on top of navy ones. Dirty underwear would have to be bagged in three layers of plastic bags and at the opposite end of the suitcase from his toilet bag. The task would take even longer tonight, as Fergus was upset at the news. Bravely trying to absorb it all, but upset nonetheless.

Mannix was upset too. Tragedy had come to visit them. A knot of dread twisted in his gut. He knew that this was bad, all right. And it was also possible that at this moment, *Mannix was the only one who knew just how bad this was.*

Heart in his mouth, he turned his mobile phone back on and waited for the signal to appear. Sure enough, just as Spike had said, there they were. Seventeen missed phone calls. Spike had been trying him for hours. Releasing a held-in breath, Mannix began to check his texts. There were only three since he last used the phone. *All from the same sender, just as he expected.* Holding his breath again, he opened them in quick succession.

Jesus.

Mannix steadied himself, feeling his knees about to buckle. He read the texts again. *Christ, no!* This couldn't be right. He was misinterpreting. But already his head was full of horrible images. He was reading too much into the words, he must have read them wrongly. But after a third and rapid scan, the meaning of the words was sinking in, their significance ever more terrifying.

As only Mannix could know, the texts had a hidden meaning. Though the messages were disguised, they had a certain logic. The awful truth was there in front of him. And yet Mannix was the only one who knew. He felt himself go clammy and he started to perspire. *This whole day had taken a terribly wrong turn.*

"Mannix!" shouted Kate from the bedroom.

He was going to have to tell Kate. He was going to have to tell her now.

"Coming," he called, as he splashed cold water on his face from the tap in the kitchen. Mannix walked slowly to the bedroom. He would tell her now. He'd somehow find the words.

"I've got something to show you," said Kate, sitting on the bed. She was holding something in her lap.

"What's that?"

He allowed himself to be distracted.

"It's a diary. It's Hazel Harvey's diary . . ."

Taken aback, Mannix sat on the bed. His stomach was churning. "I dunno, Kate, isn't that disrespectful?" He stalled for time.

"Yes, Mannix, of course it is. And in the normal run of events, I wouldn't dream of it. But whatever is going on here, it's a far cry from any kind of *normal*. A bloody far cry indeed." Kate was shaking her head.

Mannix stared at her, and opened his mouth to speak, but she continued.

"This was the book that Hazel had left behind. The one from the other night—that Du Bois asked us to take up to the apartment here, remember?"

He nodded.

"I didn't realize," said Kate. "I had no idea what it was. I had a quick flick through, I didn't mean to pry. I meant to put it down but something caught my eye. And I didn't say anything to you at the time because I felt like I was spying, and I know how much you hate gossip . . ."

What was Kate talking about? Was all of this really necessary, with everything else going on? He felt his eyes glaze over.

"Mannix, are you all right? You're sweating . . ."

"It's just that it's a bit hot in here. Don't you think it hot?"

"I'll turn down the controls. Just you read this page and the following three or four. All the entries are about the same time, all in September." Kate laid the open diary on his lap.

Finding it difficult to concentrate, he let his eyes come into focus and rest on the open page. As he followed the handwriting, he could see why Kate had been so disturbed.

Hazel Harvey had been a woman in distress. In some considerable emotional and physical distress. A surge of surprise ran through him as he read. It was all here. Verbal abuse. The punch in the stomach. Her head smacked up against a wall. A bruised throat and face. An initial reluctance followed by an inability to return to work. He read on. Hazel mentioned a friend called Elizabeth who was advising her. Advising her to go the authorities.

An able writer, Hazel clearly communicated the fear and the naked violence that was being waged against her. And yet for some reason, Hazel Harvey was reluctant to leave him. Reluctant to call time on her marriage. In Mannix's eyes, there were fewer creatures further down the food chain than men who beat their women. Hazel Harvey had clearly seen the holiday in Ireland as an effort to patch up her toxic marriage.

"Well, what do you think?" Kate came back with a glass of ice water.

"I can see where you're coming from, Kate," he said, head pounding and heart racing.

"So, are you thinking what I'm thinking?" she asked.

Mannix didn't answer. Already his head was in another place, another time. He was thinking back to his forty-third birthday. The day he ran like a scalded cat from Joanne Collins's flat.

It was nearing the end of August 2011 and Mannix was almost forty-three. Everyone had assumed he was morose because he was unhappy about getting older. Kate had noticed it. Spike had noticed it. Even the kids had noticed it.

"How's tricks? Midlife crisis, is it, Mannix?" asked cheeky Jim, the newly employed building maintenance guy.

"Listen, you little shite, don't think because you've been taken on as permanent, you can speak to your elders like that!" Mannix told him.

"Ah, sure, you'll be getting an open-top car that's too small for you next, and a bit of a young one on the side . . ."

He'd glared at Jim, who realized then that he'd gone too far. Things in Mannix's life were far from simple at the moment. This latest business with Joanne had really freaked him out. Mannix suddenly realized the damage of false expectation, the folly of living in such a fantasy. And he was genuinely fearful of where Joanne had thought this thing they had was going.

Joanne hadn't played by the rules. The rules were no commitment, no expectation. This was not a relationship. It was a thing. A sex thing. Mannix had his family. Joanne had Grace. But he had been misled. He thought about that awful evening after work. It had struck him like a thunderbolt then, just how stupid he'd been. Why did he think he'd be the one to get away with it? But there was no way Mannix could have expected *that*.

He could still see it now. The blue and white iced cake. The squiggly icing piped around the sides. Four white candles. The piped blue writing. And those three words. *Happy Birthday Daddy*. He remembered staring dumbstruck and then looking at Grace's smiling face. Poor little Grace. No three words had ever struck such terror in his heart. He'd turned on his heel and run from the flat, unable to deal with the shock. Unable to deal with the monumental leap that Joanne had made.

"You are kidding me, Manny?" Spike had said when he told him. *"Joanne Collins?"* Spike shook his head in disbelief. "Joanne Collins, of all people—that mad dancer from out in County Limerick?"

Mannix hung his head. He didn't know if Joanne was from out the county or not. He really knew precious little about her. Here's what Mannix knew: Joanne had a great body. They had a bit of a laugh together. He enjoyed the sex. Beyond that he didn't care. But poor Grace. Why did she have to be brought into it? That had altered everything.

"But I could have told you all about her, Manny. That woman has form . . ." Spike speaking sagely and shaking his head.

"What does that mean?"

Mannix had a feeling he wouldn't like what he was going to hear.

"Well, bro, she's a stage five clinger, for a start. Joanne Collins has been in and out of my nightclub for years. Desperate to find a man. Prefers the married guys for some reason. All the guys she's been with before had wives and families. Last I knew, she was with that property developer J. J. Hogan."

All the guys she'd been with before? Wives? Families? The words were ringing in Mannix's ears. Mocking him. *J. J. Hogan?* Christ, she'd been there? That guy was a tube. The more he thought about it, the more he realized what a fool he had been. So Mannix had just been another gullible candidate in a long line of liaisons?

"What am I going to do here, Spike?"

Mannix really had no feel for quite how worried he needed to be. Maybe it wouldn't be a problem. He could extricate himself gently and Joanne might be content to let things slide, upset at first, but sensitively handled, she might let him go, and after an interval, she'd be ready to move on to the next guy.

"You need to make it plain that this is over," said Spike. "I don't know what stunts she's pulled in the past but I never heard of one like this. She obviously really likes you, Manny. And it sounds like her kid certainly does."

"Thanks, Spike. Just what I wanted to hear. That really helps," he said sarcastically.

"You asked," said Spike.

"Look, I'm sure I'll think of something," said Mannix, "but do you think she's likely to cause me trouble?"

"Tell Kate, you mean?"

"Exactly."

The very thought of it made him shiver. He couldn't—no, he wouldn't—even contemplate it.

Spike appeared to give his worry some consideration. "No . . . no, I don't think so," he said. "Look, Manny, I can't say for sure but I don't think the woman is a home wrecker. I never heard of any of the other guys' wives ever finding out. But like I say . . ." He left the sentence hanging.

There it was again, that phrase, "the other guys." Mannix had known it was only sex, a bit of fun, a beer or a glass of red wine or two. So why did he feel sullied and cheap? Had he really expected this woman to be his little secret? Why shouldn't she have a past? It was a free world. Why shouldn't she sleep with whoever she wanted? And yet Mannix couldn't now get that picture out of his head. Joanne with J. J. Hogan. Loudmouthed, smarmy J. J. Hogan, who owed money to half the town.

Spike ran a hand over his stubbly chin. "I must say I'm a trifle surprised at you, Manny. I always thought that you and Kate were good."

"We were. That is to say, we are." He suddenly felt defensive. "It's just that in the last year, with the money hassles and everything, I guess I took my eye off the ball."

"Don't talk to me about hassle. I've got those psycho Bolgers breathing down my neck."

"Yeah, I guess," said Mannix. "But I do love her, Spike. I do love Kate."

"She'd have your guts for garters, Manny . . ."

"Please!" Mannix held up a hand signaling Spike to stop.

"I'm just saying."

"Well, don't."

"It's not as if you're a saint yourself, Spike," Mannix added.

"But I'm not the one who's married, Manny."

Mannix was taken by surprise. Spike was giving him that look. The look that Kate sometimes gave him. The disappointed look—the look he absolutely hated. Such opprobrium from his laid-back brother stung.

"I don't get you, Spike . . ." Mannix shook his head.

"Ah, jeez, Manny. Marriage isn't for me, even I know that. I'm not cut out for it." Spike blew a smoke ring in the air. "But you—I looked up to you, Manny. I thought you and Kate would make a go of it. You, Kate, and the kids. Hell, Manny—you guys are the only decent family I've got. It means a lot to me, Mannix, you know . . ."

Mannix sat stunned by his brother's outburst. Spike was not given to such frank exchanges. Serious matters were normally only hinted at or approached sideways. Rarely full-on.

Spike stubbed out his cigarette and looked Mannix solemnly in the eye. "I know I act the maggot. I know I play Kate up from time to time. But you're my family." He paused. "Hey, where would I go to watch my Man U matches? I enjoy those winter evenings on the couch—you, me, and Ferg. Where would I go for my Christmas dinner?" Spike laughed, half joking, half serious.

"Stop it, Spike!" Mannix's heart had started to race. "Stop painting a doomsday scenario! Kate doesn't know anything. And that's the way it's going to stay."

"Well, I hope so, Mannix. For all our sakes. You'd better sort it out, bro."

"Don't worry, I'm on it."

"Good. Kate's one of the good guys, you know, Mannix. She's a great girl."

"Enough, okay! I get the message."

Mannix left Spike's flat, grubby, dejected, and very worried. *So, was he safe?* He didn't know. He would have to think very carefully how he was going to phrase his exit speech, his get-out-of-jail-free speech.

And the way it happened, it was Joanne who made the first move. It was the second-ever e-mail she'd sent him, having agreed that she wouldn't again use his company e-mail. They had agreed to communicate by text. Perhaps by breaking that arrangement and e-mailing him again, it might concentrate his attention even more.

In the slew of e-mails in his in-box, hers was the one that clamored for attention. Mannix blinked and blinked, hoping it would melt away, be swallowed by the screen, flip and twist, invert and fade, in some fancy animation.

"We need to talk."

That's what it said. *"We need to talk."* Mannix sat at his desk, repeating the words again and again to himself.

"Give it to her straight," Spike had said. *"Give it to her straight and then get out. Don't look back."*

Mannix had replied by text, agreeing to meet her in the flat in Pery Square on one condition. It would be only the two of them. Grace could not be there. Mannix felt shoddy. How could he look that child in the eye again after running out on her surprise? How could he explain that he could never be her father? It struck him then just how preposterous the whole notion was. And again he asked himself, for the millionth time, what had Joanne been thinking of?

Mannix had enough on his plate with two kids of his own. But perhaps that was not entirely fair. Izzy generally never caused a moment's angst or bother. He smiled and tooted the car horn as he dropped her off outside Girl Guides. She hadn't seemed particularly talkative in the car tonight but he supposed he was so preoccupied himself, he couldn't say for sure.

But Fergus. Fergus made up for all the lack of demands that Izzy made on them emotionally. There were times that just being in his company, Mannix could feel his energy slowly draining away. It wasn't a thought he'd ever felt inclined to share with Kate. Her love was truly unconditional. He sometimes wondered at his own. This evening there had been yet another dimension to their troubles with Fergus. All because of that little scumbag Frankie Flynn. As soon as the business with Joanne was sorted, he'd get on to that.

His thoughts turned to Grace. Grace was a nice kid. She liked art and crosswords and baking. He remembered helping her with a crossword puzzle for homework when Joanne couldn't answer the clue. He complimented a poster she'd done in a calendar competition. She'd made him flapjacks once. But that hardly constituted being in loco parentis, now, did it? Mannix could not think of a single instance where he'd intentionally led them on. In fact, he'd always felt embarrassed when Grace was around, preferring instead to call when he knew she'd have gone to bed. No, he'd examined his conscience and satisfied himself that in Grace's regard, he had nothing to blame himself for. Whatever had happened was down to Joanne. It was her doing.

"I had Grace stay at my sister's," said Joanne, opening the basement door. "She's about the only one I could trust with Grace's meds."

Oh, great. He was at an instant disadvantage. The guilt treatment from the outset.

"Sorry," he mumbled. "I just thought it might be best if she wasn't here. After . . . after . . ."

"Yeah, I know. After last time." Joanne ushered him into the kitchen. She wore a white cotton shift dress and no shoes. "She was pretty upset, you know."

"Well, so was I." Perhaps it was best if he went on the defensive right away.

"You were?"

She looked at him in surprise, handing him a glass of red wine that had already been poured.

"Why? Pray tell . . ."

Mannix sat down at the kitchen table. He noticed then that the only light in the room was from the scattering of night-light candles flickering magically all around the room.

"Because it was never supposed to be about Grace. It was only ever supposed to be about us. And Joanne, if you really want to know, I feel really bad about it. I feel really bad about Grace. She's a nice kid and I like her."

"I know you do. And she likes you, Mannix."

The skin on her arms was taut and golden in the yellow half-light as she reached across the table to stroke his hand. He had to tell her now, before things went too far.

"Look, Joanne. I think we have to call time on this thing we have. I really think it's for the best."

She looked at him in surprise as if what he said were entirely unexpected.

"Call time? This *thing* we have? I don't understand, Mannix. Really, I don't. What we have going here is way more than just a thing. You, me, and Grace. We're a team."

"What?" Mannix heard himself croak. It was his turn to look shocked now. It was surely time for the velvet excuse, the soft-soap parting salvo. He was going to have to move quickly.

"No. Joanne. Let me stop you right there." He put a hand on her arm. With her other hand she held it there.

"Maybe in another life. Maybe if we'd met before. This thing . . . *us* . . . it's just unfortunate . . . It's all just an accident of timing." He looked into her eyes. Trying to look sincere. "But I've got my own kids, Joanne. You know that. I've got Fergus and Izzy."

"I know, Mannix. Don't you think I know that? And Grace knows that too."

Joanne was looking at the mantelpiece above the French stove. She was smiling. Mannix followed her gaze, trying to see what it was that made her smile. But what he saw made him shiver. He felt suddenly afraid.

Was it what he thought it was?

Standing up and walking closer, Mannix plucked the frame from the shelf. How had she come by this? Mannix stared at the familiar faces looking back at him. It was a photo of him with Fergus and Izzy, but there was something both odd and familiar about it at the same time. With a start, it came to him. It was the photo that he carried in his wallet of the four of them. Except that this photo on Joanne's mantelpiece didn't feature Kate. Kate had been cut out.

"Where did you get this?" Mannix asked, his voice shaking.

"From your wallet. I borrowed it and had it photoshopped," she answered blithely. She was calmly sipping wine.

Stunned now, Mannix stared at the photograph, trying to gather his thoughts.

"So you see, Grace knows all about Fergus and Izzy. I've told her all about them."

Mannix stared at her in horror.

"Grace has always wanted a brother or sister. But a brother and a sister both?" Standing up, Joanne moved in bare feet across the wooden floor and looked up at him.

"Don't you see? Don't you see how perfect this could be?"

His heart was racing. He found it hard to think. She smelled of lilies and red wine. He was in uncharted territory now. Without a compass. He was going to need to draw on all his reserves to get through this.

"Sit down," he said gently to her. "Sit down, Joanne, and let me finish what I have to say."

"Okay, Mannix, I'm listening . . ." She slurred a little. He glanced around the kitchen. There in the recycling pile next to the rubbish bin he saw an empty wine bottle. He realized then that she'd been drinking before he'd called. And quite a bit.

He was going to have to be creative. This excuse would have to fly. He was coming to the alarming realization that this woman wasn't stable. Joanne Collins was a fantasist. Flexing his mental muscles, he made a few minor adjustments to his story, a few meaningful tweaks, before attempting to speak.

She was looking at him now, her eyes dreamy and pupils large. She was drunk.

"My kids mean everything to me," Mannix began. "Just as Grace means everything to you."

She nodded and started caressing his cheek. He thought it best to let her.

"Even if I left Kate, she'd never let me have the kids. You don't know Kate, but she's one determined woman. You know the way it is here in Ireland. No matter what, the women always get the kids. I couldn't live without my kids."

"But we could be so good together, Mannix. Our own little family. You, me, Grace, Fergus, and Izzy. A perfect family."

He tried not to show his alarm, his fear. "I know that, Joanne," he said. "And maybe if things had been different, who knows? Maybe if we'd met earlier, but it's all *ifs*, *buts*, and *maybes*."

"Really, Mannix? Do we really have to settle for this? Skulking around my basement flat in Pery Square. Is that all that we are meant to have? There can be no more for us?"

"Joanne, what I came here to say, and I know that this is hard, but for your sake and my sake and most of all for Grace's sake, is that there can be no more 'us.'"

"You are *kidding*. You are kidding me, Mannix. But we can go back to the way we were before, right?"

"No, Joanne. I don't think so. I really don't. I know it's hard. It breaks my heart too. But it's the right thing to do."

"How can it be the right thing to do, for God's sake? How can breaking up be the right thing to do? I love you, Mannix. Don't you get that? I bloody love you and, God help her, so does Grace."

Jesus. This was hell. He felt like a rabbit in the headlights. How had he become embroiled in something so perverse?

"I have to go, Joanne."

Mannix removed her hand from his arm. Her red nails had been digging into him.

"Okay, okay, okay. Please, please, let's just go back to the way we were. I'm sorry I ruined it all. I'm sorry about the cake . . ."

She was sobbing now. Her eyes looked wild, mascara running down her cheeks.

"I've got to go, Joanne."

He stood up from the table.

"Okay, go, then, *you fucking bastard*. You fucking heartless bastard. Fuck off home to your cold and frigid wife and your cold and frigid life! She doesn't deserve you. I deserve you. Grace deserves you. Go on, then . . ." And wielding her wineglass, she flung the contents at him, dousing him in the scarlet liquid.

Mannix wiped the splatters from his face.

"I'm sorry, Joanne. I really am."

But she ran at him, pummeling his back. Mannix made it to the basement door, his shirt soaked in red wine. Walking up the steps she was still screaming after him.

"It was only a fucking cake. It was only a stupid fucking birthday cake!"

"Kate, put the diary way. I've got something to tell you."

She looked at Mannix. "What is it? You don't think it's Oscar Harvey? You don't think that he's the one who killed his wife?"

"Forget about Oscar Harvey and listen. You're in danger, Kate. I'm sorry but there isn't any other way to say it."

"What are you talking about?" Kate looked alarmed.

"Look, Kate, this is going to be hard," he said, "and you're not going to like it, but it's important that you listen. And after I've told you, you're going to be really mad with me. In fact, you may very well hate me . . ." Mannix paused for breath. "You're okay now," he continued, "but we need to act before anyone else gets hurt. And just so you know . . ." He felt a sudden lump swell in his throat and a wave of remorse rolled over him as he saw her stricken face. He never imagined telling her like this but he was cornered. "I want to say how sorry I am. I never meant for any of this to happen. God help me, Kate, I'm so very, very sorry . . ." He swallowed hard.

"Stop it, Mannix. You're scaring me now. Tell me what it is. Just tell me."

He started slowly. "Well, remember last March, how I went on that training course to Boston?"

She nodded silently.

"And you and I—well, not to put too fine a point on it, but we weren't getting on . . ."

There was a flicker of recognition in her eyes, followed by a flicker of something else. He watched her tense.

"Yes?"

"Well, there was this woman on the plane. This woman and her daughter . . ."

Kate's eyes narrowed but she didn't move.

"It was a nightmare flight, plane all over the shop, cabin crew in their seats, drinks flying everywhere . . ." he exaggerated. "And this woman, well—she was pretty scared, so I did my best to chat and distract her. I suppose I felt sorry for her. I suppose I imagined if it was you and Izzy. This woman's daughter was sick and she was treating her to a trip to Disney World."

Still, Kate didn't move. Not a muscle.

Mannix's heart was pounding and he could no longer look at Kate. Instead, he stared at a photograph on the Harveys' bedroom wall—a framed photograph of the giant rollers at Big Sur. He wished he could be there now. Anywhere but here.

"I suppose it was coincidence really," he said, trying to keep his train of thought. "You see, Joanne and Grace, well, they ended up in the same hotel as mine on their stopover."

"Joanne and Grace . . ." Kate repeated. She had gone quite pale.

"Yes. Grace is Joanne's eight-year-old daughter. They live in Limerick."

"I see," said Kate, her face set in grim lines.

"It wasn't meant to happen," he blurted out. "I really want for you to believe that, Kate. I'm just not that type of guy . . ."

Confused, Kate blinked a few times, and then the significance of what he was saying began to dawn on her, her eyes registering disbelief. She opened her mouth to say something but shut it again. Her eyes narrowed and pierced through him.

"What type of guy are you talking about, Mannix? Just what exactly did you do?"

Kate was going to force him to walk the plank, to actually say it. *Here goes.*

"I slept with her, Kate. I'm really sorry but I slept with that woman."

He was unprepared for the force of her surprise. Clutching her hand to her mouth, Kate heaved as if she were going to vomit, and with her other hand she pushed herself off the bed. She ran for the en suite bathroom. He listened as she dry-retched and heaved. Tempted to go and check if she was all right, he opted for the safety of the bedroom.

Moments later, she appeared. She stood in the doorway to the en suite, squeezing a tissue.

"Just once?"

"Are you okay? You look awful," he asked her gently.

"Just once, was it just the once?" She ignored him.

"No," he replied.

"I see," she said. She bit down on her bottom lip.

"Sit down, Kate."

Like a ghost, she made for the far side of the bed and perched herself on the edge, knees and arms crossed in a protective body hug.

"Do you love her?"

"God, no! No, of course I don't love her. It was only sex, Kate. I love you."

She looked at him now, her lip curling, with a look he'd never seen before. It was a mixture of loathing and disgust.

"I know you can't see that now, Kate. But it's true."

"So you're having an affair, is that what this is about? You're telling me that you're having an affair?"

"I'm afraid it's a bit more than that, Kate. It's a whole lot more serious than that."

He had her frozen attention now.

"We had a thing, yes. But it's over. At least, I thought it was—up until a week or so ago. I told her it was over a long time back. But she wouldn't let it go. I tried to tell you back then. I was going to tell you but for some reason it didn't happen. I didn't know what she was going to do, Kate. I had no idea what she was capable of. I never knew she was unbalanced. That she was a fantasist, a crazy, crazy fantasist."

"I don't know if I can listen to any more of this . . ." Kate had clutched her ears, blocking what he was trying to tell her. Her eyes were closed.

Mannix got up and walked around to the other side of the bed.

"Believe me, Kate, I wouldn't tell you any of this"—he prized her hands from her ears—"but you really need to know. I wish I could have spared you all this pain. But it's out of my hands now. I don't have a choice."

"You selfish, selfish prick." Kate didn't shout but she looked at him so blackly he wished she'd screamed her head off. "Where do you get off doing this to me? After all the years I've stood by you. I had my bloody chances too, you know."

"I'm sure you did, Kate, and you can be mad at me all you like later, but for now you've got to listen."

"Tell me, then, tell me how I'm in danger." Her voice was measured.

"Well, I saw this woman a few times in her flat and sometimes her daughter would be there. I think she got the wrong end of the stick because somehow I think she thought I was going to leave you. She had some mad idea in her head that I would be a father to her child. That in some crazy, twisted version of happy families, that they would come to live with me and Izzy and Fergus . . ."

"And me? What was to happen to me? Where was I in all of your new lovely modern family?" Kate asked, dripping with sarcasm.

Mannix thought back. For three whole weeks there had been no contact. He'd satisfied himself that Joanne had resigned herself to the fact that their affair was over. Perhaps she already had a new man. Yet Spike had no reported sightings of her in the nightclub. Still, he was happy that the texts had ceased. He'd found himself relaxing into the delicious routine of mundane family life. Then, out of the blue, they started coming again, this time more bizarre in tone. Apocryphal.

"Well, that's just it, Kate. I told her that I couldn't leave you. The thing was that I was trying to get her off my back, so I said that if I ever left you'd never let me see the kids. That I could never do that. I thought that it would work. Joanne knew how much I love Izzy and Fergus. And it seemed to work, at least for a while, but then she started texting me again. At first, I didn't take too much notice but then they started to creep me out. I thought she was only trying to scare me into meeting her again. But this past week, the texts got weirder and weirder."

"What texts are these?" asked Kate. "So that's why you've been glued to your phone ever since we arrived?"

"Yes. I could see what Joanne was driving at all the time, but I really thought that she was bluffing. She'd seemed like a normal down-to-earth woman before. There was never any indication of . . . of . . . what she was about to do. As I say, she'd never before spoken like that when I was seeing her."

Kate flinched.

Mannix was aware that in trying to explain the gravity of the situation, he was hurting Kate even more. But the time for sensitivity had passed. Kate would soon realize that herself. There was too much at stake now. Mannix pulled his mobile phone from his pocket.

There had been the initial rash of apologetic texts seeking another meeting, Joanne saying she was sorry she had gone so far. She'd never attempted the immediacy of an actual mobile call. Mannix had been relieved about that. Of course, she realized now that she was being selfish. Of course Mannix couldn't give his kids up. Joanne would explain to Grace. He'd be their secret. He'd deleted all of these initial texts.

Mannix knew that what he was about to do might seem cruel. But he also knew that it was necessary. Slowly he walked around to Kate's side of the bed and handed her the phone.

"Forgive me, Kate, but I think the only way to explain it is for you to read Joanne's texts."

Kate took the mobile with a shaking hand.

"*'Before you, there were others,'*" read Kate aloud. "*'But I know now that what we had was real. We will have all that and more again.'*"

"*'Trust in me and I will find a way,'*" she continued. "Jesus, her texts have all the charm of those tacky fridge magnets."

"I know," said Mannix awkwardly. "Read on." He sat with her as she opened and closed the texts.

"*'We will win the fight and love will be our trophy.'* This tripe is making me sick . . ." sneered Kate.

"*'I have tried loving you from afar and now I know it isn't possible. There is a way. And I will find it. Your Joanne.'*"

Kate's tone was mocking as she struggled through the texts and as the texts turned vicious, she delivered them more slowly. "*'Your wife is a BITCH. I see now what you mean. Your life must be hell, my love. Be patient. Our day will come.'*"

Mannix's felt like a reprobate as Kate was forced to read this drivel.

"*'Very soon now, we will all be together. Stay strong for me and keep the faith.'*"

She was whispering now.

"*'I see what you mean. It's lovely here in the park. I love the boardwalk as does Grace. Clancy Strand will suit us very well. Your Joanne.'*"

Kate fell silent as she scanned the next text. It was sent on Saturday. Their first full day in New York. The Harveys' first full day in Limerick.

"*'I saw the inside of your house today. Grace will love it too. Don't worry, your BITCH wife doesn't have a clue. Not long now, my love. Your Joanne.'*"

And for the first time as Kate read aloud Mannix heard fear in her voice. He wondered if she'd seen ahead.

"She was in our house?" Kate looked at Mannix. "That woman was in our home?" Kate's eyes flashed with fear and anger. "On Saturday? This was sent last Saturday, so how did she get in?" Kate stopped and thought a moment. Something had occurred to her. "The meter reader? The person who came to read the gas that we don't have?"

"I don't know, Kate. Really, I don't. But I'm guessing that it's possible . . ."

Kate resumed reading aloud.

"*You may find it hard at first to see the meaning in my method. But in time, you too will see it was the only way. I know you long to be with us. Your Joanne.*' This is freaky stuff, Mannix. I don't know what you've got yourself mixed up in but this woman writes from another planet."

There were only two more texts to go. Mannix knew that. One sent yesterday. One today. The ones that had made his blood run cold.

"*I must be brave. I know what I must do. It is the only way and it is within my grasp.*'"

Kate looked up at Mannix as she read. Then slowly she read the last one. It was a moment or so before she read it aloud.

"*It's done. It will be hard for Izzy and Fergus at first. But they will come to love me. I am a good mother. It will be hard for you too, for a few days. I need to give you space now. I know that. But after the funeral, I will come. Grace and I are busy packing. Your Joanne.*'"

Kate dropped the mobile as if it were a burning coal.

"Does this mean . . . was she the one who . . . ?"

Kate remained unable to utter the terrifying words.

It had taken Mannix a few confused and foggy seconds to arrive at the same unthinkable conclusion. But Kate had got there in a heartbeat. And the more Mannix thought about it, the more this sick conclusion was the only one that made any sense.

"I don't know, Kate." Mannix shrugged. "But so help me God, I think so. I think that she's the person who killed Hazel Harvey. It certainly looks like she's the one."

"Mistaking her for me . . ." Kate whispered.

For a few moments Mannix let the idea sink in.

Then, "That *is* what it's looking like, isn't it?" he said, forcing the point home. "Joanne had no idea that we were away. And Kate, I hate to tell you this, but Joanne had a photograph of you. Think about it—you and Hazel are both small and blond. Alike, I suppose, to someone who doesn't know you . . ."

Kate's face had drained of all color as she stared at Mannix.

"Where the hell did this psycho get a photograph of me?" she whispered.

"I think she took it from my wallet. You know that one we got taken in a studio last Christmas?"

Kate looked at Mannix as if he'd just crawled out from underneath a rock.

"So this floozy that you've been shagging, this nutcase that you invited into all our lives, she mistook Hazel Harvey for me and bashed her head in with a garden spade? Is that what you're trying to tell me?"

Mannix stared at Kate like a fool. There was nothing he could say.

"Oh, what have you done, Mannix? What in God's name have you done?" Kate said slowly.

Mannix had little doubt he'd be asking himself the same thing over and over again. Her question echoed round the silent bedroom. He saw years of angst and penance looming. But for now, the question that concerned him most was just how long before Joanne Collins learned of her mistake?

And what would she do when she learned that the woman she'd meant to kill was still alive?

Oscar

"'ve just checked on the kids. They're playing a computer game together," said Helen.

How ironic, thought Oscar—that it should take the death of their mother to bring them together. As far back as he could recall, Oscar couldn't think of a single instance in which they'd ever played a computer game together. Maybe it was the sedatives. They'd wear off soon, and Oscar wondered if he should expect a repeat performance from Jess. Though exhausted, she'd been completely unable to stop the crying. Oscar had been happy to let them both take the tablets, for the first few days at least. They had a long hard road ahead.

"Oh, Oscar, I can't take it in," said Helen. "I can hardly believe that this has happened. What are we all going to do without her?"

Helen poured two drinks. Bottled water for Oscar and a Coke for herself. Oscar knew she was doing her best to hold herself together—for his sake. Helen was bigger than him in every way and, not for the first time in his life, Oscar was immensely grateful for that. He'd allowed himself to be comforted in the cushiony warmth of Helen's bear hug.

Helen arrived on the first flight in from the States on Wednesday morning and Spike O'Brien had gone to collect her. Spike was now in the backyard, smoking and keeping company with the team of policemen who were guarding the house. Oscar wasn't sure, he couldn't put his finger on it, but there was something in Spike's body language that suggested he was keeping something from him.

"Elizabeth is in shock," said Helen. "You know I told her? Sorry, of course you do, I told you that already. I'm repeating myself now. It's all just so . . . unbelievable." Oscar heard the emotion catch in her throat. "And to think that Hazel came here to get away from everything . . . to get her head together. Elizabeth told me that she'd been having trouble."

She looked directly at Oscar now, inquiring, probing.

"You should have told me, Oscar. You should have told me. And now it's all so tragic . . . Those poor kids . . ." she said. Realizing she was rambling, Helen took a breath and squared her shoulders. "But we are going to get through this. You, me, and the kids. I'm going to be with you, Oscar, every step of the way."

"Thank you, Helen. I know that." He smiled at her gratefully and again it struck him how little he deserved her. He'd always repaid her kindness and her support so poorly. Only thinking of her as an eating machine. Not as a loving and empathetic human being.

"Elizabeth wanted to come," said Helen. "But I told her to keep her powder dry till we get back to the States. We'll need her then. We'll need all the support we can get. Poor Elizabeth has lost a very dear friend. But please tell me, Oscar, what exactly was going on at that dreadful school? What exactly did they do to our darling Hazel?"

"I should never have let her go there . . ." Oscar shook his head.

It had without doubt been one calamity after another, one great big protracted shit storm. Maybe if Hazel had never gone to that school, maybe they would never have felt the need to run away, to come to Ireland. Maybe his wife would not be lying in a body bag now. It had all started with that stupid fucking school.

"What kind of place was it?" asked Helen gently. She was leaning against the breakfast counter staring at the Halloween banner. Angrily, Oscar leaned across her to pull it down. There was no cause for celebration.

"The place was a hellhole," he spat. "There's no other way of putting it. It was one of those Impact Schools, you know?"

Helen nodded. "Armed security, strict codes, body scanners, that sort of stuff?"

"You got it," said Oscar. "Three strikes and you're out. Three black marks on your record and they kick you out."

"I knew the school was in a tough part of the city and the kids were challenging, but I didn't realize that the regime was quite that severe . . . Hazel never talked about it." Helen looked puzzled. She pulled the corners of her cardigan tightly over her bosom.

"But she wouldn't, would she?" Oscar said. "This was yet another one of Hazel's projects, another one of her crusades to make the world a better place." His voice reeked of bitterness.

"Hazel gave those punks so much of herself. She invested in them personally. It was always much more than a job to Hazel. And okay—I think that some of them may actually have appreciated it. But I worried about her, Helen. Going there every day. I know she thought she was tough but she had a real naïveté. You know what I mean by that, don't you?"

Helen nodded.

"Like she always saw the best in people, a bit like you," Oscar added.

"I try." Helen smiled sadly.

"There was this one guy—Jay Mahoney, one mean kid. Like I said—there were some real gems in that place. He gave her hell. According to Hazel, she'd been unfortunate enough to laugh at something he did in class. He waited until he got her alone one day. Accused her of disrespecting him, humiliating him. But then it got physical. That twisted punk—he hit her. And not just once."

Helen gasped but didn't interrupt. She was a good listener.

"I tried, Helen, God knows I tried. I wanted her to give the gig up. Pack up and start over somewhere else. Back to publishing. But she wouldn't hear of it. Took the whole thing as a personal challenge. She thought it would be giving in. There were too many good kids, she said. Kids who she had nurtured, who she felt were making progress. You know, Helen, you know how there was always an agenda. Somehow everything ends up getting political with Hazel."

Helen nodded soundlessly. Oscar saw her eyes begin to brim with tears. In that moment, he wished that he too could cry. But his hurt and shock were way too deep for tears. Like before, he knew the tears would come, in time. When he was able to believe that all of this had happened, for real. It seemed important to him then that Helen should know how much he had tried.

"Hazel was there for the long haul. She wasn't giving up. That first time, that first time Jay Mahoney hit her—I wanted her out of there, period. I wanted to deck the guy personally. I told Hazel then to go to the principal. I told her to file a complaint. But she made excuses. Said it was well known that Jay Mahoney was on two strikes. And apparently the only person who Jay was afraid of was his own father.

"This guy's father wanted him to graduate. Somehow, in some misguided way, my poor wife felt that telling on this guy would blight his chances in life. It doesn't matter, you know—no matter what, these guys always end up in the slammer. Oh, Helen, I cannot tell you how many countless arguments we had over that. You can imagine how fucking useless it made me feel. I got pretty mad—I can tell you. But I had to let her have her way—you know what she's like . . ." It struck him then how he spoke about Hazel as if she were there. A weight of sorrow hit him.

Helen had perched on a stool but didn't look comfortable. She slid his glass of water toward him.

Swallowing the lump in his throat, Oscar tried to carry on. "I obviously go for stubborn women, because I couldn't budge her. Not on this." He shook his head. "But you know what, Helen? The second time, I really think she may have been having misgivings. I really do. I was trying to work on that while we were here. I felt like killing the little punk myself, I really did."

"Oh, poor Hazel. I wish I'd known. If only I'd known, maybe I could have done something."

Oscar thought a moment. Could things have really turned out any different had he told her? Helen had always been a great support, but in this, he doubted she could have made any material difference.

"Do you think so, Helen? Do you really think so?" he asked.

"I don't know how much Elizabeth told you of what was going on," Oscar said, "but I know that she tried too. So that was two of us. And the reason I never told you was because Hazel didn't want me to. At first, I thought we were onto something, when Hazel took leave from the place. I thought I'd work on her. She was pretty traumatized, you know. What kind of a sick fuck roughs up a woman? And I know she never told me just how bad it was. You should have seen the bruises, Helen. I know she thought she was tough—she'd worked in the soup kitchens, she'd volunteered in the projects. But you know what? I think she found that being face-to-face with such aggression at such close quarters—I really don't think she was prepared for that. No, ma'am. Not at all. Underneath it all Hazel was a romantic, an idealist. She wasn't equipped for that place. So then she became withdrawn and moody. At first, I tried to talk to her about it. And then I tried not talking about it. Neither worked. I really wasn't sure where we were headed. And then Hazel came up with this idea of coming back to her hometown. As if that somehow was going to be the panacea to all her ills . . ."

Oscar laughed a mirthless laugh. "It's like a black comedy isn't it, though? Isn't it, Helen? Isn't it?" he said, his voice rising.

The total blackness of it all struck him again. The escape to Ireland. Into the jaws of disaster. Bubbles of anger broke at the surface. Where was the justice in any of it? It was all so bloody senseless.

Helen looked at him. "When I arrived you said the police had told you that they were following a definite line of inquiry," she said. "I don't want to press you, and I can't even begin to guess the hell you're going through right now, Oscar. But just that if you do want to talk about it, I'm here now—what happened outside, I mean." Helen sipped her Coke and waited, her eyes kind and searching.

Strangely, Oscar did want to talk about it. He wanted to tell Helen exactly what had happened, as if in the telling, it might somehow make more sense.

"It all happened so quickly," he began. This must have been about the sixth or seventh time he was going through this. Every so often, the police would return to his story and ask him to go through parts of it again. He got up from the stool, stretched his legs, and walked to the window. There was no evidence of the casual party in the park from two nights ago. The bottles and cans had been cleared away. It was bizarre to think that his wife's murder had been witnessed by a bunch of street drinkers who had been just feet away. A couple of large vans had pulled up with the letters RTÉ TELEVISION emblazoned on the sides.

"Hazel went to get the kids some candy and goodies for an evening in with a scary movie," he said. "You know how she liked to treat them."

Helen nodded.

A voice in his head said to him—*Yes, that's it. The past tense. She's no longer here. From now on, it's all the past tense.*

"Hazel was gone awhile and I was listening out for her. Hazel did the driving here. So I hear her pull into the drive and I was just over there, beyond where you are now—at the kitchen window. If you stand there, you'll see how you have a clear view to the drive below. So I'm just standing there, like, watching her, you know. Hazel was trying to put all the groceries back in bags, they'd spilled over in the trunk. Instead of bloody watching, I should have gone out to help her—

Oscar felt a spreading tightness across his chest, wondering now at what might have been.

"—It happened in slow motion," he said. "At first, I thought it was a Halloween prank. This person appears down there, just there by the gate—dressed in black with a ski mask and a hood. Someone small, slight, wearing a black cloak. I thought at first it was a kid—trick or treat, you know? Hazel hadn't heard a thing. She didn't even turn around. I didn't think much at first. I waited to see what would happen. The figure, well, it walked slowly up behind her. But there was something else I hadn't noticed in the dark. I saw a sudden flash of steel. I saw him raise the spade, high above his head. I ran, Helen, I tore down those stairs. It can only have been a few seconds, but by the time I got there it was too late. The person in the cloak was gone and I knew by looking at Hazel that it was too late . . ." He looked at his hand, suddenly realizing his fist was full of gray hairs. He'd been tugging at his hair. "It makes no sense at all, Helen. It doesn't add up, whoever he was, this person, he killed Hazel. And I don't know why. I don't know why. It makes no sense."

"No sense at all," said Helen softly. "But the police, Oscar, what was it they said—the phrase they used? 'A definite line of inquiry.' What do you think that means?"

"I'm not exactly sure," said Oscar. "But they told me they'd been speaking to the O'Briens before they left New York. There's something they know, Helen, and they're not telling us. That guy Spike, he knows something too. I can see it by the way I catch him looking at me."

"So you don't think that they think it was a random attack?" asked Helen gently.

"I dunno, Helen," said Oscar. "I was never very keen on these home exchanges. On paper or on a Web site you may very well think that other folks are like you. They may look like you but often you're surprised when they don't act like you do, when you find out that actually their value system is very different to yours. It was Hazel who set all this up, you know. She said they were professional folks, like us. Two kids, like us. A boy and a girl, like us. But what did we really know about the O'Briens? And that guy Spike, very nice and all that, but would you trust him? Really trust him? I don't know, Helen, there's something pretty odd about these people . . ."

"I think I know what you mean, Oscar. Something definitely left of center." Helen smiled. "But, then, Hazel isn't . . . wasn't exactly a conformist herself."

"And now look where that's landed us all . . ."

Outside, the sky was now an ominous gray and the water ran gray over the falls. Guys with large TV cameras hoisted on their shoulders scouted about the park, moving between the railings and the benches. Oscar quickly stepped back from the window. Oscar could still see Spike below, who was now talking to a garda policeman. The garda looked at his watch. Oscar remembered they'd said there may be something on the lunchtime news. The TV was on, but on a muted setting. Grabbing the remote from the cane swing chair, he signaled to Helen to join him on the sofa. It was now 12:55, five minutes to the news bulletin.

Once again Helen was there for Oscar in his hour of need. Just as she'd waited with him fifteen years before, as Birgitte lay dying, ravaged with cancer in the hospice. On hand again today, Helen had stood shoulder to shoulder with him as they zipped his wife into a body bag and put her in a funeral car.

Helen sat with him now in stony silence as they watched the opening headlines on TV. The opening news stories were full of economic data coming from Europe. There were lots of shots of the German chancellor and European heads of state. Somehow these news stories glided into reports of Halloween hooliganism on the streets of Ireland. With a start, Oscar realized that the bulletin had cut to a scene that was now familiar to him. Introducing herself as the midwest correspondent, a blond woman was standing with a mike in the little park across the road. The camera panned up and down the river, showing the castle and the bridges. It suddenly swung round to face the terraced house Oscar and Helen now sat in.

"Gardaí are still trying to piece together the tragic events that led to the death of an American tourist at this house in Clancy Strand on Halloween night. It appears that the woman may have been the victim of an unprovoked attack here in the driveway of this end of terrace house, overlooking the Curragower Falls."

The delivery was clear, precise, and matter-of-fact.

The reporter continued, "It is not yet clear whether it could have been a Halloween prank that tragically went wrong. Some eyewitnesses drinking in the park opposite reported seeing someone dressed in a hood and cloak leaving the scene at approximately seven o'clock two nights ago. But these reports have not yet been confirmed by gardaí. The state pathologist was on the scene early this morning and the body has been removed from the scene for forensic examination."

The camera zoomed in on the garda policemen at the gate. Spike had turned his back away from the camera.

"The woman's name has not yet been released but it appears that the family staying here were on holiday in the region and had exchanged houses with the owners for the October holidays. The owners of the house have been informed and are expected to arrive back in Shannon from the U.S. later on today. Back to you in the studio, Anne."

Oscar turned the TV off.

"Nothing about 'a definite line of inquiry' there," he said, turning to Helen. "But I guess we don't know how the Irish justice system works. It's hard to get a handle on what is really happening here."

"What did the U.S. embassy say?" asked Helen.

"They offered to send someone from Dublin, but you know what? This little house is beginning to feel so cramped with all the commotion. And I don't really want the kids disturbed any more than they need to be, so I said I'd deal with them by phone. I'm worried about them, Helen. One minute I think they're going to be okay and the next I'm afraid they're going under. They've just lost their mother. You know what? I remember when I lost Ike, and Ike was only a dog. My kids will only ever have one mother . . ." His voice trailed off. He was reluctant to give in to the well of emotion that had gurgled up inside him. There was far too much to do. He must be strong.

"I know that, Oscar, I know," Helen said, nodding.

"Spike pointed out the hotel just up the street." She tried to sound practical. "I guess we could all decamp there when the O'Briens get in? What do you think? I know your head's in a mess right now, so you can let me take care of all of that—if you want."

"Yeah, yeah, I guess so. That would be great, Helen. We sure as hell can't stay here."

He hadn't left the house for nearly two days. They had arrived here so full of expectation. And in a few short hours they'd be leaving.

Their hearts torn out of them.

A broken family.

Kate

Kate had little memory of the hours that filled that last day in New York. She knew she'd packed and tidied the apartment. *He* had changed the travel arrangements. *He* had contacted the gardaí in Limerick and told them of his suspicions. *He* had phoned Spike.

She remembered walking through the lobby, dragging her suitcase, eyes lowered, unable to look Du Bois in the face. She'd heard the confusion in the doorman's voice as they left, three days early.

Sitting on the plane home, she felt hollow inside. Dead. She and Mannix sat in a row in the middle aisle of the plane, separated by the children. Kate could hardly bring herself to look at him. There was no way of putting this one right. No brushing this one under the carpet. This was no petty theft. No stupid punt gone wrong. No feckless harebrained scheme in tatters. This was on a grander scale. This was infidelity and murder. And Mannix was guilty of both. No matter what he said, Mannix had blood on his hands now.

Kate knew that life could never be the same again. Her marriage was shot to bits. Family life, as she had naïvely known it, was over. It had all come crashing down around her ears in a way she never could have imagined. Had she slept at all last night? She didn't know. Lying trancelike and alone on the wide bed, she had listened to Mannix snoring in fits and starts in the living room. The steady sound making her more angry. How dare he relax enough to fall asleep? What kind of man was he? Where was his conscience?

Over the last twenty-four hours, Kate questioned her judgment during their years together. She'd been so foolish. And, oh, so naïve. *A leopard doesn't change his spots.* Isn't that what her mother always said? Oh, my—what would her mother say about this? Not even she could have foreseen disaster on such a scale.

Time and again, Kate had ignored or dismissed his bad behavior, the risks he took. It was what made him different. That is what she'd told herself. She'd fallen in love with his weaknesses, convincing herself that was what made him interesting. *Interesting,* for God's sake! What was the matter with her? Sure—Mannix was different from all the other men who'd ever pursued her. He wasn't staid or boring. She'd been attracted to that in the early days. Flaws were what made people interesting, she'd convinced herself.

Over the course of their marriage, Kate had seen Mannix grow increasingly unpredictable. Increasingly reckless. Mannix was the one who insisted on investing abroad. "It's a sure thing," he said. Like everything was a sure thing with Mannix. Until it wasn't. And as time went on, she found herself envying friends and colleagues with solid partners and husbands. A safe harbor was what she needed. They had kids. Responsibilities. She'd forgiven Mannix so much over the years. But no, not this. This could never be forgiven.

Kate had to face an unpleasant truth: She had gone into this marriage with her eyes wide open. She too had been reckless. Her mother had warned her. Even Spike in his best man's speech had saluted her bravery in taking on his brother. Everyone had laughed, toasting their union with pink champagne. And she had laughed as heartily as the rest of them. She'd prove them all wrong. She'd show them all. Or so she thought at the time.

What, indeed, would her mother say when she learned the whole truth? Kate had seen precious little of her mother over the last few years. Alice Kennedy came to the house for the kids' birthdays, but more often than not there would be some excuse or other when an invitation was extended. Once they had married, Alice Kennedy never overtly criticized her son-in-law again. And Kate sensed it was probably better to keep her husband and her mother out of each other's way. It hurt Kate, but it was yet another situation she chose to ignore. Another little secret she kept to herself.

Kate sighed as she stretched out a leg under the seat in front. She'd had the capacity to forgive the stupid stuff Mannix had done in the past, but he'd broken her illusion of what she thought they'd had—a solid marriage. She didn't have the capacity to forgive him that. He'd willfully and wantonly put them all in danger. He'd invited a deranged woman into their lives. Kate shivered. An innocent woman lay murdered, her skull smashed in, all because Mannix had fancied a bit on the side.

Kate's thoughts turned to Fergus and Izzy. Mannix hadn't been thinking of *them* either. He'd betrayed them all, each and every one of them. Her mother had been right after all. "Those O'Briens have the morals of alley cats," she used to say in the days before they got married. And sure enough, though it had taken long enough for Kate to realize it, an alley cat was what Kate got.

The mother in her was seething. Mannix had strayed and shown affection to another woman's child. That too she would not forgive. Over the course of the last day or so, Kate had experienced every possible negative emotion ever felt. Fury, betrayal, anger, jealousy, bitterness, and, every now and then, an overwhelming sadness at what was lost.

It came to her then that she no longer had a picture in her head of her and Mannix growing old together. She just couldn't conjure it up. She couldn't imagine it anymore. What was needed now was a different vision of her future. A vision without Mannix. And, painful though it was, she needed to reimagine it all. She would be strong. For herself and her children, she would be strong. She had made one really bad life choice. She alone could try to fix it.

She was tired now. Tired of keeping secrets. With another long deep sigh, she realized that she was actually tired of *him*. Exhausted from *him*. Even if she could ever forgive, she no longer had enough energy to go around. The energy she did have would have to be saved for herself and the children. It was over. Mannix O'Brien was out of time.

Kate needed to phone her mother. Shortly after Mannix told Kate, and though she was still reeling from the shock, Kate knew she had to phone her. This could not wait until she got back home. It would be all over the news. As Kate shakily picked up the handset in the Harveys' flat, it occurred to her that Hazel Harvey would never again hold this handset, never again have a conversation on this phone. Kate gulped. She had no idea what she was going to say when her mother answered. She was struggling to hold her emotions in check.

"Mum?"

"Kate? Kate, is that you?"

"Yes, Mum, it's me . . ." And suddenly, all her resolve, all her composure, evaporated. She was the young girl who'd become separated from her friends and missed the last train home from a concert in Dublin. She was the nine-year-old who'd been dragged off her bike by a passing truck on the way to school, whose deeply gashed leg needed stitching. The years peeled away and all of a sudden she was a sobbing child again. No longer a mother or a wife. A child.

"Oh, Mum . . ." She tried to speak but her words were strangled.

"Kate, what is it? Are you all right? Is it the kids?"

Her mother sounded alarmed.

"No, no, we're fine. We're all all right," Kate managed to say.

"You're still in New York?"

"Yes, yes." Kate sniffed, conscious that the kids were sleeping. She didn't want to wake them.

"Oh, Mum—you were right. I know you're going to say 'I told you so' and I'm so sorry I never listened to you. You were so right about Mannix. And now something dreadful has happened. Something tragic . . ."

Kate tried to get herself under control. Neither did she want to wake Mannix, who was snoring on the sofa.

"I would never say 'I told you so,'" said her mother gently.

Strangely, these words made Kate want to weep all the more.

"I've always been here for you, Kate. Whether you felt that or not. Always. Now, please tell me what I can do."

As ever, Alice Kennedy was practical.

"I don't really think you can do anything—not now, at least." Kate sniffed. "But I am going to need you over the next few weeks and months, Mum. I am really going to need you. And so are the kids."

"That's what I'm here for. You know that, Kate."

The quality of the landline was very good, and taking a deep breath, Kate began to feel slightly better.

"Mum?"

"Yes?"

"You're probably going to hear some pretty awful stuff on the news over the next few days . . ."

"I see." Alice Kennedy didn't sound too perturbed.

So Kate just blurted it out.

"Our American houseguest was murdered in our house."

There was a sharp intake of breath this time.

A pause.

"I see," her mother said. "But you and the kids are okay—you're telling me the truth now?"

"Yes, Mum. We're fine. It looks like we're going to be placed under police protection as soon as we arrive home. It's all very complicated. I'll explain when we get back tomorrow."

There was a lengthier pause this time.

"Okay, sweetheart. I don't need to know the ins and outs just yet. You just call me when you get home. I'll come as soon as you want me."

If Alice Kennedy really wanted to know, the truth was that her daughter wanted her *now*. By her side this very minute. But Kate would have to wait. She knew that from now on, there were many things she would have to do by herself. And she would. She could. Somehow, she would manage.

"Thanks, Mum. Thanks for everything," said Kate, sounding a lot more composed than she felt. "And Mum—I'm so sorry I let you down."

"Kate, you're my child and you have never let me down. Just make sure you come home safely."

"I will . . ."

As Kate quietly docked the receiver, she stretched her neck from side to side. For the first time in the midst of this hellish nightmare, she felt less alone. It had been a long, long time since she'd had an open exchange with her mother.

But then there was the fear.

Every now and again Kate had to block it out, before it threatened to fill her up and swallow her whole. It was an ongoing battle—Kate versus the fear. She could not afford to give in to it, to let it take her over.

Kate tried not to think about the Collins woman and where she was. *Just how crazy and deranged was this woman?* Had she come to the attention of the gardaí before? Often it was only in the wake of a tragedy that people realized the clues were there all the time. That there had been a history. Signs that had been ignored.

Did Joanne Collins look unbalanced to the naked eye? Was she the sort of woman you could pick out in a crowd by her strange gait or by the look in her eyes? Or had she the detachment and composure of a seasoned killer? Was it possible that she had done this before?

The masochist in Kate wanted to know exactly what this woman looked like. *What did a killer look like?* What was it about her that had attracted Mannix? Had she laughed readily at his easy charm? Had she played it up as turbulence hit the plane? Was she small and feminine or toned and athletic? Did she eat her food nicely or enjoy it with the same lust she had for Mannix? Had she chased him or had he chased her? Or did Joanne Collins simply radiate wanton abandon, sheer raw available sex, in some unhinged way?

Kate couldn't demean herself to ask. Her shattered and fragile pride would not let her stoop that low. All she could do was imagine what the woman looked like, and then, perversely, try to block out all the disturbing images she'd conjured up.

He had assured her the gardaí had things under control. Assuming they hadn't found Joanne Collins by the time they arrived back in Ireland, Kate would be put under police protection as soon as they arrived at Shannon Airport.

The gardaí knew where the woman lived. They knew where her child went to school. Surely they should be able to pick her up easily enough? Maybe Joanne Collins had gone into hiding. Maybe she was good at disappearing, at reinventing herself. Maybe they would never find her. Maybe Kate would have to live the rest of her life forever looking over her shoulder. *Stop! Stop it! Get a grip, Kate!* She couldn't afford to think like this. She had to focus.

"What do you suggest we tell the kids?" Kate asked Mannix before they left the apartment on Riverside Drive. She was gulping one last coffee, trying to muster some energy for what lay ahead. She hoped he could hear the disgust in her voice.

"About what exactly?" he asked nervously.

"They're expecting only Spike at the airport in Shannon. I would imagine they're going to find it a tad peculiar being met by the Special Branch of the gardaí when we land, don't you?" Kate was finding it almost impossible to sound civil, but for the sake of the children she knew she'd have to try.

"I'm not sure exactly . . ." He hesitated. "Do you have something in mind? Something that's not going to scare them too much . . . especially Ferg . . . he's the one who could get really upset . . ."

"It's a bit late for all that now, don't you think, Mannix? You should have thought of that before." Her voice left her throat in a monotone this time. Calm. More controlled.

"I'm sorry, Kate," he muttered. "I'm so very, very sorry . . . if only you knew . . ."

"Enough!" Kate put up her hands. She didn't want to hear it.

She looked at him now. At his sheepish expression, looking for solace. In that moment, she wanted to hurt him. Really, really badly. She wanted to reach inside herself and scoop out all the hurt and heartache and drive it deep inside him, twisting and turning it until the pain of it choked him.

She took another deep breath.

"Here's what we're going to do," she said. "We are going to have to tell them something close to the truth. Some made-up fairy story is not going to wash with Izzy. She's far too clever, so let's not treat her like a fool."

"Okay . . ." Mannix nodded.

"We are going to tell them that a mentally unstable woman has been committing random attacks in the city and that until she is caught, we are being given protection—seeing as she's suspected of being involved in the death of Hazel Harvey."

Mannix looked alarmed. "Oh, Kate, I don't know. Random attacks. A mentally unstable woman. What are they going to make of that?"

"As I said already, Mannix, you should have thought of all of that before," she replied coldly.

"And you know what?" Kate added.

"What?"

"*You* are going to be the one to tell them. And you are going to tell them now, before we leave this apartment. I'll go and call them into the living room."

Kate listened, her heart sinking, as she watched a white-faced Mannix tell Izzy and Fergus what would be waiting for them when they arrived in Shannon. She watched their little faces as they listened carefully.

Izzy said nothing at first, analyzing and weighing up this disturbing information. It was Fergus who broke the silence.

"Gardaí outside our house as well?" His eyes grew wide behind his glasses. "Will it be the Armed Response Unit with the flashing lights? You know—the special cops with guns? Frankie Flynn was bragging that it was outside his uncle's house last month!"

Mannix said nothing, looking to Kate for direction. But Kate too was flabbergasted. And for the first time since this nightmare had unfolded she felt the beginnings of a smile. A bitter smile. Could it really be that her little Fergus thought there was actually some prestige in having the Special Branch or the Armed Response Unit outside their home?

"Well, Soldier, we don't know yet," she said gently. "It may well be that this poor sick lady will have been found and arrested by the time we get home. We'll just have to wait and see."

"Wait and see, wait and see," chanted Fergus, marching up and down the hallway.

Mannix shot Kate a look, grateful that she'd rescued him.

"But why did this woman kill Hazel Harvey?" asked Izzy quietly. She was not so easily satisfied.

"We don't know that yet, Izzy," said Kate. "She's a very sick person. She must be. It may be that she escaped from a psychiatric ward. We just don't know. It's all very sad. A real tragedy. We must keep the Harvey family in our prayers. The important thing now is that we are going to be safe. The gardaí are going to look after us."

"And are they going to look after everyone else on Clancy Strand?"

Izzy certainly knew the questions to ask. Mannix looked awkward, but Kate did her best to maintain the same tone of voice.

"I guess so, Izzy. But I imagine they'll be parked outside our house."

"But . . ."

Before Izzy had a chance to ask another question, Kate interjected, "Time to go now, kids. Let's get our suitcases. Du Bois will have that cab waiting by now!"

Izzy's face set in a frown as she went to get her suitcase.

As the flight captain announced they were flying over Greenland, Kate's thoughts again turned to Oscar Harvey and his children. Poor tragic Hazel Harvey got a homecoming she never expected. A final homecoming. Kate closed her eyes. Whatever the strength of emotion she was feeling, she could only imagine Oscar Harvey's grief, the shock and confusion of his kids. Two families destroyed because of

Mannix. Kate bit the insides of her cheeks. The stupid, selfish, faithless shit. She'd had her chances since they'd been married. Guys who'd shown an interest. Who would have taken flirting to another level. But she'd ignored the signals. She'd made her choices. She was married. She was faithful.

And to think that Mannix had the audacity to try to shift the blame on her. That somehow Kate was responsible. Because they hadn't been getting on, she had forced him to look elsewhere for pleasure. That somehow Kate had a part to play in this murderous tragedy. What was the matter with him? she asked herself again. Couldn't he have found some regular slut to play away with? It wasn't like there weren't plenty out there. But no. Mannix had to pick the *nutter.*

Kate felt deep distaste as she thought of all the times they'd since made love. The duplicitous shit. Had any of his affection been real? And then it hit her. She wondered if it had happened before. How much of their life together had been a sham?

It was only sex. He kept repeating it. If he said it one more time, she'd scream. It may have been just sex to him but it was a whole load more to her. It was trust. It was the inviolability of their marriage. Forsaking all others—when she'd said it at the altar, she'd meant it. But he had let that *nutter* in and things could never be undone.

Kate thought back to last March, about the time he'd been to Boston. She tried to remember exactly what had been going on in their lives. True—they hadn't been getting on too well. There had been pressures. Money, or the lack of it. Debts. Fergus. She'd been fretting all the time about Fergus. And all the while, he'd been sleeping with *her.*

Later into the flight, Kate fell into to an uneasy doze, wishing the burden she felt could be lifted. She had no idea how things would play out when they landed, but of one thing she was certain. She had to be on her guard at all times. At every twist and turn. There was no room for complacency. There was no telling where this woman might be. Could she even trust the gardaí to protect her?

The damp light was beginning to fade as the aircraft followed the weave of the Shannon to the marshland airport. It was a landing like no other. Kate was usually happy to return home from any foreign jaunt. Not this time. As she tried to muster a smile for the kids, Kate felt sick to her stomach. They were no longer going home as a unit to the sanctuary of the family home. That too had been violated. The little terrace house that she so loved was now a murder scene.

She tried again to imagine the future without Mannix. She imagined different houses around the city, a nice small flat for her, Fergus, and Izzy. She needed to keep on imagining it, to make it real, because that's where she was headed. Then it dawned on her. Why should Kate be the one to move? The house at Curragower Falls was home to Izzy and Fergus as well. There were going to be so many adjustments in their young lives, why heap an unnecessary cruel move on them as well? If anyone was going to move out, surely it should be Mannix?

How would Izzy and Fergus react to their father's departure? It chewed her up inside as she tried to picture it. Fergus idolized his father. And how would Kate fare, cast in the role of villain, ejecting his hero from the family home? Fergus would have to be told very carefully, his father's departure sensitively executed. Kate would think of something. She had to think of something. There was a solution out there—only she hadn't thought of it just yet.

"Don't worry, Kate. It's going to be okay," said Mannix quietly as they stood at the luggage carousel. He was looking out for the suitcases with their trademark yellow twine. "Spike will be just through those doors in arrivals along with the plainclothes gardaí."

Kate didn't bother to respond. It was going to be okay for him, all right. Mannix wasn't the intended target. Kate was.

Kate thought she'd had the measure of this man. But Mannix's ebullient confidence in the face of all that had happened was staggering. Did he really believe that he could somehow smooth things over? Was he stupid? Did he *genuinely* think that things could ever return to business as usual? Mannix had a death on his hands. And yet he appeared to have little or no idea of the depth of her anger and revolt.

Three of their suitcases arrived promptly and Mannix swung

them onto the trolley as if he hadn't a care in the world. She wondered then if his behavior was part of a ruse. Mannix was nothing if not a showman. Perhaps underneath the nonchalant exterior, he was as distressed as she was.

"Mum?" Fergus was wiping imaginary dust from the camera, which he'd insisted on holding on to.

"Yes, Ferg?"

"Why aren't you talking to Dad?"

Fergus had an unhappy knack for pointing out and heightening any socially awkward situation. Tact was something she would have to try to teach him in the years to come. In fact, Kate was surprised he hadn't remarked on the silence between them earlier. She noticed now that Izzy had pricked up her ears. Izzy was definitely unhappy with what she had been told so far. She felt her daughter's dark eyes steadily fix on her. Mannix looked at her too, wondering what she'd say.

"Of course I'm talking to Dad. I've got a lot on my mind with this dreadful tragedy."

"No, you're not, Mum. You haven't said a single word to him since we got on the plane. It's not Dad's fault we have to come home early. It's not Dad's fault there's a psycho on the loose!"

Poor Ferg, always his father's champion. If only he knew.

Sharp, astute, Izzy was quick off the mark.

"It's not your fault, is it, Dad?"

Mannix looked at Izzy, flummoxed.

"Of course not, Izzy. Don't be ridiculous," chided Kate.

The words were out before she knew it. It wasn't that she was trying to protect Mannix, but she did want to protect the children. There would be time enough for the whole truth at a much later date. For now, she'd protect the kids as much as she could. Again, Mannix looked at Kate with relief. She hoped her actions hadn't given him false hope of any reconciliation. As soon as they were in private again, she would disavow him of any such notions.

"Let's go, troops," said Mannix as the last suitcase arrived. "We're locked and loaded!"

Beset by a feeling of dread, Kate followed him toward the sliding doors. Each step like walking on wet sucking concrete. *What lay on the other side of those doors?* Kate's heart fluttered and started to race. Her legs shook. Her palms perspired heavily. With each footstep, Kate's heart beat louder. *Thump, thump, thump.* Suddenly the doors were open and they were through.

Was she there?

That nutter?

Slinking through the crowd?

Faces. Faces. A sea of faces.

All looking at Kate. Kate felt her skin prickle and the hairs stand up on the nape of her neck. Someone out there was watching her. *She could feel it.* Kate scanned the crowd, eyes swiveling, darting this way and that.

Stay alert. Keep looking.

Voices called out. Kate's heart was beating wildly.

Who was that? There—at the back, behind the crowd?

That woman with the blue head scarf—she was steadily making her way toward Kate! Kate's breath came in short bursts. Kate's eyes fastened onto the woman—petrified. She was definitely headed in Kate's direction. *Kate should run! Get out of here. NOW!* But Kate was rooted to the spot. She could see the woman's lips were shiny—glistening with red lip gloss. A moment later she disappeared. Melted into the crowd. *Where was she? There she was again.* Directly in front of the man with the walking stick. Moving faster. Much, much faster—a purpose to her step. Suddenly, the woman's expression changed, her face creasing into a smile. All Kate's senses screamed. Was she smiling at *her?* Or was she smiling at *Mannix?* Kate shot a quick glance at Mannix. *How had he not noticed the woman?* She was nearly on them!

Whoosh!

Kate became dizzy as she felt the soft fabric of someone brushing by. The blood was thumping in her ears. Looking around, Kate stared as the woman wrapped herself in a tight embrace with a dark-skinned man. Relief coursed through Kate and a bead of sweat trickled down her back.

Kate desperately needed to get out of this crowd. To feel cold water on her face. *Now*. She would never make it to the exit. The sign for the ladies' toilets was there, to the right. Just a quick sprint away.

"Kate! Where are you going?"

It was Mannix. He spoke so sharply other travelers turned to look.

"Bathroom," she said, and it occurred to her that if it weren't for her kids, she'd love to keep on walking, to cut a line through the gathering of waiting taxi drivers and welcoming relatives, out through the concourse doors, to keep on walking and walking, without ever looking back.

"Quickly then," Mannix barked. "We'll wait here for you." It was the first sign he'd given acknowledging any danger.

A ball of stress had formed inside her. As Kate waited for a free cubicle, she looked around her. She wondered if anyone else in the queue was expecting a homecoming quite as appalling as hers. "Muuuum, I'm really bursting," moaned a small child, wiggling her tiny frame. "Shhh, Rosie, we're in next," said her mother.

Kate looked in the mirror over the hand basins. Her hair hung lank and there were dark circles under her eyes. Not the rejuvenated soul she expected to be on her return. Everyone else in the queue looked tired and drawn as well. Apart from the woman holding the flowers. Standing a few people behind, Kate watched as she fiddled with the petals, and when she lowered her head to smell the bouquet, Kate noticed her long ponytail beneath her woolly hat. The woman looked as if she'd been walking in the wind.

What was taking everyone so long? There were never enough toilets in these bathrooms.

A couple of ladies were applying powder at the mirror. Another young woman pinched her cheeks. As Kate waited, she unzipped her bag in search of lipstick. She turned to face the mirror, while keeping her position in the queue. As she concentrated, following the curve of her lips, Kate became aware that she was being watched.

No, she was mistaken. It was her imagination. She'd gone into overdrive.

Get a grip, Kate!

No, actually she wasn't mistaken at all. She *was* being watched. *By the woman with the flowers.*

Kate was being scrutinized. The woman with the flowers was directly behind Kate now. There was something else that jarred about her. Apart from the flowers. She was in a long winter coat, muffled up in her woolly hat and matching scarf. As if she'd come in from outdoors.

There was something odd about her.

Kate turned around and froze. She was face-to-face with her now. How sleek and shiny and perfect her ponytail was. *The woman kept staring at Kate.* She didn't lower her eyes. Not for a second. She looked Kate up and down, slowly, lingering on Kate's hands, her rings. Kate froze.

In a sudden burst of panic, Kate skipped the queue, past the gray-haired ladies and the whining child, colliding with a woman exiting a cubicle. Kate slammed the door loudly and firmly slid the bolt in place. Darts of adrenaline shot through her body.

That was really weird.

Over the rush of blood in her ears, Kate heard the indignation of those outside.

"Disgraceful! Did you see that?"

"No manners, and a little one waiting as well . . ."

Kate was embarrassed. But more than that, she was petrified.

Was it her?

Was that Joanne Collins?

Was she still outside?

Oh God! What should she do now? Kate was trapped. *But would Joanne Collins be stupid enough to come to the airport? When the gardaí were looking for her?* And then it occurred to Kate that the woman probably had no idea the gardaí were looking for her. Joanne Collins thought Mannix *loved* her. In her sick and twisted mind, what she had done was in the name of love. Why would Mannix even go to the gardaí?

As Kate leaned against the door, thinking, thinking, thinking, she knew what she should do. There was one person who would know if it was Joanne. That was Mannix, and he was outside. Kate frantically unzipped her bag again to get her mobile phone.

"Mum! Mum, are you in here?"

That was Izzy's voice!

Izzy was out there with that woman. She could be in danger! Dropping the mobile in the bag, Kate slid back the bolt and swung the door open.

"There you are," muttered Izzy. The other faces in the queue were looking strangely at her now. Kate quickly scanned the washroom. But she was gone. The woman with the flowers was gone.

"Mum? Are you all right?" asked Izzy, looking concerned. "Dad sent me, because you were taking so long."

"I'm fine, Izzy," Kate said, trying to still her beating heart. She would really have to get this under control. She couldn't transmit her anxieties to Izzy or Fergus. The woman was gone now. All she'd done was stare at Kate, and Kate had gone into a tailspin.

"Come on, Dad's going mad."

Kate's days of pandering to Mannix were done. She took her time washing her hands and splashed cold water on her face. She wiped a moistened paper towel over the back of neck.

"Mum, come on," said Izzy, as warm jets of air from the hand dryer ran over Kate's hands.

"Ready," Kate said as the machine clicked off. Kate suddenly felt a shiver run down her back. There was something there in the waste-basket at her side. She looked closely. A cello-wrapped bouquet of flowers. Freesias, lilies, and carnations. Discarded, dumped, headfirst into the waste bin.

"Let's go," Kate said, linking Izzy's arm to steady herself.

What kind of woman discarded a fresh bouquet of flowers?

"Mum, you're hurting me . . ."

Kate squeezed Izzy's arm as they walked back out on the concourse. She felt afraid again. Mannix, Spike, and Fergus were only feet away.

"You doing okay?" asked Spike gently. She let him give her a hug. After the unsettling incident in the washroom it was a relief to see a familiar face. He looked genuinely concerned.

"I've been better," she replied.

"You were a long time in there," remarked Mannix.

"Yeah?" replied Kate with complete disinterest.

"Mum isn't talking to Dad, Uncle Spike. She says she is, but she's not," piped up Fergus.

Spike looked from Kate to Mannix and back again.

"Your mum is tired and she's had a shock, Ferg," said Spike.

Kate just wanted to get out of the openness of this airport. She was frazzled. Everyone was looking at her, staring at her. Even now, someone else was headed in her direction. Another woman, headed straight for her, making a beeline for her. A serious woman. The woman was picking up her step. Kate reached out to grab Spike's arm. She felt a scream forming in her throat. But the woman was upon her . . .

"Mrs. O'Brien? Kate O'Brien?" the woman was asking.

Kate breathed out.

There were two other people with her. Two men.

"I'm Mannix O'Brien." Mannix held out his hand to the woman. "Special Branch, is it?"

"That's right, sir," said the serious woman, directing attention away from Kate, who remained mute, the blood drained from her face. Feeling stupid.

"I'm Detective Maria Nagle. And this is Detective James O'Rourke and Detective Shane Dwyer. Let's get you all home first, guys. And then we can have a little chat."

"Do you have the squad cars outside? Is the Armed Response Unit there?" asked Fergus excitedly.

"My son, Fergus," Mannix said, smiling at the detective.

"Let's get you home, young man. I'm afraid we just have unmarked cars today," she said officiously.

Ten minutes later, all the O'Briens were in one car, Spike driving.

The unmarked garda car with plainclothes detectives followed. Fergus was disappointed but he still held out hope that the Armed Response Unit would greet them at Curragower Falls.

There was a funereal feel to the convoy journey back to the house.

"The driveway to the house is still taped off but I'm sure we can use it now," said Spike, closely following the car in front as advised. "The forensics guys were there for ages. They must have everything they need by now."

"Are we going to be on television?" asked Fergus.

"I don't think so, Ferg. The TV crew moved out a few hours ago."

"Really?" said Ferg, sounding disappointed again.

"Where are the Harveys now?" asked Izzy.

God, that poor family. Kate didn't want to think about the pain they must have been going through. Those poor children. That poor man. Kate tried to block it out. She had so much pain of her own.

"I helped them move up to the Strand Hotel late last night," said a somber Spike.

"How are the Harveys doing?" asked Mannix. He sat next to Spike in the passenger seat.

How the hell did Mannix expect they were doing? They were in hell. He had swung a wrecking ball through all their lives.

"Yeah, in shock, you know," said Spike. "The kids are very quiet. Some relative arrived over from the States to look after them. Not in great shape, to be honest . . ." His voice drifted off.

Mannix said nothing.

"Are my Man U bedclothes washed?" asked Fergus into a long silence.

"It doesn't matter, Fergus," said Kate. "I'll wash them later or tomorrow. We can put another clean set on before you go to bed."

"Okay."

She hoped Fergus wasn't going to fret.

Pulling up outside the terrace house, Kate's stomach lurched as she saw all the police tape at the side of the house. Two uniformed gardaí stood at the gate. Detective James O'Rourke got out of the car in front and exchanged a few words with them. Moments later the tape was taken away and they were ushered into the driveway. One of the unmarked cars stayed out front on the main road and the other drove away.

"Can you see any blood?" she heard Fergus whisper to Izzy as they dragged their suitcases over the loose gravel.

"I'm not looking," replied Izzy seriously. Kate was not looking either. She was not going to let herself think about what had happened here.

"Here, let me take that," said Spike, taking her suitcase as Mannix turned the key in the front door. Exhausted, and happy to let him help, she glanced down at the welcome mat on the small step outside. They had been so full of excitement and joy leaving this house less than a week ago. How the world had changed in such a short space of time.

"So where is Joanne Collins?" Kate demanded after the detectives went outside. "Where the hell is this woman?"

The kids were unpacking. Out of earshot.

"I don't know, Kate," Mannix said. "Really, I don't. Don't you think I'd say if I knew? There haven't been any more texts." He looked at her with his newfound hangdog expression. "You heard Detective O'Rourke. She's cleared her flat in Pery Square. They don't know yet. Give them a chance. I'm sure they'll find her."

"Mannix is right, Kate," added Spike. "They'll find her. Don't worry."

Kate walked to the window and looked out over the falls. She looked at the water coursing over the rocks and boulders. She loved this view. But there was no way she could ever feel safe here until Joanne Collins was caught. The woman had cleared her flat and had vanished. No sign of her. No sign of her child. She wasn't answering her mobile phone and it wasn't even registering on any mobile location registers. *But she was out there somewhere.*

"It shouldn't be too long, Kate," said Spike, joining her at the window. Mannix was propped up against the breakfast counter staring into space. "I was talking to one of the lads earlier," Spike continued. "You'll be confined to the house for a day or two, just until they find her. And then you can go back to normal."

"Back to normal." Kate looked at him.

"No . . . no . . . not back to normal . . . obviously . . ." Spike stumbled. "But you know what I mean . . ." he trailed off, looking uncomfortable.

Was Spike trying to act as peacemaker here? Be the honest broker? She'd never figured him as that. Kate was grateful for the support, but if he wanted to offer practical support, there was one thing he could do for her. It had come to her in the car on the way from Shannon. It was the obvious solution. Better to tackle this sooner rather than later. A long drawn-out parting would be worse. For Fergus especially. Better to do it now. One clean cut.

"You really want to help?" she asked Spike.

Mannix listened as well.

"Sure." Spike nodded.

"Okay, so here's what's going to happen . . ."

Kate outlined how Mannix was going to leave. She would not have him in the house. He was going to Spike's. As far as Izzy and Fergus were concerned, their dad was going to help Spike with yet another electrical problem in his flat. They'd tell them that it shouldn't take long to fix and that if they wanted to, they could call around to the flat. But it would probably be better to wait until the mentally ill lady was found.

"Kate, please . . ." said Mannix, coming toward her now. "Please don't do this."

"But, Kate, are you sure?" said Spike evenly. "Are you sure you want to be the only adult in the house—now?"

"I won't be the only adult here, Spike."

Both Mannix and Spike raised their eyebrows.

"No?" said Spike.

"My mother is coming to stay, just as soon as I ring her."

Mannix sat on the arm of the sofa.

"Don't do this, Kate."

There were tears in his eyes. And for one split second, she felt herself waver. She saw his hurt. And confusion. Like he really didn't understand what he had done. It would be so easy to give in now. To cave in again. She wasn't used to seeing Mannix like this.

"Please don't do this to us."

A flare of anger suddenly welled up deep inside her. Her sympathy evaporated instantly. How could he think any of this was *her* doing? Spike interrupted before she could vent that anger.

"Manny, leave it for now. Maybe it's for the best, bro. Just for a couple of days. Come on, buddy. Throw a few things in a bag. Kate needs a bit of time to herself."

A short half hour later, they were gone. There was a lump in her throat and her heart felt like it had been ripped in two by a jackhammer. It was the hardest thing she'd ever done in her life.

"Granny's here!" said Fergus, looking out the window. He was still waiting hopefully for the Armed Response Unit to arrive. Two gardaí flanked the pillars to the driveway and the plainclothes detective sat in the car outside. Again, Fergus had surprised her. She'd thought he'd be more upset at his father's leaving, but Mannix's explanation had sat quite well with him. Of course his dad had to help out his uncle Spike.

Izzy knew that something more was afoot, but Kate would tackle that later. Much later. Dealing with Izzy was going to be a whole other project and she still hadn't decided how she was going discipline her daughter over Frankie Flynn. One step at a time, she told herself. Just one step at a time.

Over the course of the next three days, the outside world became suspended. "How much longer are we going to have to stay in the house?" asked Izzy. She had enjoyed baking scones and making cupcakes with her granny but Kate could see she was feeling cooped up and anxious to see her friend Fiona. Kate's patience too was wearing thin. *But there was still no news of Joanne Collins.* She had simply disappeared.

Alice Kennedy did her best to distract them all, and indeed, for the first few days it had the desired effect. She baked. She played cards with Izzy and Fergus, and Fergus in particular discovered that he was good at them. He remembered cards that were played. He remembered the shapes and numbers. More often than not it was her mother who would call a halt to the games, needing respite enough to boil the kettle for her endless cups of tea.

Her mother had listened quietly as Kate explained how the tragedy had come about. She listened and she never once made any judgment. There was no suggestion of gloating or "I told you so." Nothing but a heartfelt concern for Kate and the children.

When Kate asked about the Harveys and their welfare, Detective O'Rourke told her that the Harvey children had left for New York with their aunt. Oscar Harvey was still in the Strand Hotel, hoping for news of an arrest. They didn't know how long he would stay.

Kate was conflicted. She should really contact Oscar Harvey to extend her sympathy. Yet when she suggested this to Detective O'Rourke, she got the impression that it might not be advisable. The shock was beginning to wear off and he was now pretty confused and very angry. Perhaps it might be better to wait until Joanne Collins was apprehended. *If she was apprehended.*

Kate felt permanently on edge. It had been days and yet there was no progress. Not a sniff of anything. The kids were due back at school in a couple of days and Kate sensed that even though they were distracted by their granny and the comings and goings of the gardaí, they both needed some sense of normality. As did Kate. Her mother had just about washed every item of linen in the house. She'd be taking down the curtains next. As it was, she was out there now, pegging sheets on the line outside as she chatted to the young garda who'd just come on duty. She'd struck up quite a rapport with the gardaí, bringing them regular cups of tea with a side plate of scones and butter.

"Any chance of a cream cracker?" asked Detective O'Rourke, who'd come in from the car to pay her a courtesy call.

Kate looked at the kitchen clock. "It's nearly lunchtime. I was going to have an omelet. Will you join me?"

His eyes lit up.

"I don't want to put you to any trouble, Mrs. O'Brien, but if you're having one yourself . . ."

They both sat on either side of the breakfast counter to eat.

"Wants to be a detective, then?" said the detective, his mouth full. "Your young lad, Fergus. That's what he tells me anyway. He wants to be a detective when he grows up."

"Really?" Kate smiled. She'd noticed Fergus's fascination with the armed detectives. He accompanied her mother anytime she brought them tea. But it was the first time he'd ever voiced what he wanted to be when he grew up.

"It's a tough life and I'm sure you see lots of stuff," said Kate.

The detective looked up from the plate but didn't respond.

"*Where is she*, Detective?" asked Kate then. "Where on earth is she? It isn't as if it's a huge country. We live on an *island*, for God's sake—she's got to be out there, somewhere . . ."

Detective O'Rourke looked up again from his lunch. He shrugged. "She's giving us the runaround, all right, Mrs. O'Brien. We're pursuing a number of lines of investigation."

Kate wished he wouldn't call her Mrs. O'Brien. It made her feel ancient.

"And she never came to your attention before? Never before the courts on any charges?"

Detective O'Rourke looked thoughtful as he chewed his last mouthful. Slowly and deliberately, he put his knife and fork together in the center of the plate. And then adjusted them slightly so that there was an equal semicircle on either side of the cutlery. He looked at her, expressionless.

"I really couldn't say, Mrs. O'Brien. I really couldn't say."

Couldn't say or wouldn't say?

"But you must have something to go on! She can't have disappeared into thin air. You mean there's been absolutely nothing since Halloween? No one has spoken to her, been in contact with her, nothing at all?!"

"Oh, I wouldn't say that exactly," he said, taking a sip of water. "Very tasty, by the way."

"You wouldn't say what exactly?"

"Mr. O'Brien didn't tell you?"

"As you are aware, Detective, Mr. O'Brien has moved out of the house for a few days."

"Oh, yes, well . . . sorry, yes, of course . . ." The detective flushed slightly. The gardaí and Special Branch were by now aware of the personal circumstances behind the tragedy.

"Tell me what?" Kate continued.

"Well, there has been *one* sighting of Joanne Collins . . ."

"What?" Kate was stunned.

Why did nobody think to tell her?

"Yes," said the detective, looking directly at her now. "In Shannon Airport. She was caught on CCTV the morning your flight arrived into Shannon. We got your husband to verify the sighting. And it seems that it was her, all right. Filmed near arrivals. We weren't sure at first because a lot of her face was hidden from view."

"Hidden from view?" Kate repeated.

"Yes. In most of the clips we saw, she was carrying quite a large bouquet of flowers . . ."

Detective O'Rourke had left. Gone back outside to his car. Kate still felt nauseated. She stood up from the table, afraid that her stomach would not hold down the egg that she'd just eaten. But her legs shook too much to hold her. She slumped back down on the chair. This latest news had left her reeling. So her instincts had been right. *She had been right about the woman in the washroom.*

A cold chill descended on Kate. *So this is what it feels like to be stalked.* What had the woman intended to do? Had Izzy's arrival in the washroom disturbed her? And where was she now? Did the gardaí know more than they were letting on? All of a sudden Kate felt like she was a sitting duck, sitting here like bait, waiting for a sick and twisted killer to show up.

And yet what could Kate do? All she could do was wait. Kate was not in control. She desperately needed to feel in control of something. She wanted routine. She wanted her old life back. She needed to think about something that made her happy. She needed to immerse herself in something she enjoyed, or else she felt she might go crazy.

"Mum?" Her mother was in the garden, checking the washing. "I'm just going to go up to the study for a while. There are some of my students' portfolios I've been meaning to look at for ages. Is that okay with you?"

"Of course, pet. You go ahead. The children want me to show them how I make my breakfast muffins."

"Thanks, Mum. Oh, and remember, no raisins. Fergus doesn't like them."

"I remember," mumbled her mother, a peg in her mouth.

Even though the study was a bright room with its large window, Kate put on the angled silver lamp over the study desk. The November light was fading fast. She looked at the sheaf of portfolio folders that had lain there for weeks. Some of the work and the proposals were mediocre, but Kate did have some very talented students. Students whose work excited her. She'd made a mental note to personally put in a good word for one or two of them with an advertising agency she knew in Dublin. She was sure she'd be able to secure at least three decent internships.

For the next two hours, Kate went through the proposals, and looked at completed multimedia projects on the student Web site. Some of the animation clips even made her laugh. The animation companies she'd dealt with in the past would love this stuff. She could certainly forge much stronger links between the department and her old college friends who now worked in graphic design companies both in Dublin and in London. She sat back in the chair and stretched her arms. That was all very well, she thought, but these things were time consuming. She was limited in what she could do.

It was fully dark now and she could see lights over the river at the

Hunt Museum and the white trellis bridge all lit up. A warm cinnamon smell of baking wafted up the stairs along with the pleasant sounds of chatter. Kate got up to stretch her legs. As she looked over at the lights of King John's Castle, the outline of an idea came to her and she began to think.

That night after the children had gone to bed, she put her newly hatched plan to her mother. Again, Alice Kennedy was only too delighted to help. In fact, she seemed more than delighted.

"Of course you should do this, Kate," she said. "You're a capable woman. You've always shortchanged yourself."

"Well, it all depends, Mum. I could try calling him this evening. But it may be too late. It just depends on what he says . . ."

That night, alone in the double bed, Kate tried to think positively about the future. She did her best to block out all the disturbing images of Mannix, naked, making love to that woman, that killer. As on previous nights, Kate slept until four and woke with her heart racing, climbed out of bed, and peeked through the curtains to make sure the gardaí were still outside.

She was in the kitchen the following morning when the doorbell went. Her mother was reheating the breakfast muffins and they smelled good. Next, she heard her mobile ringing. Kate's heart skipped a beat. Izzy was answering the door. The sound of the door shutting again. No talking. Two sets of footsteps coming up the stairs. Izzy's and someone else's . . .

It was Detective James O'Rourke. This time she knew by his face.

"We have some news, Mrs. O'Brien . . ."

"Yes?" Kate's heart was in her mouth.

"Look, I know I shouldn't really be telling you this." He paused. "But a woman and young child fitting the descriptions of Joanne and Grace Collins were just detained a couple of hours ago trying to board a ferry in Larne, up north."

"Oh, thank God! Thank God!"

Kate slumped against the pillar at the breakfast counter. She was beginning to wonder how much longer she could carry on. Kate suddenly felt as if she had been cut free of a giant boulder that was threatening to pull her under. They had her! They had had Joanne Collins, at last! They were safe!

Detective O'Rourke was smiling as he patted Izzy on the shoulder.

"Yeah, our colleagues in the PSNI tipped us off. A few lads from Pearse Street in Dublin are already on their way across the border. I'm leaving shortly myself to meet them on their return to Dublin and I'll be escorting them down here to Henry Street to make the formal arrest."

"Did something happen?" A bleary-eyed Fergus appeared in the kitchen doorway. He was in pajamas and not yet wearing his glasses.

"Yes, Soldier! The police in Northern Ireland have caught the very sick lady. So we can all relax again. We're safe."

Kate's mother hugged her tightly.

"Does that mean you're all going away now?" Fergus asked Detective O'Rourke. He sounded disappointed.

"Well, son, I need to be on my way, but the gardaí outside will swing by throughout the day until a formal arrest is made."

Fergus nodded.

"Does Oscar Harvey know?" asked Kate quietly, over her first rush of elation and relief.

"Yes, Mrs. O'Brien. I've just come from the Strand Hotel."

The detective looked about the kitchen, his eyes coming to rest on the tray of muffins that just came out of the oven. "Great smell," he said.

"Here, I'll wrap a few for your journey," Alice Kennedy offered.

Five minutes later Detective O'Rourke was gone.

It was a happy breakfast. Relief came over Kate in huge waves. As each wave washed over her, she felt herself relax a little more. Her shoulders felt less hunched. The knot in her stomach had slackened and the tight feeling across her chest was easing off.

"So the gardaí are gone now," said Ferg. He sounded disappointed.

"That's right, Ferg," said Kate.

"And Dad? When is he coming back from Uncle Spike's?"

All eyes turned to Kate.

"We'll see, Fergus. I'll have to talk to Dad today. I don't know how things are going in the flat. We'll just see."

Kate was clearing up after breakfast, alone in the kitchen, when her mobile rang again. It was Mannix.

"Hi, Kate, it's me. You've heard the news?"

"I have," she answered.

"So that's a relief, isn't it?"

"Yes, Mannix. More than you will ever know . . ."

"Kate, I'm sorry I put you through this. If I'd had any idea."

"Let's not go over old ground, Mannix. It's over. They have her. I'm okay. The kids are okay too."

"Can I come over? I'd love to see them. I really miss them."

Kate thought a moment.

"You know what? Okay. They need to see you too. But not today. Mum is here just now. Come tomorrow. Come tomorrow for lunch."

Mannix sighed but he sounded grateful.

"Okay, Kate. See you tomorrow. About one."

"Fine." She hung up.

Kate went out to the garden, where her mother was busy hanging out socks.

"Oh, don't bother with that, Mum. I put them in the tumble dryer."

"A bit of fresh air is lovely, though, don't you think?"

"I suppose. Listen, that was Mannix on the phone. He's coming over for lunch tomorrow."

"That's fine, pet. I'll make myself scarce. In fact I may go home in a while. I'd better check my post."

"Of course, Mum. Absolutely. You do that."

"By the way, did you make that phone call last night?"

"Oh, I did, Mum." Kate smiled now, remembering.

"And what did he say?"

"He said that they hadn't had any luck with their recruitment campaign, and no, they hadn't appointed an assistant head of department yet."

"So the job's yours, then?" her mother said excitedly.

"On one condition." Kate smiled again.

"What's that, then?"

"That I join him for a steak and a bottle of Châteauneuf-du-Pape!"

"That's wonderful news, Kate."

For the second time that morning, her mother threw her arms around her.

An hour later, Kate waved off her mom, who was accompanied by Fergus and Izzy. They were looking forward to playing with the old train set in the attic of their granny's Ennis Road house. A warm feeling came over Kate as she watched the three of them leave. Kate had been to hell and back. But she had her kids. It looked like she had a new, if more demanding, job. Her mother would help out with Fergus and Izzy. It might all just work out.

Kate had another brain wave. She knew exactly what she was going to do with Izzy. Exactly how she'd teach her the lesson the child so desperately needed. With Alice Kennedy's help it was all falling into place. It was the ideal way to teach Izzy that actions had consequences. As Kate went back upstairs to the study, her step felt lighter on the stairs. Things might just turn out okay.

It was early afternoon before Kate cleared her in-box of all the e-mail that had piled up in her absence. Even though Kate wasn't due back in the Art College until Monday, she wanted to have a clean slate before starting her new job. She also sent a few e-mails to Simon Walsh to show him that she was already thinking about her new position. As far as Kate knew, Simon wasn't aware of the recent upheaval and tragedy that had visited her. He certainly hadn't mentioned anything. Kate wasn't surprised in the slightest. Simon lived in a dilapidated Georgian house by the river in Castleconnell with his Irish wolfhound. He brewed his own heavy-duty beer, listened to classical music, and liked his own company.

Looking up from the desk, Kate rubbed her eyes, and noticed that a gentle rain had started to fall outside. Better get that washing that her mother had pegged on the line. Running down the stairs, she stopped off at the tall cupboard in the hall to grab the washing basket. She jammed the door open with the doorstop, so it wouldn't slam behind her in the wind.

The wind had really picked up and Kate thought the better of pairing the socks as they came off the line. She could do that later. There were Fergus's T-shirts with the transfers of the Empire State. Izzy's Hollister sweater. And so many sheets! Where had her mother found all these sheets to wash? As she dragged the Manchester United duvet cover off the line, a stray gust of wind caught the fabric and it billowed over her head. Kate wrestled with the yards of fabric, flailing to free herself. She eventually managed to drape it into a manageable rectangle over her arm before laying it on top of the basket.

A pocket of dry and shriveled leaves had blown into the hallway as she entered the house again. And there on the stairs were more leaves. And also smudges of mud going up the stairs. How did they get there?

Kate's pulse quickened as she continued up the stairs. Was Mannix back? *Why could the man not wait until tomorrow, like she'd asked?*

The sound of the radio came from the kitchen. Her mother had left it on. And Kate could hear the sound of the kitchen clock as she stood outside the kitchen door. But nothing else. Slowly, she walked in, tightly gripping the plastic washing basket.

The cane swing chair. Someone was in the cane swing chair in the window.

Swinging back and forth.

Back and forth.

Kate's breath stopped in her throat. It was someone with her back to her. Someone in a long coat and jeans. Kate could see a ponytail and a woolly hat. A long sleek ponytail.

Slowly the chair twisted around.

It was her.

"Hello, Kate," she said.

Kate could no longer hold the washing basket. She felt it slip. She heard a thud as it hit the floor and turned over.

It was her.

The woman from before.

She had something in her hand and she was smiling.

Mannix

With a heavy heart, Mannix put his mobile back in his pocket. He supposed he should be grateful that Kate was even answering his calls. If it weren't for the kids, he suspected she'd let his calls ring out. He'd have to wait until tomorrow now to see the kids.

As he sat alone in his brother's flat, he looked around. Mannix had been here three days already and he wasn't due back at work until Monday. Is this what the future held for him now? How much longer would he have to stay here? A damp pair of jeans, a damp hoodie, and three pairs of underpants lay drying over chairs in front of the gas fire. A framed photo from Christmas two years ago sat on the mantelpiece. Izzy and Fergus on Spike's knee. Spike was wearing a Santa hat. A fly buzzed over the empty plastic cartons from the Chinese they'd had last night.

He'd fancied some breakfast, but when Mannix opened the fridge, all he saw was a stack of single-portion macaroni and cheese ready meals and some dodgy-looking slices of corned beef. Last night's whiskey had left him parched, and the milk was two weeks old, so he couldn't even have a cup of tea. His head throbbed violently. He wasn't sure if the hazy fug was due to his hangover or the lingering veil of cigarette smoke.

How did Spike ever get any woman to come up here?

Mannix shuddered at the state of the bathroom. But the evidence was all there. Obviously Spike managed to pull. The bathroom cabinet housed an open carton of condoms. A tube of lipstick and a clear blue bottle of eye-makeup remover sat on the toilet cistern along with a big bottle of toilet bleach. The seal on the bleach had not been broken.

He shouldn't complain about his brother. Spike had been a shoulder to cry on over the last few days. How he wished he were at home, at his own breakfast table, watching Fergus pick the crusts off his toast, listening to Izzy's dry remarks. Christ, how he wished he could turn the clock back.

Of course he knew he deserved no sympathy. Mannix knew all of this was his own doing. Yet he found it difficult to accept that the havoc that had been wreaked was solely down to his appalling judgment of character. Other guys got away with it.

If he'd had even the slightest sniff that Joanne Collins was this crazy, this out-of-her-tree, there was no way Mannix would have put his family in danger. No way he'd have put the Harvey family in danger either. There was no way in hell he'd have even touched her.

He'd been so stupid. It wasn't even as if he'd held any affection for the woman—even before he realized she was completely off the reservation. It really, genuinely had been only the sex. But Mannix knew that as a defense, as an argument, that would not wash with Kate. Sex and love were too closely linked for her, whereas for him, they were two different things.

Mannix allowed himself to think about the infidelity, but he found it very difficult to think about what had happened to Hazel Harvey. It was almost too much for him to contemplate, the role he'd played in her death. There was no way he could distance himself from it. He knew that ultimately he was responsible for the death of another human being but he was having difficulty registering the enormity of such a charge.

"If I'd never met that woman, Hazel Harvey would be alive today." He'd looked Spike in the eye last night as he openly acknowledged it for the first time.

"Top up?" Spike had asked as he poured himself another whiskey.

"What's he like, Oscar Harvey?" Mannix indicated that he would have a small drop more.

"A nice guy." Spike plopped another generous measure into the chipped mug. "Maybe a bit of a stiff, but, you know—a regular guy."

Well, he wasn't a regular guy anymore. He was anything but. The guy was now a widower. Mannix felt a massive stab of guilt.

"*She* was a nice woman, Hazel Harvey," added Spike, unprompted. "Posh type of girl. I'd say she might have had problems with her nerves, though. A bit on the jittery side."

"Jesus, Spike. Why in hell did I ever talk to Joanne Collins? I *hate* talking to people on planes. I never do it. Why did I just not stick to my book?"

Spike shrugged.

"What about the kids, Spike? What am I going to do about my kids? I don't want to be a weekend dad. They deserve more than that."

"The kids love you, Mannix. Kate won't interfere in that. She's a good woman. She wouldn't turn them against you."

"You're talking like it's all over, Spike. Like she's never taking me back. Don't you think she could forgive me? Give me another chance?"

"Straight up, Mannix? I really don't know. She's hurting. You can see that. You can certainly give it a go . . ."

Mannix felt morose but not quite numb enough for sleep.

"She has her mother with her now. That woman never liked me," he said bitterly. "Never thought I was good enough." He let another glug of whiskey burn the back of his throat. "Although, you know what, Spike? I guess I've proved her right. Haven't I?"

Spike looked at the clock. It was 3:30 A.M. All was quiet downstairs now, the nightclub had shut an hour ago.

"Manny, do you mind if I head to bed? The sleeping bag is over there on the sofa for you."

"Yeah, you head off, Spike. Sorry for boring the arse off you again . . ."

He didn't even make it to the sofa, falling asleep where he was, drunk and uncomfortable. He'd never felt worse in his life.

It was midafternoon the next day before Mannix mustered up the will to shave himself. As he scraped the three-day-old stubble in the grimy mirror, he felt a vibration in the pocket of his cord jeans. A text. He wiped the foamy residue with the towel that hung under the basin. It smelled of perfume. He looked at himself in the mirror. Slightly more human. Only just.

Wriggling his hand into the taut pocket, he retrieved the mobile. The text was from a number he didn't recognize. His hand still wet and slippery, he opened it.

Jesus Christ!

A shock wave sizzled through him. It took an instant to scan but in that instant his blood ran cold. He blinked and looked at it again. *This simply could not be.* It was a hoax. Was it someone's sick idea of a *practical joke?*

"So sorry you had to wait this long. It could not be helped. Good things come to he who waits. The waiting is nearly over. The BITCH is alone. This time I shall not hesitate. We shall have what we deserve. All my love, J."

Stunned, he read it again. It didn't make any sense. O'Rourke had told him she was in custody. He hadn't dreamed it up. Heard it with his own ears. She'd been picked up along with Grace Collins by the PSNI. *And yet this had the terrifying ring of truth.* The same syntax. The same crazy tone as the previous texts. Was this really Joanne? *Was she still out there?*

There was no time to procrastinate. He had to act. And fast. He couldn't take any chances. He punched the keypad of his mobile. It was ringing.

Ring, ring. Ring, ring.

No answer.

It went to voice mail. "This is Kate O'Brien from Limerick School of Art and Design. I am currently on annual leave. For any urgent queries please contact department head Simon Walsh. Otherwise leave a message after the tone . . ."

Shit! Why was Kate not answering?

"Kate—it's Mannix. Look, something's turned up. Can you call me urgently, please? This is serious. Call me as soon as you get this, Kate. Please. Do it now."

Mannix hung up.

Next, he rang the landline.

No answer.

Where the hell was Kate?

He had to get over to the house.

Now.

Christ alive! The thought that Joanne Collins could be on the loose . . . No—he couldn't think like that. He couldn't panic. He'd have to run. It was more than a mile away. *How long would that take him?* It was a long, long time since he'd managed a four-minute mile. Okay, so he could manage eight minutes tops if he really went for it. Hell for leather. But would he be in time? His head was pounding. His heart was pounding. That hangover was certainly kicking in—it was really vicious now.

Mannix grabbed the damp hoodie and quickly zipped it up. *Where the fuck were his shoes?* The flat was a tip. He couldn't see them anywhere. No time. No time. He grabbed a pair of Spike's white running shoes inside the front door.

Mannix is out on the street now, running as fast as he can. Onto Patrick Street . . . up past St. Mary's Cathedral . . . acid and bile reach his throat . . . down Nicholas Street . . . his head throbs madly . . . down toward the castle . . . he gets a sharp pain across his chest. His body screams for him to stop. He can't afford to stop. Terror keeps him going.

You've got to get there, Mannix. You've got to stop her!

Sweat is pouring out of him. He's panting heavily. He can taste last night's whiskey in his mouth. Whiskey and fear. He tries to find another number on his mobile as he runs. It's hard to scroll and run. He can't stop. No time to stop. Passersby look warily at him. He probably looks like a scumbag who's just committed a robbery. Just another scumbag on the run.

Where the hell is that number? He knows he put it in his phone. There!

He has it. *O'Rourke*. He dials the number.

O'Rourke answers. Thank Christ!

"Detective O'Rourke?" Mannix hardly has the breath to talk. He doesn't need to.

"A bit of a hiccup, Mr. O'Brien," O'Rourke cuts in immediately.

Mannix keeps up the pace. He's nearly at the castle now. It must be five minutes since he got the text.

"The two persons of interest detained by the PSNI, well, it appears that the young girl is Grace Collins, all right. But it appears the woman accompanying her was not her mother . . ."

Oh, God . . .

A massive surge of adrenaline rips through Mannix's body.

"It appears that the woman accompanying her is her aunt, Sheila Collins. They were on their way to relatives in Glasgow. Are you there, Mr. O'Brien?"

"I'm listening," Mannix answered, panting, blood roaring in his ears.

"So, Mr. O'Brien, it would appear that Joanne Collins is still at large. I'm on my way back from Dublin, but Henry Street has been alerted to send a squad car down to Curragower Falls right away."

Right away? Right away? Right away may still be too late . . .

"Oh Jesus . . . Oh sweet Jesus . . ." Mannix's voice is rasping now, sweat dripping into his eyes as he crosses the road. "I've just had another text from Joanne Collins . . ."

O'Rourke goes silent.

Beads of sweat fall into Mannix's eyes as he spots the gable end of his house coming into view.

"Don't worry. We're onto it," says O'Rourke. The phone goes dead.

Mannix blisters a path up the strand. *Thump, pound. Thump, pound.* Spike's shoes cut into the backs of his heels. A band of pressure tightens across his chest. He listens out for sirens. His eyes search for flashing lights. Strange. It looks like the street outside his house is empty. No flashing lights. Not a single squad car. Not a single garda. What the hell is going on? That dipstick O'Rourke had said that they were onto it.

Mannix snatches a look at the park across the road. It too is completely empty.

Should he wait for the guards? Or should he—

The front door to his house is open.

His sweat turns cold on his skin.

Sweet Jesus. Don't say it's too late. He cannot be too late. Fear snakes all around him. His heart in his mouth, he tears up the stairs.

A cry of terror! Mannix grips the banister. Another piercing cry—

Oh God! Mannix feels his blood is curdling. He stumbles at the top. His chest is about to explode. Now a muffled sound. *What the hell?* He lunges into the kitchen.

Jesus Christ!

He is winded. He can no longer move. He is paralyzed. His legs are heavy, rooted to the spot.

"Mannix!" she says softly, turning around.

Her eyes are glassy.

"I knew you'd come . . ."

She sounds spaced. Out of it.

He wants to go for her—to launch himself at her, to grab her wrist. But he stops himself. Too risky.

"Joanne?" He tries to sound calm, matter-of-fact.

"You didn't doubt me, did you?" she says dreamily, almost trancelike.

He wonders if she's been drinking.

What should he say? It could all be over in an instant. He has to think of something good to defuse this.

"Is this really the way you want us to start out, Joanne?" He is surprised at how he hides the panic. He sounds okay. "Do we really want this hanging over us?"

Her hand slips a little and she appears to think. He has her attention.

Kate.

Oh God! He can hardly bear to look at her.

Her eyes are wild with fear. She looks at him in terror, her nostrils flaring as she tries to breathe. She tries to shake her head.

"Stop, BITCH!" Joanne hisses suddenly.

Mannix recoils in shock.

Joanne is clamping Kate's mouth with one hand. With the other, she points the bright steel of a serrated knife against Kate's neck. It glints—flashes of light dancing in the gloom.

Christ! What has he unleashed? What the hell has he invited into their home?

Keep it together. He has to make this good. HE JUST HAS TO MAKE THIS RIGHT. Overwhelmed by a basic instinct to protect his wife, Mannix gulps and sucks for breath. He needs to get them out of this. He needs to talk this crazy woman down. The air in the room is crackling.

He can do this. He can do this. Just don't look at Kate.

He will reason with Joanne.

"If you do this, they will take you from me—"

"No, Mannix, darling, you are—"

"They will take you away from me and Gracie and—"

"Stop it! Listen to me, Mannix!"

"We will never be together. Not the way you want, the way you deserve."

"It's the only way, Mannix. She has to go. Believe me, I've thought it through—" Joanne's eyes have come into focus again. But there is steel in her voice.

A ghastly white has spread across Kate's face.

Where the fuck were the gardaí? Where the fuck were those muppets?

"Don't do this, Joanne. It's wrong . . ." He's pleading now. Mannix knows he sounds pathetic. He's running out of ideas.

"But your children?" Joanne looks confused. "She needs to go, Mannix. If she stays, the bitch will take them from you . . ."

Kate wildly tries to shake her head.

"SHUT UP, BITCH!!" Joanne spits, her eyes flashing. "I've heard enough from you today. And it's all fucking lies!"

Mannix stares in horror.

Slowly Joanne moves. Oh, so slowly, she punctures the skin,

scoring a wavy red line down the side of Kate's neck. Joanne moves in closer, staring at the jagged score mark, examining the minute detail of her handiwork.

"Mmmm . . ." she says to Mannix. She takes another look at the blood as it starts to soak into the white of Kate's lace collar.

"So the bitch bleeds red just like the rest of us—"

Joanne cocks her head suddenly, as if listening to something, and abruptly she starts to sing:

> *"Roses are red,*
> *Violets are blue,*
> *Your mother was good-looking,*
> *What happened to you?"*

She throws back her head and laughs, still gripping on to the knife— a cruel, mirthless, mental laugh.

Mannix is terrified.

Reason with this woman?

He is cold to his core. It hits him with full force. Joanne Collins is completely out of it. Completely and totally disconnected from reality. Mannix doubts if she has even heard a thing that he said. Kate's eyes are frantic now. All he needs is a couple of seconds to distract Joanne, just a couple of seconds.

"Gracie? Would Gracie like to see her mother like this?" It was a gamble.

"SHUT UP, MANNIX. You're too soft on this little woman here, you're just too—"

"I'm not, Joanne, I just want to do this right."

He's more petrified than he's ever been in his life. She's completely unhinged. How did he not notice before?

Right away. Right away, O'Rourke had said. *Where were the bloody gardaí?*

"*She* had her chance." Joanne looks at Mannix coldly. She's looking at him, at least. He needs to keep her focused on him.

"*She* doesn't love you like I do . . ."

Mannix feels a rising panic. He cannot hold her off much longer. Now she turns to Kate.

"My turn now. Mine and Gracie's. Grace deserves a father. And Mannix loves her. Don't you, Mannix?" Joanne swings back to him. "You love Gracie, don't you?"

"Of course I do. That's why I want to do this right. This is not the way—"

"You know where my Gracie is now?" she interrupts.

Mannix shakes his head.

"With my sister. Visiting cousins in Glasgow. They're gone to IKEA to pick out stuff for her new bedroom. I had Kate here give me a guided tour this time!"

How long had this woman been in his house? With his wife?

"It's time." Joanne's tone changed. "Say good-bye to the BITCH, Mannix. Say good-bye to the little bitch . . ."

He cannot wait another second.

"NO!!" He lunges, reaching for Joanne's wrist.

Startled, Joanne stumbles against the breakfast counter, *but still she has the knife.*

"It's for us, Mannix!" she screams, righting herself, her face contorted with rage and disbelief. She lashes out, reaching again for Kate. *But Kate is free!* Kate darts away, grabbing the empty knife block as a weapon. Mannix grabs the glass paperweight that keeps the bills. He swings it high.

"*Mannix?*"

Joanne does not understand. He sees that now. He smells the alcohol.

"Drop the knife, Joanne!"

"YOU DON'T GET IT, DO YOU?" she is screaming. "It's for *us* . . . you, me, and the children . . . because I *love* you."

"But *I don't love you*, Joanne. I never have." He says it forcefully. "I love Kate. Joanne, stop this now, before anyone else gets hurt . . ."

Her eyes register disbelief.

"I don't believe you . . ."

She really thinks he's joking.

"Joanne, STOP IT now. You're not well. You've been drinking . . ."

He can see Kate out of the corner of his eye, still brandishing the knife block. Her eyes still crazy with fear.

"I have NOT been drinking. YOU FUCKING BASTARD!! YOU FUCKING TWO-FACED BASTARD! You're just like all the rest!"

Mannix feels it in his shoulder first. And then his arm. Short, sharp, agonizing jabs. He drops the paperweight. He feels the warmth and wet of blood.

"STOP! STOP IT!" Kate is screaming.

It was all too late. Too late now for the gardaí . . .

Joanne is slashing him now, moving too quickly for him to grab the knife. He reaches out again . . . she slashes . . . the pain is hot and searing.

THUD!!

Kate brings the knife block down hard across Joanne's head. Mannix hears her groan. The air forced out of her. In slow motion, Joanne slumps and moans, facedown, the knife skittering and clattering across the floor.

The rush of feet pounding up the stairs!

Three uniformed gardaí rush into the room.

About fucking time!

No rush, lads.

A garda races over to Joanne. He braces his knee on her back. Roughly, he pulls her arms back, and deftly he slips a set of cuffs over her wrists. Two other gardaí are pulling Joanne to her feet. She is groaning now, blood coming from the gash on her head, trickling down the center of her forehead and down the length of her nose.

Mannix staggers against the breakfast counter, clutching his bleeding arm. He is gasping, reeling with the shock of what he invited into his home. Kate is ashen, she's still clutching the knife block.

"You disappoint me, Mannix," says Joanne as the gardaí bundle her toward the waiting car.

"You're just like all the rest, Mannix," she says softly. "You *really* let me down."

It had taken a month for the puncture wounds in his forearm to heal, two months for the tendons around his thumb to knit back together properly, and nearly three months of repeated physiotherapy to get any decent mobility back in his shoulder.

His colleagues at work had looked at him with a mix of sympathy and curiosity. Even now, Mannix could still sense the nudging and the sidelong glances as he passed the rows of cubicles on his way to the watercooler or the kitchen. Brendan, his boss, seemed to treat him with a newfound caution.

No one knew exactly what had happened in the house at Curra-gower Falls. There were rumors, of course. But no one knew exactly. An American tourist on a home exchange had been murdered. Mannix and his wife had later been attacked by the suspected murderer. The woman was on remand in Limerick Prison awaiting trial. Mannix had certainly provided them with enough lunchtime gossip for quite some time to come.

Mannix was keeping his head low. It was time to knuckle down. He'd been responsible for enough heartache to last a lifetime. He'd had his walk on the wild side. After the gardaí had taken Joanne Collins away, Kate had collapsed, a sobbing wreck, shaking uncontrollably in his arms. And it had come to Mannix just how close he'd come to losing her forever. He would never forget that feeling.

These days, Mannix found himself nodding enthusiastically at strategy meetings. He found himself agreeing with Brendan and even making suggestions for the new vision statement for the department. He volunteered to go on a number of steering committees. He im-mersed himself entirely. He didn't feel the need to rush home at night to Spike's bachelor flat.

The guys were happy to see him back in the rowing club. It was nearly light enough now in the mornings to take his scull out on an early tide before heading into the plant in Raheen. Mannix started running again. And every now and then, he called in for a pint to the Curragower Bar. He found it hard, though. Not being able to walk home around the curve in the road afterward.

Christmas had been hard. He'd had fun with the kids and Spike. He'd shared a few laughs with Kate and thought himself perfectly civil and amiable to her mother. But after dinner and all the games of cards were over, he and Spike had to leave. Back to an undecorated flat with three Christmas cards on the mantelpiece.

Alice Kennedy walked his kids to school and walked them home again. Kate thought it best that Fergus adjust to a clear routine as soon as possible. So rather than popping in and out to see them unannounced, he saw them on Monday and Tuesday evenings, Saturday mornings or sometimes the whole day Saturday, and every time there was a Man U match.

Fergus still thought it was a temporary arrangement. It was taking a long time to sort out Uncle Spike's flat, especially now that there'd been a fire. A month into his stay, Mannix put a waffle into the toaster and fell asleep, pissed, as it caught fire.

Izzy was philosophical.

"You're not moving back ever, are you, Dad?"

She knew that what had happened had something to do with him. But she had stopped asking. They were feeding the swans outside St. Michael's boat club. It was something they'd done together since Izzy was little. She felt she'd outgrown this pastime. But she indulged him. "It's okay, Dad. I'm not Fergus. I can handle it. You and Mum are getting a divorce, right?"

It was a shock to hear her say it.

"Things are a bit complicated, Izzy."

There had been no talk of divorce or even of a formal separation.

"Yeah, the standard adult response." She threw another piece of crust. "Dad, I know you love me and Fergus. Fiona's parents are divorced and she sees her dad all the time. So much that he annoys her!"

"Let's just see what happens, Izzy."

"Play it by ear, is that it, Dad?" She cocked her head and looked at him. "Isn't that what you always say . . . ?"

"I guess so, Izzy. I guess so." It seemed as good a strategy as any.

Mannix still held out some hope. Dum spiro, spero—*While I breathe, I hope*. He'd rarely listened in Latin class, but the old adage suddenly popped into his head. Unlike Oscar Harvey, Mannix at least had an outside chance of his wife coming back to him.

Mannix shuddered as he thought of Oscar Harvey. He would be forced to meet him face-to-face at the trial. But that was some way off. He wouldn't think about that now. Neither did Mannix allow himself too much time to dwell on little Grace. He preferred to think the alleged affection she had for him was all in her mother's twisted mind. Grace was better off with her mother out of the picture—she had an aunt who sounded like she cared for her.

"How's Fergus doing?"

Sometimes it was easier to ask Izzy than Kate. Somehow his questions didn't seem so loaded when he asked Izzy. And his daughter shot from the hip. She'd tell him straight.

"At school, you mean? Or in general?"

"At school, I guess." In general, Fergus seemed okay.

"Well, all the messers want to hang out with Fergus at break time now. And there was a fight yesterday—about which team would have Fergus in goal, so I guess he's okay."

"I see . . ." Mannix wasn't sure he wanted Fergus hanging out with the messers. But to be sought after as a goalie must be another dream come true for Fergus. His son had two left feet.

"And Frankie Flynn? Is that tosspot leaving him alone?"

"Yeah, Frankie . . ." Izzy looked puzzled for a second. "I don't understand it, really. Fergus said Frankie offered him one of the Mars bars he robbed from the off-license his mother works in. It's all a bit weird to me."

But Mannix understood it perfectly. Having the gardaí outside the Curragower house hadn't done Fergus's reputation any harm at all. In certain circles it had been enhanced. Frankie Flynn was treading warily around Fergus now, no doubt thinking he hadn't had the measure of him before. Fergus was the geeky posh kid whose family had drawn adverse national media attention, whose home had been a murder scene. Oh, yes. Mannix got it, all right. Despite being the geeky posh kid, Fergus had come through some unspoken rite of passage.

"And yourself, Izzy?" asked Mannix. "How did you get on in Dublin during the week?"

Izzy threw the last scrap of bread to the fast-approaching swans. Then slowly and deliberately she turned to Mannix and threw her eyes to heaven.

"Really, Dad. Did she *really* have to do that to me?"

"Well, yes, Izzy. I think she did. Your mother only wants what's best for you." Mannix thought it best that they both sing from the same hymn sheet.

"I know, but a young offenders' institute? C'mon, Dad . . ."

Mannix knew where Kate was coming from. As she'd said herself, it would have been a wasted opportunity not to bring Izzy. Kate was going anyway to give a presentation on behalf of the Limerick School of Art and Design. Why not take Izzy and show her where the kids who took a wrong turn ended up?

"Izzy, I don't think you realize how close you came to being there yourself. Just because Mum and I are the only ones who know what you did . . ." Mannix felt a bit of a hypocrite. Talk about the pot calling the kettle black, yet he knew he should back Kate up. Izzy looked at him, her dark eyes serious now.

"Dad, what I did was nothing. Not a patch on those hard-core kids. Some of them in there had actually killed people, for God's sake! And they were staring at me like *I* was the one who was the freak!"

"Well, you know, Izzy. Things can so easily get out of hand. Some of these kids could have been just like you, where things didn't turn out so well. The next thing they know their whole life is upside down and they find themselves in Oberstown."

"Yeah, yeah. I hear you, Dad." Izzy sighed theatrically. "Stop going on about it, please. It's not going to happen again, okay. Ever."

He believed her. From what Kate had said, she had been pretty damn silent on the journey home. The message had rung home loud and clear. A swan swaggered up the slipway, unhappy that all the bread was gone. It looked a touch aggressive. Time to go.

Mannix slung an arm around Izzy's shoulder. "Come on, Izzy, let's go. It's getting dark. Mum wants us back in time for dinner."

Tonight, it was just the four of them. Kate's mother had gone to a bridge conference. And for a couple of happy hours he forgot that he no longer lived in the house. It was spaghetti Bolognese and cookie dough ice cream.

"The kids seem to be doing okay," he said to Kate in the hallway.

Kate appeared to think.

"You know what, Mannix? I've come to realize something. I can't wrap the kids in cotton wool. I can be a first line of defense but not a bulletproof shield. Sometimes those bullets are going to get through. And when they do, we'll deal with it. That's just something I'll have to accept."

"I'm here to help as well," Mannix said lamely. He hated it when she spoke as if she were a single parent.

There was no response.

"Thanks for dinner," Mannix said as she accompanied him down to the front door.

"My pleasure," Kate said, smiling, as if the two of them were friends.

"See you on Saturday, then." He hovered on the step, wondering if he could hazard more. The evening had gone well.

"Saturday it is," she said. She was already closing the door.

Probably best to leave it.

He waved his hand in salute, and turning on his heel, he heard the door firmly click behind him. He walked down the driveway and out onto Clancy Strand. He turned left, passed the Treaty Stone, and turned right onto Thomond Bridge. A lone fisherman wrestled with his line.

"Are they biting tonight?" Mannix asked casually as he passed by.

"Had one a second ago," came the reply. "You should have seen it! An absolute beauty. The catch of my life. I've just bloody gone and lost the catch of my life . . ."

Mannix shrugged and walked on.

"You and me both, pal," he said. "You and me both."